the Rose Quilt

A Steve Walsh Mystery

MARK PASQUINI

C&T PUBLISHING

Text copyright © 2018 by Mark Pasquini

Photography copyright © 2018 by C&T Publishing, Inc.

Publisher: Amy Marson

Creative Director: Gailen Runge

Editors: Kate Homan and Liz Aneloski

Cover/Book Designer: April Mostek

Production Coordinator: Zinnia Heinzmann

Production Editor: Jennifer Warren

Photo Assistant: Mai Yong Vang

Cover photography by Lucy Glover of C&T Publishing, Inc.

Published by C&T Publishing, Inc., P.O. Box 1456, Lafayette, CA 94549

Library of Congress Cataloging-in-Publication Data

Names: Pasquini, Mark, 1950- author.

Title: The rose quilt : a Steve Walsh mystery / Mark Pasquini.

Description: Lafayette, CA : C&T Publishing, [2018]

Identifiers: LCCN 2017033113 | ISBN 9781617456350 (softcover)

Subjects: LCSH: Murder--Investigation--Fiction. | Quilting--Fiction. | GSAFD: Mystery fiction.

Classification: LCC PS3616.A84 R67 2018 | DDC 813/.6--dc23

LC record available at https://lccn.loc.gov/2017033113

Printed in the USA

10 9 8 7 6 5 4 3 2 1

Dedicated to the
Memorial Day quilt group:

Katie Pasquini Masopust

Holly Cunningham

Terry Robertson

Acknowledgments

In appreciation of Roxane Cerda and Kate Homan, without whose help and support this book would never have seen the light of day.

Prologue

Mrs. Alice Chandler stood in the open doorway of her Georgian mansion. The blue dress draped her tall, erect frame, the softness of the wool offset by the severity of the dress's lines. It had a square-cut neckline, and a chain of pearls encircled the woman's wattled throat. A black shawl covered her squared shoulders, fending off the cold. She had a long, lined face and iron-gray hair and eyes. Her wide mouth was untouched by cosmetics, and her button nose was so small her late husband had teased her that part of it must have been lost. Mrs. Chandler met every guest at the front door, her bearing stiff and formal, on the edge between European social mores and the American concept of equality. Even after all the years of wealth and a prominent social position, she was still the daughter of her nouveau riche parents, who felt that hosts should welcome their guests properly upon their arrival. A slight, self-deprecating smile flashed across her lined face at this thought. She tried to relax her bearing but suspected she was succeeding only partially.

The house was made of native stone from the family's quarry and had been built by her father-in-law on a small hill. The hill overlooked the company town of Chandler on one side, while the farms occupied the rest of the surrounding area. She mused that she was much like the house, tied to the hill, her foundation the responsibility she felt to everything around her. Another flicker of amusement touched her face as she wondered whether the rigidity of the house had seeped into her bones.

The occasion for the night's gathering was to make plans for the A. J. Chandler Memorial Flower Show for 1923. She still missed her husband and remembered the easy manner with which he could greet a grizzled farmer or a French diplomat. With either, he was a lifelong friend in a matter of minutes. The mist that blurred her vision for a moment was not caused by the cold, blustery wind.

The drive up to the Chandler mansion had been heavily sanded by the staff. Even with the gritty covering, automobiles tended to slide on corners unless the drivers were careful and slow. The March evening was dark, with low clouds and a light snowfall.

The butler met each vehicle with a slight bow and an umbrella. Jeremy Smythe had gotten over his discomfort at being addressed by his Christian name. He soon realized that the Chandlers were egalitarian Americans and preferred the more personal form of address. When he had gently tried to correct her, Mrs. Chandler had patted his arm and said, "Do not be silly, Jeremy."

Professor Lech Poltovski arrived first, using Baker's Taxi Service. Mr. Chandler had brought him over from Austria-Hungary, just before the Great War. He was small and bent, with a tremor in his hands and an obsequious manner, looking far older than his years. He carried a large portfolio with him. He nodded. "Good evening, Mrs. Chandler," he said with a bobbing head. She greeted him and touched his hand in passing. As he hurried to the sewing room and to warm his hands at the fire, she thought of the man's tentative proposal a few months earlier. There had been several invitations of marriage since A. J.'s death. She suspected that her suitors were more interested in her money or the Chandler empire, but Professor Poltovski was the first who wanted citizenship. An amused chuckle was followed by the thought that she must talk to her attorney, Nicolas Martin, about his application.

Hard on his heels, an old black 1916 Saxon Roadster arrived, driven by a thin, mousy woman. The car was showing its age. Mrs. Mary Flowers accepted Jeremy's help with a nod. When she passed her hostess, her "Good evening" was muted. As she hurried by, Mrs. Chandler thought of the unfortunate incident with the committee funds. Perhaps Mrs. Black had been right about removing her, but Mrs. Chandler believed in redemption and had no regrets about her course of action in the matter.

The Joneses rattled up in their stake-side 1918 Ford truck with "Chandler Nursery" painted on its doors. The solid rubber rear tires had holes drilled through them from side to side to soften the ride. Barry and Wanda Jones ignored the umbrellas and marched up to the front door, stamping their boots to rid them of snow. They shed their heavy work coats after greeting Mrs. Chandler and stepping inside. Both were dressed in wool shirts and work pants. Mrs. Chandler studied the younger woman for signs of unsteadiness and was pleased at their absence.

A Ford Depot hack on a 1914 chassis, the only other taxi in Chandler, slid to a stop an inch from the silent, frozen fountain in the turnaround. Mrs. Chandler took a half-step and raised her hands to her breast in alarm. Mr. Chandler had loved the sight of the cascading ice on the center carvings. He told her that the moonlight on the frozen water looked like suspended diamonds. Every year, they would have to replace burst pipes, but he said it was worth it to be able to give her the largest wedding ring in the world every winter. She shook her head and mentally accused herself of being a sentimental old woman for continuing the tradition.

The hapless taxi driver was suffering a blistering lecture from the birdlike woman in the passenger seat. "I have never endured such rude and uncouth behavior in my life. Mr. Jackson, if you desire my future custom, you will mend your ways. You will return here at nine o'clock sharp. Do you understand me? Nine o'clock." The tiny figure slapped the driver's offered hand and climbed out of the hack under her own power. Mrs. Emma Black raised her own umbrella, interfering with the one extended by Jeremy. She jerked hers impatiently from the tangle and marched up the walk. Her manner changed abruptly when she reached her hostess. She showed a wide, frozen smile and offered a too-familiar greeting: "Well, good evening, my dear Alice. A bitter night, but we must start, and a little inconvenience can easily be ignored for the greater good." She ignored the hovering maid's effort to take her coat and hat until Mrs. Chandler said, "Yes, Emma. I hope you are not too inconvenienced by the weather. Susanne, please help Mrs. Black with her coat and show her into the sewing room."

The other passenger was helped down by the driver, who looked as if he would be more than happy to forgo the little harpy's future custom. Miss Anna Carlyle paid Harry Jackson for the ride and gave his arm a sympathetic squeeze. She was rewarded by a tip of his cap and a "Thank you, ma'am." The plump woman availed herself of Jeremy's covering and entered the house with a nod to Mrs. Chandler.

"I sent the preliminary application in today, Alice. We must be patient, however. Rome was not built in a day, and the committee is much slower than the Romans."

Mrs. Chandler's expression softened, and a low laugh followed the smile to her lips. "Thank you, Anna. I admit I am nervous. I have no trouble managing the Chandler enterprises but am feeling butterflies because of a simple application. And you really did all the work of developing the hybrids."

The sewing room had originally been a sitting room when Peter Chandler built the house. Mrs. Chandler had converted it to its present use in 1917 when she decided to sponsor the flower show and create the first quilt.

Mrs. Chandler moved around the long, cloth-covered table, which had chairs lined on the far side. Six pads of paper with two pencils each were arranged along the edge. There were pitchers of ice water and glasses on matching silver trays within easy reach along the center line. Behind her, above the chair rail, thick cork covered a portion of the wall.

A light double clap brought the attention of her guests. "Please be seated, everyone." Mrs. Chandler spoke in a mild voice edged with steel that took command of the room.

"I would like to thank all of you for coming on a night such as this. This will be a short meeting so that all of you can get back to your homes before the blizzard strikes," said Mrs. Chandler.

At Mrs. Black's sudden movement, Mrs. Chandler held up her hand. "Emma, I will have a driver available for you if we should break before Mr. Jackson has returned."

The small woman's mouth tightened. She was resentful at being forestalled and had difficulty keeping silent, but she rarely scolded Mrs. Chandler as she did the others.

"On the tablets in front of you, you will find a copy of the abbreviated agenda for tonight's meeting. Primarily, we need to choose the pattern for the quilt. All of you have, presumably, brought your ideas. Second, a color palette will be presented. I was planning on having Professor Poltovski and Mrs. and Mr. Jones present their plans for the layout for this year's show. However, due to the inclement weather, we will postpone that item until our next meeting. Are there any questions?" She nodded to the three who had been scheduled to present. "Please accept my apologies."

She moved to the table at the end of the wall, which contained stacks of cloth from prior years and a wooden box of wrist pincushions. Mrs. Chandler slipped one over her hand and returned to the cork. She picked up a piece of paper and pinned it to the board. The pattern drawings were always black and white. The sketch showed five bouquets of roses, one near each corner and a larger one in the center.

"Anna, do you have one?" she asked.

The plump woman held out a folded paper to Mrs. Chandler. It was opened and pinned to the wall. The drawing showed an oblong with a large rose in the center, which radiated five stems ending in smaller versions of the central flower.

"Emma?"

Her offering consisted of a stylized Greek urn with a bouquet of lilies symmetrically arranged in it. There were detailed Greek-style figures visible between the heavy meander borders decorating the urn.

"Mrs. Flowers, what have you to offer?" The question was delivered in an unconsciously cool voice.

Nervously, Mrs. Flowers extended a sheet of paper.

Her design consisted of four concentric frames with spaced roses sandwiched between them.

"As always, we will not criticize any of the drawings but will select one in toto or create a new drawing using combinations of elements from several," Mrs. Chandler said, studiously avoiding glancing at Mrs. Black.

The committee members studied the board and discussed the designs among themselves. They returned to their seats when Mrs. Chandler said, "Does anyone wish to use one of the presentations as it stands?"

Mrs. Black squirmed in her chair, raising whispers from the black bombazine fabric of her dress. She raised her hand quickly. "I am sure that you have all noticed that there is only one classic design. It is formal, symmetrical, and tasteful. It would give dignity to the quilt and a sense of order and elegance. The fine lines of the urn go beautifully with the floral arrangement. The elegant designs on the urn are ordered and classical."

Miss Carlyle spoke up forcefully. "We had nearly the same style last year. Wasn't that the fluted vase with a bouquet of flowers?"

Mrs. Black huffed, "An orderly, classical design never loses its appeal, Anna."

Mrs. Chandler hid the smile on her lips by bowing her head and laying out a blank sheet of paper on the table. "Does anyone else want to keep one of the drawings as it is?" she asked, looking along the table.

Mrs. Flowers tentatively raised her hand, prompting a quirk of the eyebrows from Mrs. Chandler. "I like Anna's rendering. Could we add a frame, soften the curve of the branches, and add a leaf or two to each branch?"

Mrs. Jones added, "Instead of four small roses going to the center of each side, I would add another set of four between those, but on shorter branches."

Mrs. Chandler asked, "Anna, will you draw it up for us, please?"

Mrs. Chandler traded positions with Miss Carlyle, who took a small pouch out of her bag, extracted an artist's charcoal pencil, and began to draw. Strong, bold lines created the frame. Quick, sure strokes sketched the central rose and four sweeping lines to represent the branches, each ending in a smaller version of the central rose. She added four shorter curves and ended each one with a small rose. She added narrow diamond forms at random to the branches to represent the leaves. When she was finished, she pinned it up on the board.

Mr. Jones tapped his blunt fingers on the table and offered, "The leaves. I'd make them look a little rounder, sort of like real leaves."

After a murmur of agreement, Miss Carlyle softened the foliage.

A few moments later, Mrs. Flowers said, "The center doesn't feel right. Would another border on the outside of the inner roses define the center—accent it?"

The professor raised his hand and said, almost apologetically, "The inner roses—maybe buds instead?"

Miss Carlyle bent over the table and began to draw. She pinned up the new picture. The committee saw an outer border with roses at the compass points. Inside of those roses was another, thinner border. In each corner was a stylized rosebud. The center contained a larger rose with six petals. Randomly from between the petals came the branches in a clockwise flow to attach to the small roses and buds. Three leaves were attached randomly.

"Not so good," Professor Poltovski observed in his heavy accent. "Not buds; back to roses is better."

The rest of the committee expressed their agreement at the restored design, though Mrs. Chandler noticed that Mrs. Black's was tepid. She tapped a fingernail on the table to bring order and continued, "Now, let us decide on the general colors."

Mrs. Flowers said, "The roses, of course, will be in shades of red—possibly each petal a different shade—and the branches and leaves shades of green? I noticed, too, when I was in the print shop at the mill that there was a bolt of olive cloth with magenta roses on it, which might be used for the border."

Mrs. Black stated with a hint of acid in her voice, "Certainly. That is obvious and needn't even be stated. As to the border, the whole committee will decide on that." Mrs. Flowers ducked her head in embarrassment. Mrs. Black had never lost an opportunity to crush her since the scandal.

Another fingernail tap from the hostess silenced the attack by the small, acerbic woman. "The only question is which colors for the interior and border, which Mary might have solved for us. First of all, we have a large quantity of cloth from past years. I think a light background would highlight the flowers, and, since there is such a quantity of remnants, that a somewhat scrappy quilt would be in order.

I am having the backing material printed in the Chandler Mills print shop. Professor kindly helped me with the Latin. It is a dark background with magenta flowers labeled with their Latin names in a yellow-green tone."

She turned to Mrs. Flowers and nodded her head in acknowledgment. "I also noticed the remnant from the bolts ordered by the Midwest Furniture Company and had the backing printed with the same colors." Her tone had a note of finality. "Further, I think Mary's idea is excellent regarding the border, and, if I recall correctly, there is a sample that we printed with smaller flowers in the same color scheme that the company was also considering."

After a few minutes of desultory discussion, the olive green and magenta were selected for the border and white and pale gray tones for the background. Mrs. Black was noticeably torn between continuing her pecking at Mrs. Flowers and agreeing with Mrs. Chandler on the color scheme. Soon, all the background colors had been extracted from the piles of cloth and scattered across the table.

Miss Carlyle returned to the piles of cloth and brought out several other swatches. "I think the background is a little too bland. Here are some light greens and slightly darker grays that might bring a little snap without overpowering the red and green roses." She arranged her new suggestions on top of those that were already down. Then she laid some deep reds and greens on top.

Mrs. Chandler looked at the faces around the table. Mrs. Black, as usual, looked as if she wanted to find fault with something—anything. Miss Carlyle stood with a self-satisfied look on her broad, heavy face. Mrs. Flowers gave a jerky nod of approval, with sparkling eyes. Mrs. Jones twisted her mouth and looked pleased with the palette. The men merely shrugged their agreement.

Mrs. Chandler suggested that the seamstresses—herself, Miss Carlyle, Mrs. Black, and Mrs. Flowers—meet separately to choose the actual cloth for the quilts.

Jeremy entered as Mrs. Chandler was calling for the committee to adjourn for the evening. "Mrs. Chandler, I took it upon myself to retain Mr. Jackson. He is in the kitchen, waiting to convey members of the committee back to Chandler."

Mrs. Chandler took her place by the door to wish her guests a safe trip. When everyone had departed, she walked back to the sewing room to review the drawings and sort through the material on the table.

Francis, who had been waiting impatiently for the committee to adjourn, walked in to speak with her, but she waved him away. "Mother, I must talk with you. It is very important," he insisted.

She turned to him, catching his angry stare before he suppressed it, her face calm. "Francis, I know what you want to say. My answer has not changed. You managed to get yourself into this—this mess, and you will resolve it by yourself. This family will not squander any more funds on your peccadilloes, nor will you have access to the funds in your trust. I do not want to hear anything more on the matter." Her flashing eyes and rigid posture communicated finality. Her red-faced son glared at her for another moment and spun around. He exited the room, slamming the door.

Mrs. Chandler's shoulders slumped. She stood for a little while before straightening and slowly turning back to the table. While she was absently fingering the swatches, she heard the front door. Mrs. Chandler quickly crossed the room and stepped out into the hall.

"Silene!" she called at the slim figure rushing up the stairs.

"I'm tired, Mother," her daughter called over her shoulder. "You can lecture me in the morning." The exasperation was plain in her voice.

Mrs. Chandler caught the sound of a high-powered car driving away. She wondered who it had been tonight. Probably Dean, but it could have been any of Silene's rich, spoiled friends. Suddenly feeling her 69 years, she paused and sighed, listening as the sounds of her daughter's passage faded.

Slowly, she walked back to the sewing room. After closing the door, Mrs. Chandler leaned her lined forehead against the dark wood. She thought briefly about Catherine, the meek daughter she had sent to South Carolina, hoping the experience running the cotton farms would put some steel in her spine. Catherine looked more like a Chandler than the other two adopted children but had none of the fire of A. J. or herself. Her thoughts drifted to Paul Sullivan, who had gone along as her manager and to make sure Catherine did not make any egregious mistakes. Mrs. Chandler realized that the capable young man undoubtedly resented the demotion from manager at the mill.

Suddenly losing interest in the quilt and feeling tired, she murmured, "Oh, Andy, why did you have to leave me? I do not understand our children, and I am weary of fighting them."

✂ Chapter 1

An arm stretched out from the tangle of blankets and backhanded the jangling alarm clock. It clattered from the battered mahogany record cabinet that served as a bedside stand and onto the floor, where it wheezed to a stop. A groan issued from the bed as the blankets were thrown back. Steve Walsh, lead investigator for the Connecticut State Police, slid his pajama-clad legs over the side of the mattress, and his feet searched the floor for his slippers. He raised himself upright and stood with his eyes closed for a few seconds. His right lid slowly opened before immediately squinting closed again against the shaft of early morning June sun. Another groan and stretch completed his morning exercise.

He fumbled for his flannel robe as he jammed his feet into the slippers. Tying the belt, he sighed. "Two more reports and I can sleep in a quiet cabin in the pines. Come on, Steve. Snap to." He headed toward the bathroom, scratching his tousled hair and yawning from deep down.

The mirror on the slide-in metal cabinet did not give him much encouragement. Wide-set green-flecked hazel eyes stared back from a triangular face. Below his auburn hair was a broad forehead with thin brows. The high cheekbones were smooth and framed a thin Roman nose over a thin-lipped mouth. Stooping his lean six-foot frame to bring his head into full view in the mirror, he raked his hand through his hair. He brushed his teeth to get rid of the coating of sleep. While he was trying to one-hand the lid on the tooth powder at the same time, the tin slipped off the porcelain sink and dumped its contents on the worn floor. Wiping the dusting of polish off the tile floor, he muttered through the foam in his mouth, "I really hope this is not a sign of what this day is going to be like."

Having splashed cold water on his face and rinsed his mouth, he felt that he might survive the day. He made his way to the kitchen, where open-faced cabinets with a clutter of dishes and various-sized pots stared at him. He stared back. The small covered tin garbage can lined with newspaper next to the sink was overflowing and ready to be emptied. He was glad he took most of his meals in restaurants and did not have to worry about smells and other unpleasant residue. Most of his trash was paper and rinsed tin cans. Boxes and packages of food sat behind the door of the base of the Hoosier cabinet. Most of these provisions had been purchased to impress Susan with his domesticity. At the thought of her, he felt like a knife had been twisted in his stomach, even after all the years since she had left.

With almost religious reverence, he crossed to the stove and picked up the battered and blackened coffee pot. Moving to the sink, he dumped yesterday's sludge into the cluttered sink and rinsed the enameled pot and basket. He worked the top off the container of grounds and spooned several heaps into the basket, tapping each one to the proper level. With the water level at the exact mark, he lit a burner on the small Chambers stove and set the pot on. Steve now considered the most important task of the day complete.

While the coffee transformed itself from water into ambrosia, he looked with distaste toward the job at hand on the claw-footed round oak kitchen table. A squared collection of completed reports, neatly labeled in manila folders, stood at the left end. Steve reluctantly slid his eyes to the right edge, where a precariously stacked heap of unfinished reports, in the form of notebooks and loose papers, threatened to avalanche onto the cracked linoleum below. He wondered what a skull doctor would think regarding the contrast. The disordered material on the right would probably be an example of his own disorder, while the left side represented the neat possessions of some other entity. *Good luck, Freud,* he mused.

"Go away," he almost snarled to the right-hand pile. He should get a dog, he reasoned. Then he could pretend he was talking to something besides himself. Then he could gauge whether he had really gone around the bend based on when he began to expect an answer.

Steve had never been a morning person, and he hated paperwork. Even in the military, chasing spies and saboteurs, he was a field man who preferred pursuit and danger to sitting at a desk scribbling. His military file contained several dings regarding his failure to submit timely paperwork. This reminded him of the major he had served under in the Great War, who brayed with laughter when he observed, "The army may march on its stomach, but the intelligence service marches on its paperwork." Steve sighed and swore, for the millionth time, that he would keep up with it in the future to avoid marathon sessions like this. Steve suspected that Bob Crowder, chief of the Connecticut State Police, expected him to forgo his anticipated vacation rather than finish the hated task before he left. Steve admitted he was tempted but swore he would not give his boss the satisfaction. The vacation was not as important as actually taking it. Bob had a habit of finding a big case whenever Steve planned a vacation. The value of putting on a show of independence overrode the loneliness of idling around by himself.

Stalling, he lit another burner and set the toaster frame over the low flames. He unwrapped the loaf of bread from the bread box; a trace of mold dusted the bottom. He paused and shrugged before slicing off two pieces. A quick flick of the knife and the offending lightly fuzzed crust was gone. He carefully laid the bread on the toaster and was satisfied with the look of the dark brew he saw through the observation bulb of the coffee pot. The debate about getting a clean cup was settled when he realized that all his cups were in the sink. He emptied the dregs from the one he had used the prior night and rinsed it. *I read somewhere that hot coffee is a great disinfectant,* he lied to himself. As he took his first satisfying sip, the smell of burning toast overpowered the odor of the coffee. He quickly turned the slices over and swore as he burned his fingers.

Luckily there was a clean plate in the cupboard. He slathered the toast with strawberry jam of uncertain age that he found in the icebox. He emptied the drip pan while it was on his mind so it wouldn't overflow. When he sloshed water onto himself, he vowed that he would get an electric refrigerator the moment he returned. Staying away from the table, as if he were afraid the paperwork would attack him, he ate his breakfast leaning against the counter. He considered washing up but realized that the passing thought was only another delaying tactic. Anyway, the cleaning lady, Mrs. Colletti, was due for her weekly dusting and polishing session. *I would hate to disabuse her of her conviction that no man can take proper care of himself,* he justified.

Then he thought about getting dressed, but he knew that this was just one more excuse. With a fresh cup of coffee in hand, he drifted back to the years he had spent in England working as a military liaison for the United States. He had been recruited and given a leave from the state police. Because of his knowledge of languages—Steve spoke German and Dutch and knew enough French, Italian, and Spanish to get by—he was approached by one of his law school classmates who had joined the intelligence service. He had laid out the military's need for agents in the European theater. The Great War was just starting, and the Germans had spy cells in England. Steve had been sent to Great Britain as part of a team to work with British and other Allied agents. Their job was to uncover German plots related to their own countries. His English counterparts treated espionage as a game, but they had been able to shut down many cells of the German spy service.

He had infiltrated multiple groups and interviewed members of others. His efforts had uncovered several plots and plans, including the Kaiser's belief that if he landed a division of troops in New York, an uprising of German-Americans would conquer the United States and bring it to the side of the Central Powers. Steve wondered how they would have fared in the Five Points section of New York City. Kaiser Wilhelm would have had to be careful about stirring up the boys there. A regiment of the toughs from the slums of New York could probably have been in Berlin in a week without raising a sweat.

His eyes fell back on the precariously stacked files, and he grabbed one before he could find another excuse for delay. For several hours, he worked furiously to finish his reports on the last and most intricate cases and add them to the neat stack.

Steve turned the burner off under the pot, which perfumed the air with the sharp odor of boiled-away coffee. He went through a new coffee maker every few months, it seemed. He showered and spent a few minutes packing his large leather suitcase, towel wrapped around his lean hips. Steve was glad he had remembered to pick up his laundry the day before. He carefully placed a linen suit, shirts, ties, handkerchiefs, socks, and underwear in the bag. He added a pair of deck shoes in a storage bag and, finally, a casual shirt and a pair of denims, perfect for the Poconos in June. After scraping the beard off his face with his straight razor and brushing his teeth again, he added his toilet kit to the bag and dressed carefully in a light gray summer suit with a tan shirt and brown tie.

He picked up the suitcase and looked around the apartment to make sure that nothing had been left running that would burn the place down or flood it out. Satisfied, he packed the files in a scuffed briefcase. He paused as he stepped into the living room and gave the room an approving look. It was a homey, lived-in space, with the surrounding walls lined with the books he had collected over the years. Leather-bound sets of the classics, a set of encyclopedias, textbooks, law books, and miscellaneous novels. The furniture had been there when he bought the flat, and he had found it surprisingly comfortable. The overstuffed chairs facing the fireplace; the large chesterfield, which sat like a dowager under the window; and a floor lamp positioned for easy reading had become old and familiar friends. He idly wondered if he had kept the furnishings because Susan hated them.

After parking the suitcase by the door, ready for a quick grab on the way to the train station, he checked his billfold, stepped outside, and started to lock the door behind him. Stooping, he picked up the paper lying on the doorstep. A quick glance at the headlines showed that the murder of Mrs. Chandler was still top news. *I pity the poor sucker that gets this one,* he mused. *But it would be interesting—a house full of suspects and a high-profile victim. The thing smells of politics, though. Good thing I'm on vacation.* He folded the newspaper and dropped it into his briefcase and locked the door.

He started down the stairs but reversed after going down two steps. He let himself back in the apartment and wrote a quick note to the housekeeper, informing her that he would be gone for two weeks. After looking around again, he stepped out and descended to the street. He took a deep breath of city air. He took in the faint smell of smoke, the perfume of the bright flowers from the building's planting beds, and the homey scent of the local bakery. Steve stepped to the curb, where he flagged down a passing hack to take him to the office.

Chapter 2

The edifice that housed the Connecticut State Police was old and slightly decrepit. The bricks were soiled with years of dirt and soot. A tarnished brass plate by the door notified the public that the building housed the official offices of various governmental departments, including those of the Connecticut State Police. The double doors opened onto a large lobby with polished marble floors and two rows of pillars. The seal of the state of Connecticut was inlaid in the floor, and a massive reception desk stood at its center. The security officer, large and sloppy in his uniform, nodded a greeting as Steve headed toward the elevator. Charlie, the ancient elevator operator, sported a gray beard that reminded Steve of a merry-faced Santa. The moment the inspector entered the car Charlie began talking. Steve ignored him. The old man never expected any reply; he just loved to talk, and Steve tuned him out. Going over the list of tasks to be completed before he took off for the Poconos, he ignored the chatter and exited the car at the Connecticut State Police floor. He walked through the office, accompanied by the usual din of jangling telephones, voices, and chattering typewriters.

Halfway across the floor, Steve saw Jerry McQuarry and James Morgan approaching. He nodded and received an antagonistic glare from McQuarry and an answering nod from Morgan. Morgan slowed to give McQuarry room to move, but Steve remained in the center of the aisle. Stubbornly, both refused to give an inch; their shoulders collided. Before either could react, Morgan stepped between them.

"I will meet you at the car, Jerry," he said mildly.

When the big, craggy-faced man hesitated, his partner continued forcefully, "Jerry. Don't push it. Just bring the car around."

Hard brown eyes looked from Steve to Morgan and back. McQuarry shifted the unlit cigar clamped in his teeth. "Watch yourself, college boy," he muttered. "Ain't nothin' special about you." He stalked off.

"Sheesh, Steve. Give a little. You know he's busted up because you got the promotion he thinks he deserved. Back off until he cools down."

Steve looked at the older investigator. "He won't ever cool down. And he's about as far up the ladder as he will ever get. He's too free with his fists and the word is out. I'm tired of walking on eggshells around him, and his last little stunt is going to get him booted if he tries it again."

Steve watched Morgan as he walked out the door. McQuarry resented not only Steve's promotion but also his education. McQuarry was an old-fashioned cop who had no scruples about how he got information, and it had hurt his reputation with the brass. Lawyers knew his temperament and played him when they had him on the stand. He had a vindictive streak a mile wide. Steve had recently arrested a small-time hood and was playing him for bigger fish. Evidence disappeared, and they had to let the informant go free. Steve had reason to believe that McQuarry was responsible, but there was no incontrovertible proof. He turned and continued across the office.

He smiled and greeted Mrs. Ida Clark, Bob Crowder's Cerberus. She had been a fixture in the office for as long as anyone could remember. Her brittle personality and biting tongue could reduce even the most hardened investigator to a trembling mass. However, she looked at the officers as her family and protected them like a mother wolf. Steve knew that no word of the incident with McQuarry would get to their boss. She gave him a crisp nod and snapped, "Chief Crowder has been waiting for you." For her, that was a friendly greeting. *One of these days,* Steve thought, *she is actually going to say, "Good morning."*

He ambled into the chief's office and dumped the stack of folders he had retrieved from the briefcase onto the worn old oak desk. The lanky inspector sank gingerly into the ancient wooden guest chair, which protested at any burden. He adjusted the four-in-hand knot on his tie and said cheerfully, "There you are, Chief. Paperwork is done and I am off to the Poconos this afternoon." He patted his breast over the pocket containing the tickets. "Two weeks with nothing to do and all day to do it."

His boss carefully laid down his cigar in the overflowing ashtray, ignoring another drift of ash that avalanched onto his stained blotter. His square face was lined with worry— a common sight. Steve wondered whether he was born with that expression or if it came with the job. Bob was overweight, and his black wool suit was rumpled. His shirt collar was unbuttoned under his spotted tie. He rarely fastened his vest, which was kept together by the watch chain that stretched across his swelling stomach. Chief of the

Connecticut State Police was a political position, and he was under constant pressure from the governor and legislators from both parties. Steve thought this could be the reason for his appearance and his need for the stomach powders that were never far from his hand. The only time Steve had seen him in a pressed suit was when he was headed to the legislature to fight for funds.

Bob leaned back in his cracked leather chair, causing it to creak and groan. "The Poconos? Too crowded this time of year. Elbow-to-elbow people, shrieking kids, noise all day long and half the night. You would hate it," he growled, running thick fingers through his thin hair. Bob leaned forward and twined his sausage fingers together. "I have a much better place for you to go. Not many people, quiet town, great fishing, friendly folks. You'll love it," he continued with a faint wheedle in his voice, trying to sound cheerful. He had no idea what the fishing was like in Chandler, but it was all he could think of as an attraction.

Steve sat up straight, immediately suspicious. Bob often reminded him of a troll trying to convince the villagers that they would be happier after they had been eaten. "I hate fishing. You know I hate fishing. What are you up to?"

"Oh, come on. Chandler is a great little town. And you should get a pole. Fishing is relaxing, and you know you need to relax. You are wound tighter than a watch spring," Bob said innocently. "You have been working too hard. That's not good for your health."

"Ah, so that's it," said Steve disgustedly. "I read the papers, you know. This is about the Mrs. Chandler murder. You want me to investigate her murder on my vacation. What gall. Well, get someone else. You have a dozen people sitting around playing pinochle all day long. Get one of them. Find another fall guy. Hey, what about McQuarry? He could beat up a couple of society folks. He wants my job; let him show you how good he would be." Steve rose and headed for the door. He knew that he was just putting off the inevitable. Steve admired and liked Bob, even with all his faults, and he knew what a mess this was. The Connecticut State Police were getting this dropped in their lap because it was such a hot potato that the locals did not want it. Already three days had passed since the killing, and the more time that passed the more difficult a resolution would be. As he strolled toward the door, these thoughts caused him to tune out the chief.

"Steve, STEVE," Bob shouted. "I need you. No one else can do this. Can you imagine Nelson, McQuarry, or Morgan trying to handle this? The press would have them spilling their guts and letting everyone know just what and how we are investigating this. Then the politicos would be second-guessing us and getting in our way."

Steve knew that when the editors of the various newspapers found he was on a case, they understood that they wouldn't get any news from him. He was known as "Stonewall" to the media, ever since, as a rookie, he had let slip something that had allowed a suspect to go free through the timely "passing" of an important witness.

Bob continued in a wheedling tone. "This is going to take a delicate hand, an experienced hand. The best I got," he said soothingly, picking up his extinguished cigar. He scratched a match on the underside of his desk and puffed the cigar alight. "This is big. Think about it: the biggest noise in that part of the state, huge power in the party, lots of moolah, all of that. Only you can do it," he repeated. "The locals have asked for our help."

"No, no, no." Steve waved a hand as if to knock away the cloud of words. He knew this was political dynamite, but he was Bob's cleanup man. "They have asked for our help because they don't want to get in the middle of a mess like this. I haven't had a vacation since I mustered out of the army in 1919, and I got that only because I took two weeks to get back here from New York. No, I am taking this one. Every time I try to take some time off, something comes up and I am the only guy you trust to handle it," he finished theatrically. He wondered what concessions he could get out of Bob and how far to push it. "Find. Someone. Else."

Bob bowed his bowling ball of a head. In almost a whisper, with a hangdog look, he pleaded, "As a favor to me?" Glancing up for a second through his bushy eyebrows to gauge Steve's reaction, he hurried on. "Look. I will give you three weeks, paid, if you will just do this for me. I took you under my wing. I thought we were tight. Your dad and I are old friends. I brought you on board and … " Bob trailed off, causing Steve to wonder if he had just remembered the relationship that existed, or did not exist, between Steve and his father. From the look on Steve's face and the narrowing of his eye, Bob realized he had made a mistake by bringing Thomas Walsh into the conversation. He decided on a new tack: "Didn't I save your job while you were serving? Didn't I give you a promotion when others thought you were too young to be senior grade? Didn't I keep the politicos off your back when you got too close to that club thing? Didn't … "

"Oh, you are pathetic," snapped Steve disgustedly, deciding that the game had gone on long enough. Another week of vacation was probably the best he could do. "Get off your knees. You are one sorry example of a beggar. I'll do it. Not because of this pathetic display, but 'cause I want you to stop before I upchuck in your wastebasket."

The chief became all smiles at once. "Great, great. Now, there is a train leaving at four this afternoon. Go home and get packed. I'll have your ticket all ready and waiting. I made, uh, will make reservations at the Chandler Hotel. Best of everything for my star investigator. This will take no time at all. Then off you go—three weeks with nothing to do except collect your pay."

He paused as if a thought had just struck him. "And don't get suckered by the Chandler daughters. One's a looker, and you know how you get around a pretty woman."

Steve felt the flush rise from his collar. "What's that supposed to mean?" he asked defensively.

"Come on. When you first came here, you had the reputation for tomcatting around with every pretty face. Then you got tangled up with Susan, who treated you like dirt. Then Julie, who dropped you like a hot rock when she got tired of you. Between them you became a monk. You're a monk now. You can't have a normal relationship with a dame with a diagram and instruction book. You think I haven't heard the stories?"

Steve fumed. "You have no idea what you are talking about." His response sounded lame even to himself. Bob's analysis came close enough to the truth to sting.

On a scratch pad, Bob wrote down a name and said, "Contact this guy. He's the head of the Chandler Constabulary. He will let you know all the details. The murder room is roped off and ready for you." He was actually trying to sound jolly, Steve noticed. The pressure must be bad for him to pull the cheerful boss act.

"Constabulary? Don't they have a decent police force?" asked Steve.

"They are company police. The company and town hire American veterans for their watchmen and officers. Very patriotic. You may even find some old friends there," Bob said enthusiastically, rubbing his hands together. "The old man lived in some place when he was a kid where they had a constabulary, and he called his officers that. Don't give me or Captain Daniels a hard time—just find him and get his help. No, wait. I'll send a telegram and he'll meet you at the station." He escorted Steve to the door, patted him on the back, and did the bum's rush on him by gently pushing him out and closing the door before the exasperated investigator could think of any other questions to ask or anything else biting to say.

Steve stood staring through the frosted glass with "Robert Crowder, Chief of Investigations" printed in gold leaf on it. The chief actually thought he had manipulated him. Steve was tempted to take out his .45 and empty it into Bob for his audacity and go on vacation anyway. He mentally tossed a coin; heads for the train and tails for shooting his boss.

He wished his mental coin did not have two heads.

Before heading to the train station, Steve picked up his suitcase. He took a taxi to the *Hartford Morning Post* offices. There, he exchanged greetings with Bobby Ecks, the elevator operator, who looked too young to be out without a sitter. They chatted about the chances of the Red Sox and the

Yankees for the rest of the season while Steve took the elevator to the third floor, where the editorial staff was housed.

He rapped quickly on the news editor's door. At the shouted invitation, he entered the smoke-filled room. Calvin Johnson was a small man who looked like he never combed his hair and always had a cigarette pasted to his lower lip, where it flapped when he spoke. He reminded Steve of Rumpelstiltskin with his white beard; long nose; and thin, hunched body. That is, if Rumpelstiltskin had worn thick horn-rimmed glasses. Steve had never seen him with his tie cinched or his vest buttoned or his sleeves unrolled and fastened. Two gold cuff links sat in the unused ashtray on the right of the cluttered desk. Smashed cigarette butts littered the linoleum floor, and he was constantly brushing ashes from his shirtfront. Steve thought of Calvin as mussed, while he considered Bob slovenly. He wondered if politics, long hours, and dealing with bad news were a cause of dishevelment.

Calvin had been the news editor for the past twenty years and had very nearly gone to jail for writing scathing editorials critical of the Wilson administration during the Great War. He had tiptoed around the Sedition Act like a tightrope walker over Niagara Falls. He had been under investigation when the act was repealed in late 1920.

Steve hung his hat on the tarnished brass rack next to Calvin's battered fedora and suit coat.

Calvin was on one of the four phones that sat on the battered mahogany desk. He held up a finger and continued taking notes, phone pinched between ear and shoulder. Steve walked around the desk and pulled a bottle and glass out of the bottom drawer. Collapsing on the red leather couch, which was worn to softness, he poured himself a drink and lit a cigarette. He listened to his friend talk about the latest scandals in the big-city police departments around the country. With bootlegger money flooding the streets, there was no end of opportunities for payoffs from the top to bottom of law enforcement organizations. He had even heard that the gangs derisively considered the term "copper" to mean that the police could be bought for a penny. From what Steve could overhear, Calvin's paper was preparing a series on the issue. Law-and-order editorials were always popular in election years, and this was an election year. He thought about arguing the matter with his friend but knew that he would get nowhere. Corruption was a favorite topic with the publisher when the opposition party was in power.

Calvin put down the receiver and removed his glasses and tossed them on the cluttered desk. He looked at Steve with a vacant stare, processing the information from the call.

After a few minutes, Calvin pulled out another glass and held it out. "You can at least offer me some of my own booze. Put your asbestos pants on, old buddy. Looks like the usual fire-and-brimstone "criminals are running the prisons" editorials and stories are coming down the pike. Orders from on high. You might want to move to Europe, but it's going socialist. The angle this time is that the new federal bureau is going to get involved and be the avenging angels, sending all corrupt officials—theirs, not ours—to perdition. Unless, of course," he continued cynically, "there is a change in administration, and then we will rail against false accusations. If, that is, we all don't get blown up in the next war a couple years from now." Calvin was disgusted by what he considered the United States's bumbling steps on the world stage. Wilson got the country entangled in the Great War after promising during his reelection campaign to avoid it, and Calvin was positive the government would not be smart enough to avoid the next one.

As Steve poured him a generous dollop of booze, he commented, "As an officer of the law, I should arrest you for failing to observe the Volstead Act."

"Bah. I've had that bottle for years. A Christmas gift from '06 from my dear, departed mother. Besides, who else would let you just drop in and help yourself? What do you want? I'm busy. Unless, of course, you have a hot scoop for me?" His large ears seemed to perk up in anticipation.

"You never had a mother," Steve quipped as he moved to the guest chair by the desk. "You were born in a vat of newspaper ink. How is your mother, by the way? Still a pistol? I've got to get up there and see her again." He continued, answering Calvin's question: "I will have. When I get anything, I'll make sure that you have first crack at it. Now, what do you know about the Chandlers?" Steve asked, freshening his drink before taking another healthy swig.

With an absentminded look, Calvin answered, "Yeah, right. I won't hear from you until the thing's done. But I want it first, an exclusive." He grunted at Steve's nod, knowing it was the best he could expect.

He continued, "Mom's fine. Still a hoot and driving the wife nuts. Insists she's a vegetarian or something. She wants to know when you are going to visit her." The editor leaned back in his chair and closed his eyes. He took a few minutes to organize his eidetic memory. Calvin could remember anything he had ever read or heard, but it might take him a little time to find out where he had filed it.

"Old Josiah Chandler was a clerk in a shipping firm that ran into financial trouble. He had some savings, which he loaned to his employer in exchange for a share in a shipload of trade goods headed to the West Coast and China. When the ship returned, the old man was rich. The owner of the firm retired, and Josiah bought him out. He built the firm into a small powerhouse with a fleet of ships and contacts in San Francisco, Shanghai, Hong Kong, and India. He expanded to the European trade before he died.

"His sons, Peter and Paul, inherited. Religious family. One clause of his will forbade any involvement in the slave trade. Paul died in a storm off the Azores. Peter decided to diversify and bought the current estate along the Connecticut River. He built a big old pile of a house and settled his family there. He hired a manager and retired. He ended up a big noise in the Abolitionist movement and pulled the political strings from the background. The family has carried this on ever since.

"He left everything to his sons, George Washington Chandler and Andrew Jackson Chandler, born twelve years apart. G. W. died during a voyage to the South Seas or maybe running the Confederate blockade. This left everything to his brother, since he had no kith or kin.

"A. J. decided to expand again and started the Chandler Mills, Connecticut Quarry, and Chandler Lumber, along with an expanded farm and breeding complex. Married Alice Jordan in 1875. The marriage joined the fledgling Chandler Mills with the long-established and nearly bankrupt Jordan Cotton operation. Cheaper raw materials. A few government contracts during the Cuban war, and

Chandler Mills and Shipping exploded. The company town of Chandler and a dyeing/printing factory were built around 1890. Huge contracts during the Great War. The medical packs they developed set them on the good side of the Medical Corps. They were branching out into a clothing factory, based in New York.

"A. J. was addressing the company managers in June 1916 when he suffered a heart attack. He lingered for a few days at the Chandler Hospital and died of a second attack. The missus took over without missing a beat. She sold the clothing manufacturer. For a profit. Revamped some of the existing operations, making the company much more profitable. Beat back three takeover attempts by big mills in South Carolina and Georgia. Burned marriage proposals by the bushel basket.

"They had three adopted children, Francis Dubreuil, Catherine Mermet, and Silene. All named after tea roses. The old man was gaga over them, kids and flowers, both. Last year Mrs. Chandler turned over operations to the three of them. Francis got the mills, Catherine moved to South Carolina to run the farming operation, and Silene is head of merchandising and sales. The old lady kept the political power *and* the purse strings. Nothing gets done that affects that area without the blessing of the Chandler political machine. State and federal representative and senatorial aspirants owe their positions to her. She was a heroine during the influenza epidemic.

"Three nights ago, during a meeting of the committee of the A. J. Chandler Memorial Flower Show, they were having a quilting bee to make the annual A. J. Chandler Memorial Lap Quilt, which was to be the best-in-show prize … "

Steve interrupted for the first time: "The old lady was sewing on a quilt?!? For a flower show?"

Calvin gave him a pitying look. "You should get out once in a while, Steve. This is the biggest show in the state. Sponsored by Chandler Mills in memory of Mrs. Chandler's husband. The story is that he would have loved to duplicate one of the great gardens of the world—Versailles, Fontainebleau, Westminster, wherever. He had some famous designer come in and design and build something a little smaller. He would sit on the back porch, which is an acre of granite, sandstone, and marble, and enjoy the view. The missus, early on, made him a lap quilt to keep him warm on those cold Connecticut nights. She was big on quilts—learned from her grandma down in Georgia or South Carolina or somewhere. Anyway, that is the grand prize for the show. When the committee broke up for the evening, she returned to the sewing room. When they looked for her, she was found lying by the quilt wall with a pair of shears in her back. Nobody was around. Nobody heard anything. Nobody saw anything. I imagine Bob Crowder has finagled you into investigating this and your vacation is on hold," he finished, opening his eyes and putting on his glasses.

"Yeah. Any connection between the two deaths? The old man and her?"

"Nah." Calvin lit another cigarette from the stub that was endangering his lower lip. "His was a heart attack, and she was murdered. There was nothing strange about his death and everything about hers. A lot of witnesses for him and none for her. I never heard of shears in the back being natural causes or an accident."

"Anything else you can tell me? Any trouble with the kids? Resentment, fighting among themselves?"

"Kids were unhappy that she still held the reins, but enough to kill her? No clue." He grinned. "You can get more information on the family when you get down there. Julie Boroni is there covering the flower show, and she knows all about them." Calvin laughed knowingly as he finished.

"Julie, huh," Steve grunted. She was a tall, slender honey blonde with deep blue eyes, a great sense of humor, a smoky laugh, and a driving ambition to be a top-flight news reporter. The two of them had been a hot item until Julie started getting visions of "something old, something new, something borrowed, something blue." Steve, who had been allergic to commitment since Susan had dumped him and run off with a Wall Street trader during the war, had put the brakes on and had told her he still wanted to be "friends." A slap, some tears, and a quick exit resulted. She was coldly polite when they met. Steve was giving her time to get over it, but the clock was still ticking on that one, and he had a suspicion that it was not going to work out for him.

After he had wrung Calvin of all he had, Steve hurried out of the building and picked up his suitcase from the reception desk. The doorman waved down a taxi in front of the building. Steve looked at his watch, shoved his suitcase in, and told the driver to step on it because he had a train to catch.

Chapter 3

Steve Walsh, running late, shoved a bill into the cabbie's hand, told him to keep the change, and rushed to the ticket window. Unfortunately, he was behind a stout businessman who was arguing with the counterman. Steve gently shouldered him aside and asked for his ticket over the businessman's vocal disapproval. He sprinted for the train.

He spent the time before supper in the club car going over his notes. A scanty meal of Dover sole, steamed carrots, and creamed potatoes in the dining car was eaten alone. As he once more reviewed what he knew of the murder, his sinking feeling that it was going to be ugly was reinforced. Too many tentacles of the political world were wrapped around it. When a local jurisdiction gives up control, it is usually because of politics, and Mrs. Chandler had been a power in the state. Give him a clean, quiet gangland murder anytime. For all his skill with politicians, Bob Crowder was feeling trapped. He was looking for a scapegoat before he took on that role himself. Steve knew that Bob would sacrifice him to save his own skin—regretfully, of course. Friendship went only so far with Bob. He had a wife and three kids, so Steve knew he would not fall on his sword for anyone. Bob was more practical than noble.

The rhythm of the iron wheels over the joins of the rails lulled him into a state between sleep and wakefulness. His mind drifted to Julie. He saw her as the young woman he had first met as a cub reporter. Her blond hair had swung in a loose mane around her fresh-scrubbed face. He had just finished a long and difficult case with a nasty, killing band of bootleggers. The Volstead Act had just been passed, and the competition for bootlegging territory had been fierce and sudden. An Irish gang and their Italian counterparts had engaged in several shoot-outs, and innocent bystanders had been hit. The press was howling for blood, and the case had gotten a high profile. Steve had led a dedicated team of officers from the Connecticut State Police and stopped the war.

Julie had taken it upon herself to write the story in order to get out of another assignment she had been given, a column on cooking, in which she was providing recipes and advice for the paper's readers. Her print persona was that of a fifty-year-old grandmotherly woman. Even then she had a driving urge to get into the meat of reporting: exposés, murders, and other high-profile pieces. She had faced Steve down with enough gumption and intelligent questions to impress him. Instead of his usual snarl and silence in response to the press, he had accepted her invitation to dinner and a story. It had not hurt that she had the rangy build and blue eyes that had always stirred something in him.

Her story had gotten ripped to shreds, figuratively, by Calvin, who sat her down and told her two things: to do the job she was assigned and to get the schoolgirl journalism out of her system before she tried something serious. Calvin had ripped her copy in half, literally, and told her that when she could tell the same story with half the words, he might possibly read another piece she wrote. The dressing down was brutal, but Steve knew his friend was impressed with her potential. She had kept her job.

With the pain of losing Susan just starting to fade, he had taken Julie out a couple of times, just to drop a few hints into her shell-like ears, of course, about where the news was. Over the next few years Julie had gotten serious, but Steve was still gun-shy. All along, he tried to convince himself that he was bachelor material and he would play the field, even though he was seeing Julie exclusively. He liked her a lot but felt the situation was getting too close to serious, and he had tried to lower the temperature. Steve hoped she understood his views and would handle the situation professionally. The fact that he did not understand his views meant that he could not communicate them to her. Maybe he should rethink his feelings about marriage.

He sat up quickly enough to startle the attendant behind the refreshment counter, where he was polishing clean glasses. Steve rubbed his eyes and slammed the door on his thoughts. He did *not* need to be wandering down those roads. His fun-time, girl-in-every-town bachelor's life was *not* going to be altered by maudlin thoughts. That is, when he found the time to start assembling this harem. He was *not* looking for a wife and kids and a white picket fence in the country. He came close to convincing himself of that.

The train pulled into the Chandler station in a cloud of steam and screeching brakes. Steve exited and assisted a lady in mink. Her smile gave him a spark of hope, until he realized it was for a tall, wealthy-looking man whose suit probably cost more than his monthly salary. "Your day still hasn't improved any, Steve," he muttered as he retrieved his suitcase.

The almost palatial station, built of dressed stone under a slate roof, stood proudly across the platform. Freshly painted window and doorframes gleamed white in the slanting evening sun. Neatly stacked baggage and freight waited. Uniformed attendants assisted debarking passengers with their baggage, while the stationmaster quickly and efficiently unloaded the freight. The foyer of the station opened into a well-lit room with a grilled counter and a waiting room with padded benches rather than the splintery specimens that Steve was used to. The notices were neatly arranged and, at first glance, appeared more artistic than utilitarian. The arrival/departure slate markings were almost calligraphically drawn. Steve was impressed.

From the station doorway, Steve saw a short, blocky man in an impeccably tailored dark green uniform standing by the exit door across the waiting room. A blank face was topped by short, dark hair. Steve observed a slab of nose, slightly off-center from a poorly set break, between deep, shaggy brows and a neatly clipped mustache. One ear was misshapen, and the man's large hands were scarred. Steve realized that he was looking at a former pugilist. His compressed lips were almost invisible and his posture rigid. An aura of disapproval radiated off the statue-like figure.

The patch on his shoulder identified the Chandler Constabulary, and a silver shield shone on his left breast. A black patent-leather belt held a pistol in a holster with the flap down, pouches for ammunition, and a pair of handcuffs. He held a flat-brimmed, campaign-style hat modeled on the military cover issued during the Great War. His shoes shone in the bright illumination of the train station.

He stepped up and introduced himself as William "Buck" Daniels, captain of the Chandler Constabulary, in a flat, unfriendly voice. "I have a car outside," he said after a brief handshake and a stiff exchange of pleasantries. They went through the station, and Steve put his bag in the back seat of the 1919 Pilot sedan, which had a logo on its front doors matching the design on the captain's shoulder patch. They climbed into the vehicle and settled into the seats.

"Where to?" asked the captain.

Steve sighed. He had gotten up early to finish the reports, been running around all day, and was tired. "Has the crime scene been locked down?"

"Yes," the other replied, staring straight ahead through the windshield. "As soon as I got there. Then I called the county sheriff, and he said not to touch anything. Technically, he has jurisdiction over this because Chandler is unincorporated. It's a little confusing to an outsider. Basically, the Chandlers run the county as their own fiefdom. What they decide is rubber-stamped by the County Council. They wanted the town and officers as independent as possible. The Chandler Constabulary is considered an auxiliary force to the sheriff's department. Our town council doesn't pass anything unless it is reviewed by the county attorney. Like I say, probably confusing to an outsider.

"Anyway, the sheriff said he would get someone from the State Office down as soon as possible." His voice carried an edge of irritation.

"So, the sheriff didn't want anything to do with this either," observed Steve. "Looks like it's more of a hot potato than I figured. Well, you did the right thing. Too bad you aren't incorporated and don't have a full organization here. We could have kept the whole investigation local. Oh, well, did the county handle the preliminary investigation before calling us in?"

"Yes. They took photos and dusted for prints. The body was removed to the county morgue, and their coroner should have performed the autopsy by now. Sheriff Duggan told me that the reports would be forwarded to the state."

Steve snorted. "Then they called us in to do the investigation here in Chandler. Duggan must be not only nervous but running scared. I hate politics in an investigation." He glanced at Buck. "You and I have to get those reports before they get lost in the maze in Hartford. We'll use your boys for local scut work, if you don't mind. I don't want any of the sheriff's people around if they are thinking more about avoiding bad press than solving this thing."

He paused for a second. "There probably isn't anything in the reports, though. Thinking about it, if evidence was there that pointed to a killer or if the autopsy had any surprises, the sheriff would have stepped in to nab someone and grab the glory. Right now, I will assume that no one is identified and the cause of death was the stabbing. We do want to get the lab and autopsy reports, though, just to be sure."

"Inspector Walsh, we may … "

"Steve. Call me Steve, 'cause I have a feeling that we are going to be working together for a while. Damn that Bob," he finished in a mutter.

"Okay, Steve." Buck sounded a little more relaxed and turned toward his passenger. "Now, we are a small department. There are only twelve of us, and two are night watchmen at the mills. We usually only handle drunks on Saturday night, vandalism, and truants. Murder is out of our league, and I really do appreciate you coming down. And your attitude. Whenever there was a need to bring in the county, for bootleggers or hijackings or what not, we were pretty much treated as idiot children."

Steve twisted around in his seat, fished out a cigarette, and lit it with a match he flicked alight with his thumbnail. He opened the window and flipped the burnt match out. "Let's clear the air, shall we? You are here on the ground. You know the players and the terrain. The worst thing I could do would be to twist your tail and end up having to cover a lot of territory I shouldn't have to with you sitting like a grumpy bear in the background. I will be running the show; don't have any doubts about that. You have trouble with local or state yahoos; I will take care of it. You and I are going to work on this together, if you're willing. Otherwise, stay out of my way or I will hammer you like a tenpenny nail for hampering my investigation." He took a drag and blew the smoke out of the corner of his mouth toward the half-open window while locking eyes with Buck.

For the first time, Buck showed an expression other than that of an Easter Island statue. With a grin he held out his hand again. "Inspector Walsh, you have a team. Now, where to?"

"If the crime scene is secure, I could do with a decent feed, a drink, and a bed. Train fare is a little sparse for my tastes. I am supposed to have a room booked at the Chandler Hotel. Does it have a restaurant, or is there a decent one nearby?"

Buck started the car and drove through well-ordered streets lined with elms, surrounded by freshly painted black ironwork dotting the sidewalks. The houses were all in a light brown color that closely imitated the tint of the station.

Windows, doorways, and porch rails gleamed white. The homes were of different layouts to fit different-sized families. There was not the feel of a typical company town. Steve saw an air of pride in the village that attested to the goodwill of the contented residents. Children's toys were scattered in many of the yards, and trees with tire swings shaded the homes. The business district consisted of buildings of quarried stone—the material used at the station—well-lit streets, and stone planters with flowers and wrought-iron benches at intervals. There was a hardware store, several churches, a variety store, a shoe store, and a haberdashery, among other businesses. The retail spaces generally had office or living space above.

The city hall sat in the center of the plaza, facing south, its cupola topped by a statue of Josiah Chandler, as Buck informed him. The library, with its gardens, faced the government building. A large grocery covered a long block to the east. Along the north side of the plaza was a six-story building with "Chandler Hotel" on the marquee. It seemed surprisingly large for a town the size of Chandler. The final side of the plaza was taken up by the Chandler Constabulary building. It shared the block with a theater/auditorium displaying colorful posters advertising Douglas Fairbanks's *Robin Hood* and *When Knighthood Was in Flower*. A line of customers was queued up at the brightly lit ticket booth, where a young woman was dispensing tickets. There were uniformed doormen stationed at the entrance. Buck drove slowly around the city hall to give Steve a good view.

"Pretty fancy for a small-town theater," observed Steve, rubbernecking.

"The Chandlers believe that their employees are human, unlike a lot of mill owners. Grandpa Chandler saw a lot of company towns that were little better than shacks and saw how much trouble there was from Reds and agitators and dissatisfied employees and decided to try something else," Buck said with pride.

"The family uses the rents to keep things nice. The mayor and city council run the town, and they always got together with Mrs. Chandler to plan new projects or repairs," Buck said earnestly.

Steve glanced over to find that his companion was sincere and, moreover, appeared to believe in this theory himself. *Not just a run-of-the-mill company thug,* he thought. *Good.*

Buck parked in front of a "No Parking" sign. At Steve's raised eyebrows, Buck grinned and said, "Perks of the office." Steve exited into the summer night, cooled by the Connecticut River that reflected the shimmering sunset of gold, red, and orange. The uniformed hotel doorman greeted them, passed Steve's bag to a bellhop, and ushered them through the outside door. Buck led the way to the front desk on the right, across a wide lobby. On the left, Steve noticed the opening to the restaurant and a three-seat shoeshine stand. A cigar counter and a newsstand flanked the elevator cage opposite the revolving front door.

"Hi, Pete," Buck said to the clerk. "Got a customer for you. This is Inspector Steve Walsh from the State Police. You have a reservation for him."

The scrawny man behind the desk stuttered, "Y-y-yeah. We-we've got a room s-s-saved for h-h-him. S-s-sign here, s-s-sir."

Steve added his name to the register and gave the bellhop his key and a two-bit tip. He then followed the captain through the lobby to the restaurant. They were given a table in the corner, led there by a tuxedo-clad maître d' who handed them menus and left with a polite smile. Steve looked around and saw a real restaurant: muted lighting, crisp table-cloths on the well-spaced tables, and full table settings. Not like the hotel coffee shops of his experience. The dark walls and tasteful furnishings showed that a professional eye had been used in selecting the decor. *The Chandlers were definitely not typical,* he thought.

Steve decided on his choice and turned to Buck. "Let's clear the underbrush out, shall we? Do you have any suspects in mind? I understand that there were a half-dozen people from the show committee. Several servants. The three kids. Those were in the house. What about others? Unhappy workers from the mills? Any agitation from the Reds or radical union people? Any strangers in town? How many people can really be listed as suspects?" He took out a notebook and pencil from an inside pocket of his jacket.

Buck shook his head. "I would bet that none of the Chandler people here in town could be guilty. Unless there is a secret reason that someone hated the old lady. I'm sure it would have gotten around."

The waitress approached, and Steve ordered a steak, baked potato, and vegetables. "Just coffee, black, May. Thanks," said the captain.

He turned back to Steve. "There are a lot of strangers in town. Mostly for the flower show and the Regional Agricultural Fair. Mostly, at this point, those are vendors or carny people. A week from now, there will be a lot of fairgoers swarming the town. But Mrs. Chandler had a wall built around Chandler Hill, where the house stands. There is broken glass cemented on top, and it is pretty hard to get in. There are gates through each side, but all were locked. I checked. I can't see why any stranger would want to kill Mrs. Chandler anyway. She still had her jewelry and nothing was missing from the room or body. No easy getaways and the main road is on the other side of town. There is an old farm road, but the dust from a car would linger, and it is a long way to walk from where it hits the main road.

"Same thing with the workers. A long time ago, Mr. Chandler said he would pay the going wage of any other cotton mill in the state. There was no reason to resent the company. They never had to strike to get any demands met.

"Mr. and Mrs. Chandler kept the town nice. The rents and profits from the different businesses, whether the company owned them or they were rented out, were reasonable, and they went back into keeping the town. There is a council and mayor who make decisions, and they are all elected by the citizens—women too, now that the Nineteenth Amendment was passed. Some places, the workers are kept in virtual slavery, always owing the company store, but here that isn't the case. Most of the fruit, vegetables, and meat are produced on the farms on company land."

"They own farms?" queried Steve, feigning ignorance of Calvin's information. He was willing to hear things he already knew rather than have his informant skip something that might later turn out to be important.

"They own several thousand acres. Mr. Chandler's grandfather bought it years ago with profits from his shipping company. Mr. Chandler expanded in a new direction.

They already had the farms, quarry, and timber operations. Cotton was cheap after the Civil War, and he built the mill.

"Then there is the pin. It seemed to point to someone in the house," Buck finished.

May brought his meal, and Steve liberally salted his steak and vegetables. He added slabs of butter to his baked potato, but before he took a bite, he paused. "Tell me about the pin," he said.

"When she was found, she was lying under the quilt wall. She had reached up and shoved a pin into the quilt. Probably from the pincushion on her wrist. The pin was in the backing cloth, which had flowers and writing in Latin printed on it. It was called something like 'Giardino Latino,' according to Mrs. Black, head of the committee."

"What's this 'quilt wall' thing?" Steve asked.

"Part of one wall is covered with cork. Apparently, they pin the pieces of the quilt—squares, I think they're called—there so they can see what it would look like before they sew it together. Last week they put it together. This week, they were doing the finish work for the show next week. Then there is a big unveiling at the Chandler mansion, where all the swells get together to ooh and aah and have something to eat. Then the quilt is taken to the flower pavilion, when the show starts, to be put on display until the awards are given."

Steve nodded and took a drink of water, grimacing. "Are you sure there isn't a speakeasy around here?"

Buck laughed. "Not in this town. You had better bring it yourself if you're thirsty."

"Barbarians!" he muttered. He regretted emptying his small flask on the trip down. "All right. This dying clue. Does it point to anyone in particular?"

"It points to everybody, in a way. The main color of the backing cloth was black. Mrs. Black is the executive secretary of the flower show. Latin points to Professor Poltovski, who teaches ancient languages at the college. And the rose part points to Miss Carlyle, who is in charge of setting up the floral displays at the show and is a botanist, and to Mrs. Flowers, the treasurer. The translation of the name, Latin Garden, points to Mr. and Mrs. Jones, who own the local nursery and provide all the plants for the displays, though that is a stretch. Oh, and the pin was shoved through a printed tea rose, and all the children were named after tea roses, Mr. Chandler's favorite."

"That would make me want to kill my mom," muttered Steve, taking another bite.

Buck took a refill from May and continued, "Do you want to go up to the house, then?"

"Nah, I'm beat. If you have the place bottled up, I'll look it over tomorrow. Are the kids there? I may as well start with them."

"Francis and Silene are there, but Catherine is here in the hotel. With her husband." The way he said it made Steve look up and arch an eyebrow. "Catherine ended up marrying her manager," Buck continued. "The one Mrs. Chandler transferred from here to run things and make sure that Catherine didn't tangle things up. Mrs. Chandler didn't have too much respect for the girl's judgment, and, the rumor is, there was some trouble that the family bottled up. They came up here to tell the old lady about the marriage, and she didn't take it well. Threatened to cut her out of the will and fire the girl and Paul Sullivan. For all her generosity,

Mrs. Chandler liked to have control over things, including her children's lives."

"I don't suppose she has another alibi besides her husband?"

"No. They had room service, and the waiter didn't see her either coming or going," replied the captain.

"Tomorrow, can you pick me up in the morning at eight o'clock? I want to go over the place." Steve took the last bite of steak and pushed his plate away.

After his meal he took his leave of Buck. Steve retrieved his key from the desk, asked for a wake-up call at seven o'clock in the morning, and took the elevator to the top floor. He stopped for a second when he saw the bright brass plaque next to the entry, which read: "Presidential Suite." He opened the door and stared around in surprise.

Steve was used to small, dark, cheap rooms when he traveled for an investigation. Water-stained walls and broken-down furniture were more the norm than the comfortable, airy environment of the room in which he stood. The suite was as big as his flat, maybe bigger. This one had marble floors, two rooms, and a bottle of champagne in a sweating ice bucket. A fruit basket and a gaily wrapped bottle of Canadian whiskey sat on the large round table in the center of the living room. A card read "Welcome" and was signed "Julie" in a familiar masculine hand with six hearts and a single arrow piercing all of them. When he turned the card over, he saw, in the same scrawl, "Really, it's me. Calvin. Remember my scoop. Ha ha."

He snorted at the sick humor and used some of the ice from the bucket to fix himself a drink. He downed it before putting on his pajamas and going to bed. As he drifted off, he wondered when Calvin had managed to get the bottle and note delivered.

Chapter 4

The wake-up knock came too early for Steve. He communicated with monosyllables until he had had his first cup of coffee in the hotel restaurant. While he nursed it and waited for his toast, bacon, and eggs, Buck walked in looking neat and cheerful. Steve gave him a good morning grunt as he sat down.

"You look like you had a rough night," Buck said with a laugh in his voice.

"Mornings should start at noon," Steve muttered.

"Well, we have a full day. Mrs. Black left a message with my wife. She wants to talk to you right away. Actually, she insists—no, demands—that she talk to you immediately."

"Okay. Did she give you any idea what she wanted?"

"No. I am only a lowly constable. You are a lofty state inspector and are in charge, so she wants to talk with you and you alone. I told her to come to the house at nine this morning, but she will be there at eight thirty, I'm sure."

Once Steve's breakfast arrived, he directed all his attention to his plate. Buck ordered coffee and chatted with the locals at adjacent tables. By the time Steve had wiped up the last of the egg with a scrap of toast and finished his third cup of coffee, he was finally feeling human. He signed for his meal and dropped off his key at the front desk. The two men left the hotel and walked down the street to the constabulary building in the morning sun, a light breeze tugging at Steve's coat. They drove off in Buck's official vehicle, directed to the Chandler house.

The mansion, Chandler House, stood at the top of a low hill overlooking the town, farms, and mills. It reminded Steve of the country Georgian homes he had visited in England. It was unadorned, a rectangle with a steep roof and jutting dormers. The stone was the same local material evident in other buildings in Chandler. Sunlight sparkled off rows of windows, and Steve thought it looked ready for the members of a hunt club to come pouring around the corner, following a pack of dogs encouraged with horns. The lawn was elegantly manicured, with tastefully placed trees and brilliant patches of flowers. A white gazebo stood on a wide expanse of grass. The manor and grounds were surrounded by an impressive stone wall, and there was a guard hut of the same material next to the main gate. Behind the hut was a small cottage. An old man, hoeing in the diminutive vegetable garden, waved a salute to the captain when they motored past.

As they drove up the long, curving drive, Steve observed, "They must have been afraid of something if they needed this huge wall. Reminds me of some of the castles I saw in England."

Buck explained with a slight trace of amusement in his voice: "During the '20–'21 recession, Mrs. Chandler took the workers who would have been laid off and set them to constructing the wall. Mr. Chandler was always joking about adding a wall and moat. She had some working at the quarry she reopened; some she had haul the stone on company trucks. She made sure no one was laid off. Even if the Harding administration hadn't cleaned up the mess so rapidly, I think she would have kept it up with projects until the depression had ended or she went broke. The old guy is Huskins, the retired head gardener. Mrs. Chandler installed him here at the gatehouse when he couldn't handle his job anymore. Like the other workers who have been pensioned off. There is a string of cottages down near the farms, and Mrs. Chandler gives the farmers a little to keep an eye on them. A boarding house in town provides rooms for others. I think there are around 20, 22 pensioners now."

"You mean the Chandlers pay the upkeep on these people?" asked Steve.

"Yup. As long as they want to stay, and they will pay for the plots when they pass. A. J. Chandler had a sign in his office that read: 'People are not a disposable commodity.'"

Buck went on, passionately, "During the influenza epidemic, Mrs. Chandler had one of the lines at the mill produce muslin for masks, which were issued to all workers and their families. During one period, the Chandler Hotel was turned into a hospital, and she spent twelve to fourteen hours a day as a volunteer nurse."

"Wow," was all that Steve could think of to say. It was a rare employer who would take care of workers who were past their time or sick. He was convinced that Buck was a member of the choir. "Okay. I understand. The Chandlers aren't your typical robber barons."

Buck drove around the sparkling fountain in the center of the graveled turnaround and parked. The fountain had a square stone base two feet tall. The center featured a series of three tiers, topped by a stone mermaid holding a shell from which the water flowed. Lily pads floated on the water, with small orange and white fish darting among the roots of the plants.

The officers were met at the door by the uniformed butler. "Welcome, gentlemen. My name is Jeremy, Inspector Walsh," he informed Steve in a clipped British accent, with a slight bow. He took their hats after welcoming them in that upper-crust tone Steve had become familiar with during the Great War.

Steve stopped and took a minute to stare. He was standing before a large mahogany table with intricate carving around its edge. A beautiful round lace cloth with a Georgian silver bowl containing a flower arrangement stood in its center. The large marble-floored foyer spread out around him, its green and white squares gleaming with the care showered on it. Directly opposite the front door were two wide, sweeping staircases leading to the second floor. The banisters were an open invitation for any child. A wide landing connected the staircases at the midway point, from which they continued on in opposite directions. On the ground floor, halls extended to the left and right. Their front walls were lined with wide windows harboring stone benches between them. The opposite wall of each hall contained antique furniture, and a suit of armor stood guard halfway down. Sunlight streamed through the windows, raising highlights on the wood and steel. There were two doors leading off each hall, and both halls ended at double doors opening onto the terrace. Directly ahead, another wide corridor led between the staircases to another set of doors onto the terrace. More doors lined each side of the main hall.

"Impressive, isn't it?" said the captain with a grin. "I always like to see the first reaction. At least your mouth didn't flap open."

"Probably would have if I hadn't seen some of those English country homes. This is small potatoes compared to the ones that house the Duke of This and the Earl of That," answered Steve.

The captain led the way to the first door on the left, where a constable sat in an ornate chair next to the door, presumably stationed there to ensure that no one entered. She was dressed in the same uniform as Buck, and Steve looked at her in surprise.

"So, not all of your constables are veterans, then?" he asked.

Buck gave him an amused look. "Steve, meet Constable Ruth Beckstrom. She served overseas in the United States Army during the war." Ruth stood and snapped a smart military salute. "Ruth Beckstrom, Signal Corps, Female Telephone Operators Unit, United States Army, sir." She dropped her hand and held it out to him. "I served in Southampton, England, and Chaumont, France. I trained under Grace Banker in Camp Franklin, Maryland, before being deployed with the American Expeditionary Force. I am one of the Hello Girls. After the war, we were treated as redheaded stepchildren, but I consider myself a veteran."

Steve extended his hand, and she gave it a short, sharp shake. "Captain Steve Walsh, United States Military Intelligence Liaison. Stationed in London." He grinned and continued, "Didn't have much in the way of training. Got shanghaied by an old law school friend who needed someone to hold his hand."

Ruth gave him an appraising look and said with a teasing smile, "You can hold my hand any time." Her cherubic face and friendly eyes caused Steve to take another look at the whole package. She was five feet and a little, and the uniform hid what he guessed to be a tidy figure. Her heart-shaped face broke into a full grin, and the dimples showed on her full cheeks. Pale blue eyes sparkled and seemed to draw him in.

Buck's laugh was almost a roar. "Careful, there. Her fiancé is a Golden Gloves champion and tougher than wet leather."

Steve snapped back to reality and colored. "Pleased to make your acquaintance, and I look forward to working with you." He shot a glance at Buck. "At a comfortable distance," he added.

Ruth gave a little laugh. "Oh, Gino wouldn't hurt a fly. You know that, Buck." She turned to Steve. "He's a flyer with the Gates Flying Circus. He's in the Midwest, performing for the next three weeks." She blushed at the implication that her statement indicated an invitation.

Buck stepped in to cover her embarrassment. "All right, back to business. I have had someone here since I got the call about the murder and sealed the room to everyone except for the sheriff's men."

Buck pulled a knife from his pocket and pushed the button to flick open the six-inch blade. He slit the large square of paper attached to the door and jamb and depressed the lever.

Steve stood in the opening and turned around to face the hall. He studied right and left and then gazed out the window in front of him for a few seconds. Anyone in the drive would be able to see the door, especially with the hall lights on. He turned and entered the room. It was large, with a fireplace on the right wall flanked by floor-to-ceiling built-in bookcases. Directly ahead, pictures, plaques, and knickknack shelves covered the walls. Below them were a reading area, a dower chest, and a record console. On the left side, a cork wall held the quilt. A long table stood back from the wall, chairs lining the near side. Overstuffed armchairs and sofas were scattered around the center of the room in a conversational arrangement.

Steve studied the quilt. His familiarity with quilts consisted of the spreads covering the beds that his mother, his grandmother Mimi, and their friends had created on winter nights. As a child he would listen to the conversation of the women who gathered to sew fair entries and birth and wedding gifts. Usually, the quilts consisted of square blocks made of pieces of old cloth. On occasion, they would experiment with other styles—Log Cabin, map, stars, and other patterns. Steve smiled as he remembered the women sitting in a circle chatting, their needles flashing in the firelight. He was ever ready to run errands: fill coffee cups, replenish the cookie plate, gather scraps. His smile faded when he recalled his father's silent disapproval of his participation in what he considered women's work.

He shook the memories out of his mind and admired the flowers on the wall. It looked more like a picture than a quilt.

The surfaces were filmed with fingerprint dust, left by the sheriff's office investigators. A piece of torn notepaper lay on the floor next to a splash of blood three feet from the door. A sturdy table stood next to the door. It contained a silver tray with thimbles scattered on it. There was another tray with scissors laid out neatly according to size. A space showed at the end of the graduated row, the large end. Lastly, there was a large thread box, decorated with the words "Chandler Fine Thread" in gold, containing three glass-fronted drawers and another narrower drawer at the top. When Steve opened several of the larger drawers, he saw they contained spools of thread organized like a rainbow. The top narrow drawer held packets of needles of various sizes.

Another table along the quilt wall held precut swatches of cloth. Obviously, these were ready to be used for the quilt, though it looked to Steve like the quilt was finished. An ornate low-sided box held two rows of pincushions that could be worn on the wrist, attached with an elastic band.

Several more ragged pieces of paper led to the foot of the quilt wall, each marking a dark stain. Buck stated, "She was stabbed here, by the door. We figured that the killer panicked and got out, fast. He or she probably thought this was like in the stories or moving pictures—one stab and the victim was dead. In this case, Mrs. Chandler managed to crawl the ten feet to the quilt and take a pin from her wrist pincushion and jam it in the quilt before she died."

They crossed the room as he outlined his theory. Steve took a closer look at the quilt fastened vertically on the wall. A lower corner had been folded up to expose the backing cloth, on which another paper scrap had been tacked. This had a hole torn in the center and was marked with the word "pin." There were six oblongs of cloth stuck along the top and next to the folded-over section. They matched either the olive and magenta border or the pale swatches of the background. He lay down on the polished wooden floor and reached up. "How long were her arms?" he asked.

"Well, we estimate the pin was about at her farthest reach if she was raised on her elbow," Buck answered.

The inspector got to his feet and dusted off his hands and carefully brushed his suit with his pocket-handkerchief. He shot his cuffs and turned to Buck. "She knew her killer," he mused.

"Yeah. That's what we think. If she didn't know him or her, Mrs. Chandler would have ushered them in and the killer would have been in front of her. But she must have led them, because there was no reason for her to move further into the room and then step back or to turn her back to the room and face the door. Also, try to pick up another pair of scissors from the tray without making a sound. We had three men and a woman try several times and none of them could do it. From that, we determined that the murderer hadn't snuck in on her.

"Now, I can only go by my experiences with my mom, but when she was angry and wanted to end the conversation, she turned her back on me and concentrated on something else. That would give the murderer his, or her, chance to stab Mrs. Chandler. I figure that the killer said something and used the sound to cover when he grabbed the shears."

Steve picked up a pair and put them back. "Good thinking." He looked around the room again, his glance touching on the door. "Wouldn't the rest of this committee have heard the voices?"

"Probably not," answered Buck. "They were mostly out back on the terrace or in the dining room talking. I had to shout before the constables I stationed out there heard me, when I tested that theory."

Steve pointed to the chairs scattered in front of the table. "Were those chairs like that when you got here?"

Buck thumbed through the notebook extracted from a breast pocket and found a diagram. "A couple of them have been nudged a little, but none of them were moved more than a couple of inches, if that. Why?"

"I just thought that if one had been knocked over and blocked her off from the door, she might have had a reason to crawl to the quilt instead of out the door."

Glancing again at his notebook, Buck said, "She was hurt pretty bad. The rest of the committee were too far away, in the dining room or out on the terrace. That's through the foyer and down the center hall. Even the servants were back there or in the kitchen, downstairs. Jeremy and Susanne and Annette, the maids, were serving and keeping the buffet full or pouring refreshments. Cookie was in the kitchen." At Steve's interested look, he continued with a grin, "No. Tea, coffee, sodas—that kind of thing." He laughed at the inspector's faux shudder.

Steve asked, "All right, who was where during the time Mrs. Chandler was gone from her guests? When was that, by the way? And how long between the time she left them and when they found her?"

Flipping pages until he found the timeline he had prepared, Buck answered, "They broke up in here at about eight o'clock. They adjourned to the dining room, where the buffet was set up on the sideboard. The plates, utensils, and napkins were at one end and the food laid out at the other. The middle had candles and flowers and decorations.

It was the usual: those little cakes, macaroni salads, finger sandwiches, custards, and so on. Mrs. Chandler didn't eat anything, according to the rest, just made some chitchat. Made the rounds and made sure that there was enough of everything and everything was running smoothly. Most of the others figured she was there for fifteen to thirty minutes.

"Usually she went back to the sewing room to look at the quilt after the group had finished. No one knows what she planned on doing. You know, make changes to the quilt, finish up a stitch or two, or consider what to do next or whatever." Before Steve could ask about the rest of the committee, Buck proceeded: "The rest of them loaded up their plates and either sat at the table or wandered onto the terrace or around the gardens. And nobody kept track of anyone else, especially. No one stayed the whole time with another person. Mrs. Black went into the little area behind the dining room where the silver and dishes were kept. I almost checked her bag before she left. Miss Carlyle visited the powder room, upstairs. You get the idea. It was like any get-together—everyone was wandering around, like I said, and no one was keeping track of anyone else. At least, that they admitted to.

"From the dining room, you can, and just about all of them did, exit onto the terrace. Once outside, you can swing around the house and reenter the house from either end of the gallery along the front windows. There is also a door to the terrace from the ballroom, through which you can get to the main corridor across from the dining room. The bathroom is upstairs.

"As close as we can tell, it took only two, three minutes to stab Mrs. Chandler and beat it. I don't think anyone who was here can be out of the running for killer."

While Buck was talking, they had walked down to the main hall. Steve gave a cursory glance into the dining room and made a circuit out the back, onto the terrace, around the left side of the house, past the ballroom, and back through the corridor door to the sewing room.

Suddenly, a whirlwind burst through the front door. It was hard to see who was wrapped in the heavy black coat, though it was a warm day outside. Buck groaned as a tiny woman charged toward them, shedding the coat on the floor. She was followed by Jeremy, who picked up the garment. "Inspector, Inspector. I need to talk to you."

The captain turned to Steve. "Mrs. Black."

"Excuse me, sir. She was rather forceful, and I tried my best," the butler informed them calmly.

Steve ignored the little bantam who kept trying to get his attention. "Thank you, Jeremy. Is there somewhere we can conduct interviews?"

"Yes, sir." He bowed them to the other end of the corridor. "I readied the morning room for just that purpose. If you will follow me, please." He led them past the foyer to a sitting room. "Mrs. Chandler used this as her private office," Jeremy informed them.

Steve held out a chair for Mrs. Black in front of the desk. "Please, stay here, Mrs. Black."

He moved toward the door, but the woman jumped out of the chair and began to follow him. Steve spun around and pointed a finger at the chair. "Sit down. Stay there. If you don't, you can wait your turn to talk to me. Sometime this afternoon or even tomorrow. Maybe." He spoke to her much as he would a disobedient puppy. He had met these insistent types before and knew that he had to show them who was the boss immediately.

Under his stern look, she returned to her seat with tight lips and stiff shoulders. With a sniff thrown in Steve's direction, she hoisted herself into the chair, clutching her oversized leather bag tightly in her lap.

The inspector quickly closed the door to muffle Buck's snicker. "Are we all done with the crime scene? Got anything else in your little book?"

"No. You are stuck with talking with her. Good luck. I don't envy you."

"You can only hope, friend," Steve said, taking a firm grip on his arm. "You are not leaving me alone with her. As you insisted, you are part of this investigation, and that means you sit in on the interrogations."

He turned to Jeremy. "Is Mr. Francis Chandler ready to talk with us yet?"

"No, sir. Annette just brought his breakfast and newspapers up to him. He rings when he is dressed and ready for them. Normally, he requires a half hour for breakfast, sir. He informed me that he would be ready for your interview when he finishes. And Miss Silene does not arise until later in the morning," Jeremy said, answering Steve's next question proactively.

Steve grunted. He had wanted Mrs. Black to wait and stew in her own juices.

Chapter 5

The captain shook his head with what looked like dread and followed Steve. He moved a chair next to the door and sat. Steve rounded the Louis Quatorze desk and took a seat. He looked up, unconsciously expecting to see the door directly across the room in front of him. The desk was off-center, and it struck him that there was an inordinate amount of space to the left. He mentally shrugged the thought off and turned his attention to Mrs. Black.

Perched on the edge of her seat, Mrs. Black reminded Steve of the crows he had seen in his father's fields. They were the same shiny black. The woman's dress was black bombazine and made a whispering noise whenever she moved. Her eyes brought to mind round ebony stones as she stared at him with her head sitting on her scrawny, tucked neck. A midnight hat, with a long, matching feather, covered her head like a helmet. Even her hands were covered by dark lace gloves. Her face was the only part of her that was not her signature color. It was pinched and scrunched tight in an angry expression, and Steve wondered if the expression was permanent or passing.

"Now, Mrs. Black … "

"We need to be able to finish the quilt. We have only this week until the Chandler flower show starts, and we will not have any time to work on it after the fair starts on Monday," she interrupted.

Steve tried not to smile. Even her voice sounded like that of a crow's. "Of course. Captain Daniels and I are almost done with the room. You may use it after I give it one more look. But you will have to wait until this evening." She was prepared to continue the argument, and his ready agreement was unexpected. She sat frozen in surprise, her mouth open and finger raised to emphasize her next point.

Before she could recover, Steve pressed on. "Mrs. Black, what can you tell me about the night of the murder? Where you and the other members of the committee were between the time you broke for the night and the time the body was discovered?"

"Oh," she croaked. She paused for a moment to collect her thoughts. "We worked until eight o'clock. I wanted to continue, but Alice felt we should break for the evening as we had been laboring since five o'clock. We all adjourned to the dining room, where a delicious buffet had been prepared for us. Alice mingled with everyone and then, as was her custom, returned to the sewing room. She liked to review our labors, to decide which of us were holding up our end of the job and which were not." From her tone, Steve thought it likely shirkers would be shot. "I wanted to go with her, but she insisted, as always, that she wanted a solitary moment to herself. I did not understand her reluctance to have me along. After all, I am the executive secretary of the show, and I would never intrude upon her thoughts." Her furrowed brow visually expressed her puzzlement at Mrs. Chandler's refusal.

"I can understand your confusion, Mrs. Black, but let's stick to that night. We are trying to figure out who could have done this. Can you remember seeing anyone heading back to the sewing room between the time Mrs. Chandler left the dining room and her body was found? Why did you go looking for her, anyway?" asked the inspector. He could understand, even after the short time he had talked with her, why Mrs. Chandler preferred to be by herself—or at least not with this woman.

Mrs. Black tugged down her skirt, smoothing it over her bony knees. "No, there is no one whom I remember observing all evening. Mary Flowers, Anna Carlyle, and I went looking for Alice to take our leave. That was almost nine o'clock. I remember because Jeremy had asked just a minute before if we had seen her. He wanted to ask her if anything else was needed for the buffet, and he hesitated to disturb her in the sewing room. Poor man—he just cannot seem to think for himself. He should have been able to see that no one was taking refreshment any longer. Some people say that they hired him out of pity. He seems very incompetent, and I do not know why Alice retains him."

Steve cut in. "Yes, Mrs. Black, please keep to the subject."

She sniffed and let out a little *humph*, which made it clear that she did not appreciate being interrupted. "Well. Let me see. Yes, I spoke with Anna Carlyle while I was supping. I had a petit four and a cucumber sandwich. I thought the bread was not as fresh … "

"Mrs. Black," snapped Steve, exasperated.

Another sniff. "Anna and I did not speak for long. Professor Lech Poltovski wanted to ask her about something. Some people say that Anna was extremely angry with Alice. She is a botanist, you know. Anna, not Alice, of course. Anna developed a rose hybrid that she was attempting to register. Alice had a desire to develop her own hybrid. They worked together and created several beautiful plants. But some say Alice insisted on having her name, exclusively, on the registration application. Of course, she provided the funds, so it was only appropriate that Alice attach her name to the registration. Some people say Anna was heard speaking inappropriately about Alice regarding this. Very disloyal, if you ask me."

Again, Steve interjected himself in Mrs. Black's irrelevancies. "So, Miss Carlyle and Professor Poltovski were together for the rest of the time until you went looking for Mrs. Chandler?"

She gave him an irritated look. "Certainly not," she stated emphatically. "I saw the professor exiting the dining room onto the terrace a short time later in her company. Some people say he was a suitor for Alice's hand. He did not take the rejection calmly. I've heard he took an oath to make her sorry. I think that he was too young for her, too stuffy. Very sour, he was. Some people say she insisted on bringing him over from Austria-Hungary and he misinterpreted her attentions, at least some people said he did."

Buck jumped in, startling her when he spoke up from his seat behind her. She had forgotten all about the constable. "Did you see Mrs. Flowers at any time during the evening?"

She put her bird claw of a hand against her chest and twisted around to glare at him. "Oh my goodness. You startled me, Captain Daniels." She turned back to Steve and directed her answer to him. "Mary Flowers took a plate and just piled food on it. I was under the impression that she had not eaten for a week. *A week.* I can understand that, however. Some people say Mary was caught trying to abscond with show funds. That Alice, who was an experienced accountant,

I might add, went over the books and found a discrepancy. Some people say Mrs. Flowers, a widow, you know, was addicted to gambling. And there is a dog-racing establishment in East Bowling. Some people say she went there to gamble, and she was using money from the flower show."

"Doesn't, um, didn't Mrs. Chandler have more control over the finances for the show?" Steve asked, confused as to why Mrs. Flowers was still the treasurer, if she was dipping into the till.

Mrs. Black again tugged at her skirts. Steve decided it was a nervous habit. "Oh, no. Alice would deposit funds to the account at the conclusion of the previous year's show. That was to allow for expenses throughout the year. And Alice had too good a heart and was too trusting. She always believed in redemption. I informed her that this would be a mistake, and for once Alice did not heed my advice. Usually she does, you know. Alice always depended on me to help guide her. But Alice allowed Mary to return to her post. Some people say Alice contemplated prosecution at some future date. And I always kept a close eye on my pocketbook, I can tell you.

"Mary went out immediately to the terrace after she completed her repast. Barry Jones followed her out. Some people say Barry is a womanizer and that he propositioned Alice a year after her dear husband passed. Some say they knew each other prior to her marriage and that one of the children, I do not know which one, is the fruit of their liaison, and that is why she insisted that they adopt. Some people say he wanted to renew their relationship, and she threatened to force him out of his nursery by canceling his lease on the property."

Buck interrupted. "So, could someone say that all the children could be Mrs. Chandler's?"

Mrs. Black seemed to consider this for a moment, unaware of Buck's sarcasm. She tilted her head to one side. "No-o-o, I do not believe so. The other two were adopted because she and A. J. were unable to have any of their own. At least, I suppose so."

Steve spurred her on with, "And Mrs. Jones? Did she see this?"

"Of course. She did not seem to care. Some people say she has a drinking problem and only cares about her next cocktail. I heard that Alice knew and threatened to cancel their lease if she continued in her dissolute behavior. As for her husband, some people say Wanda prefers that Barry take his dalliances away from her, if you understand me." Her look was prim and disapproving.

As tired as Steve was of listening to this wellspring of gossip, he continued his questioning. "What about the children? Were they around that evening?"

This gave Mrs. Black another direction for her venom. "The children were ungrateful. They were given everything and were a frightful disappointment to A. J. and Alice. Some people say Francis Dubreuil has a gambling problem, also. He vacations in Havana, and everyone knows what goes on there. That is why he is still in Chandler. Alice does—did— not trust him out of her sight. Some people say that is the reason he attempted to produce woolen cloth. Alice would not give him any money, and that was the only method by which he could satisfy his addiction—by taking some of the money for that or by getting paid some of it back as bribes. A. J. Chandler tried to incorporate him into the mill, but some people say A. J. had to threaten to eject Francis from the family and have him provide for himself before Francis would agree to join the firm when he matriculated … "

Steve held up a hand to stop the flow. "If I understand you, both Mary Flowers and Francis Dubreuil had gambling problems."

Mrs. Black looked offended. "Well, it *is* a common problem. And a sizable number of persons suffer from it."

He waved her to continue.

Another nervous tugging of her clothing. "Catherine Mermet is incompetent. She was exiled to the South to handle the agricultural side of the enterprise. Some people say she was involved with a common lout from one of the farms, and Alice could not face the shame. Once ensconced in South Carolina with a manager to act as the actual administrator, she continued to wallow in her shame, some people say, and not only had a forbidden relationship but also compounded it by actually marrying him. And I tried to warn Alice about her activities, but she, uncharacteristically, did not heed me."

"Who did she marry, again?" asked Steve. He wondered how Mrs. Black knew what was happening in South Carolina but did not feel it was worthwhile asking. Not only did it seem unimportant but he was avoiding another long, rambling explanation.

"Why, Paul Sullivan, of course." At Steve's blank look, she continued impatiently, "The manager. At least this time, she had the decency to find a more suitable choice. He had some education, and his family did not still grub in the dirt. However, he was unacceptable to Alice, and some people say she swore she would modify her will and sever all relations with them."

"And Silene?" encouraged Steve.

"Silene is an embarrassment," sneered Mrs. Black. "She is a flapper. A *flapper*. She wears scandalous clothes, listens to jazz music, and has cut her hair so that she has the appearance of a boy. And she smokes. In public. She frequents dens of iniquity where she listens to inappropriate music, drinks alcohol, and stays out to all hours. Some people say she indulges in opium and other disgusting practices. Some people say she is a—a—a loose woman. Some people say she was seeing Barry Jones, and Alice found out and threatened to disinherit her," she finished with a whisper and a quick, darting look around. "That was another reason for her antipathy toward Barry Jones."

"And you, Mrs. Black? What did you do that night? Were you in the dining room all evening?" Captain Daniels asked from his seat by the door.

"Me? Oh my! Alice and I were the last to leave the sewing room. We were having a difference of opinion on the hanging tabs. I wanted the darker material that matched the border, and she was inclined toward a contrasting lighter material that matched one of the shades in the interior of the quilt, accented with a rose that matched those in the quilt. The others were divided."

Steve asked, "Didn't Mrs. Chandler have the final say?"

"Oh, no," she replied. "Alice was always considerate of other people's feelings. We all discussed it and were going to leave off deciding until tomorrow evening—well, this evening, now—when the quilt was to be completed."

"Let's go back to after Mrs. Chandler returned to the sewing room."

"I remained in the dining room all evening. I remember that Susanne, that is one of the maids, served tea, and I enjoyed a cup of Earl Grey with lemon, no cream."

"So, you never left the dining room all evening?" queried Steve, pressing.

Mrs. Black hesitated a moment. "I may have stepped into the adjoining storage area. I was inspecting the crystal, china, and cutlery. Some people say you cannot trust the help to polish or adequately clean. Nowadays, the help is extremely slipshod in their duties."

"So, no one saw you for a period that night." Steve did not think that Mrs. Black could be the murderer. She did not have the strength to inflict the wound that Buck described killed Mrs. Chandler, but he did want to shake her superior attitude.

"Well, not that I am aware of. However, I am sure that someone noticed that I stepped away and to where." After delivering this confusing answer, she began to fidget. With a pointed look at the watch pinned to her dress, she asked, "Do you have any more questions for me? I have an appointment in town."

Steve looked at Buck. "You have anything else for Mrs. Black?"

"Not a thing. We know where she is if I do." He gave the woman, who had hopped out of her chair, a broad smile. "Will you and the committee be here working on the quilt this evening?" he asked.

Mrs. Black answered, "Of course. We still have an amount of work to do." With that, she scurried out the door and demanded her coat from Jeremy in an imperious, shrill tone.

With a deep sigh, Steve shook his head and leaned back in the chair. "Some people say that she is a nasty little rat of a woman."

Buck replied, "Some people say she can give me a head-ache. I feel I need a bath after that. I wonder how much of what she told us is true."

Chapter 6

Steve rose and stretched. "Looks like everyone had a reason to stick a pair of scissors in Mrs. Chandler, according to the genteel Mrs. Black. Now, at least, we have something to talk to the rest of our suspects about."

Jeremy appeared at the door. "Will there be anything, gentlemen?"

"How about some coffee, Jeremy? This looks like it is going to be a long day. A long, long day. And could you provide lunch at around eleven thirty? Nothing big, just some sandwiches," asked Buck.

"And a couple of beers, if you got 'em?" said Steve, hopefully.

Jeremy smiled and shook his head slowly. "I am afraid not, sir. The madam forbade spirits on the premises. I will have something prepared for you for luncheon, and the coffee will be here in a few minutes."

A knock on the door announced Francis. His whipcord frame was dressed in a smart three-piece double-breasted brown suit, with a gray-and-brown striped tie in a Windsor knot over a crisp white monogrammed shirt. His dark hair was held in place with pomade, and he wore a thin, clipped moustache. He had a round, broad face with high cheekbones and dark brown eyes that looked almost black in the right light. His face bore a carefully cultivated air of calm boredom. Steve noticed the black mourning ribbon encircling his right sleeve between shoulder and elbow.

"I hope I am not too early?" he said neutrally.

They assured him he was not, and Steve asked Jeremy to bring another cup.

The butler bowed and departed.

Steve introduced himself and shook the moist hand offered him. "I have been sent down to investigate your mother's death. Please, accept my deepest sympathy."

Francis gave a quick nod, seated himself in the chair recently vacated by Mrs. Black, and crossed his legs while smoothing the cloth of his impeccably tailored trousers over his knees.

Steve seated himself and turned his notebook to a fresh page. "Mr. Chandler, can you please outline your movements that evening from about seven thirty to eleven p.m.?"

"I was at work," he answered in a plummy voice.

Steve waited for him to elaborate. When Francis did not continue, Steve prompted, "Did anyone see you there? Were you in a meeting with someone?"

"The old man, the watchman. He had been in Cuba with Roosevelt." He twisted and looked a question at Buck.

"That would be Mr. Haney," the captain supplied.

Francis turned back, and Steve proceeded, "Was he in sight the whole time?"

Francis adjusted his tie. "No."

Steve ran his fingers through his hair in a sign of annoyance. He hoped all the witnesses would not be as difficult as his first two. "Mr. Chandler. Can you please elaborate?"

With a look of supercilious surprise, he said, "I am answering your questions, am I not, Inspector?"

With a sigh, Steve nodded and continued, "How long was Mr. Haney not in sight?"

"I do not keep track of him. I was in my office working on the production schedule. I noticed him when he was on his rounds on the mill floor once." He leaned back in his chair, folding his hands calmly in his lap.

Something about Francis's lack of emotion tickled a thought, but it disappeared before Steve could grasp it.

There was a discreet knock on the door, and Jeremy entered, followed by two maids wheeling a cart bearing a coffee service. The interview paused while the butler lit the tea candle under the warming stand and arranged the service. He poured while the shorter of the female servants served the three men. The taller, redheaded maid offered a silver tray with a silver bowl of sugar, a silver creamer, and silver coffee spoons.

Steve continued after their departure, "Chief Daniels, is Mr. Haney one of your deputies?"

"Yes, Haney is one of the watchmen. He has rounds every hour."

"How did you hear about the murder, Mr. Chandler?" Steve asked, returning to Francis.

Francis turned to Buck. "Wasn't it that young officer with red hair and a scar on his chin?"

Buck looked at Steve. "As soon as I heard, I sent Constable Brook to get Mr. Chandler."

Steve nodded and turned back to Francis. "Later that night at the house, after things had quieted down, did you hear anything odd or out of place? I'm wondering if the murderer hid in the house somewhere and snuck out after everyone had gone to bed."

"No."

"How were relations between you and your mother?" Steve sprang on him.

Francis tilted his head and a quick smile skipped across his face. "Our relations were good. I loved my mother, and I was miles away at the time some madman murdered her. We had insignificant differences, of course, but nothing of importance. We agreed on the direction of the company, and she was pleased with my management," he answered in a slightly amused tone. Steve wondered if he was playing with them.

"Like the investment in wool?" Steve asked mildly.

Francis's lids lowered to partly cover his eyes, and he answered calmly, "My mother and I discussed and resolved that issue."

Steve flipped a page in his notebook as if looking for something. "Mr. Chandler, I understand you vacation in Cuba. What do you like about Havana? I have never been there, myself. Maybe I'll go, one of these days."

Francis's lips tightened for a moment, and he leaned carefully forward. His eyes were steely as he answered in a slightly mocking tone, "I enjoy relaxing on the beach. I sail and fish. I like Cuban food. At night I visit the casinos and enjoy a drink or two. When I leave, I pay my bills and do not leave any scandals behind.

"Inspector, I do not like the direction of your questions. You stated that you are investigating my mother's death. You are hinting at a problem between my mother and me. If you even dare hint to the papers that anything untoward was between us, my lawyers will have you in court so fast you won't have time to put on your hat." Francis sat back, his face blank.

Francis's attitude puzzled Steve. Why would he treat the investigation like a game? There was an undertone of mockery and condescension that was jarring for a grieving, loving son. He filed the thought away to mull over later when he and Buck were alone.

Steve leaned back in his chair and sighed. "Believe me, Mr. Chandler, I am not making any accusations at this time. However, I will pursue any pertinent line of questioning, and I don't pay any attention to threats. Neither do I talk to the press during an investigation. Thank you, Mr. Chandler. If we have any more questions, may I have some more of your time?"

"Certainly, *if* you leave your insinuations at the door."

Both men rose. Francis shot his cuffs and left with a nod to Buck.

Buck poured refills and took a sip. "He always was a cold fish, but that whole thing seemed staged, somehow. Maybe it's the contrast with Mrs. Black. I don't know," he observed.

Steve tapped his teeth with the end of his pencil. "I get the same feeling. Something is out of whack."

"Steve, you don't really think he had anything to do with the murder of his mother?"

"No, it looks like he couldn't have done it unless he was able to get out the door and sneak back when Haney was in his cubbyhole."

Buck shook his head. "When someone is in the watchman's office, he can see Mr. Chandler's office and Mr. Chandler sitting at his desk. Unless the interior blinds are drawn," he finished thoughtfully.

"If necessary, I'll look the mill over, but I don't think there would be anything to it," observed Steve. "Still, there is something about his attitude that doesn't fit. There was almost a challenge about him. Just a feeling I have." He shrugged and asked, "Do you think Silene is ready to talk to us yet?"

Chapter 7

Light footsteps sounded in the hall, and a moment later in walked a tall young woman with bobbed, tawny hair and a black, close-fitting dress that reached a scant two inches below her knees. She had a broad brow and heart-shaped face narrowing to a square chin with a small cleft. Green, smiling eyes looked out from under perfectly arched brows. Her patrician nose topped wide, thin lips colored with pale pink lipstick. Steve cleared his throat and realized that she looked subtly like Julie. He quickly swept that thought from his mind.

The woman greeted Buck absently but looked Steve over from the top of his head down to his shoes as he stood in front of the desk, hand extended. Her lids dropped to half cover her emerald eyes as she finished her appraisal.

She shook his hand with a firm grip, using her full hand, not just the fingertips as many women did. Her grip lasted longer than necessary for politeness, and she met Steve's eyes with a speculative boldness. "I am Silene Chandler. You must be Steve Walsh. Very, very pleased to meet you," she said in a husky voice. Silene released his hand when she saw the flush creep up his cheeks. A low laugh accompanied her to the chair, which Steve held for her. She sat at the front of the seat with a faint smile curving her lips.

Steve circled the desk and took his seat. He felt that his collar was too tight but suppressed the urge to tug on it.

Regaining his composure, he asked, "Miss Chandler, could you tell me your movements on the night your mother died?"

"Yes," she answered, her smile broadening into a friendly, teasing grin.

After a pause, Steve continued, "Yes, what?"

"Yes, I could tell you what my movements were on the night Mother died."

Another pause. Steve sighed, forcing calm. "Then will you please do so?"

The girl got up and walked around the desk to take a seat on the corner. She crossed her legs, exposing more leg than Steve was comfortable seeing on a possible suspect. She leaned over in front of him, took a cigarette from the box on the desk, and waited for him to light it. She arched her well-groomed eyebrows, her light smile challenging. He reached for the large silver lighter and extended the flame. He was beginning to get irritated. Silene bent down, cupping his hand, and inhaled the cigarette alight. With her left arm under her chest, she rested her right arm on her left hand and pulled in a lungful of smoke. Grinning at Steve, she exhaled. "You're cute."

She scratched a dimpled knee with well-manicured fingernails, drawing Steve's eyes.

"Now tell me, cutie," she said, stubbing out the barely smoked cigarette in a large purple glass ashtray. She rested her right elbow on her knee and tucked her chin into her hand, leaning over. "Are you married? I didn't notice a ring, but you men don't like to advertise when you are out of sight of the wifey."

"Miss Chandler," Steve began.

"Oh, call me Silene. I don't like to be so formal with good-looking men. Do you want to take me out for dinner and a little dancing tonight?"

"Miss Chandler, will you please sit in the chair. I have no interest in turning this into a social occasion." Steve's face was a stern mask.

She made a moue with her lips. "Now, don't be that way. You look like you don't mind having a little fun once in a while."

He stood up and looked at an amused Buck. "Can I borrow your handcuffs? I am going to arrest Miss Chandler as a material witness and take her to the holding cells at your station. There she will stay until she decides to cooperate."

Silene's attitude changed immediately. With narrowed eyes, she straightened and said in a low, shocked voice, "You wouldn't dare."

"Yes, I would. If I have to I will take you up to Hartford to a real jail, and I will fight every effort to get you out. That would be highly embarrassing to you and would probably cause a fracas with my boss for me. But I don't really care. I have been fired before, and I think the opposition party will make a huge play with the situation.

"Alternatively, you can stop the vamp act, and I will stop the hard-boiled detective act. Then we can get on with this like real adults."

Silene rose, spine stiff, and circled the desk to return to the chair. She settled in, crossed her legs, and said in a cold voice, "I left the house right after dinner at, oh, about six o'clock. Miles and Margot Steen-Masterson picked me up, and Dean Williams was with them. We went to a little place south of here where we, well, could dance. About ten o'clock we left and had a bite to eat, and then we went out again. I returned around eleven o'clock and found the place in an uproar."

"So, you were with Miles, Margot, and Dean all evening?"

"Most of the time. I needed some air and borrowed Miles's convertible and drove around for about an hour."

Buck interjected, "Most of Miss Chandler's crowd goes down to Harrotsville to The Firehouse. There is a speakeasy in the basement. It is about forty-five minutes from here. I will check with the three of them to verify."

"Are we done here?" asked Silene icily.

"Unless there is anything else you can tell me that would be pertinent to the investigation, I think so," answered Steve. "Thank you for your time." He spoke equally icily. "Oh, how were the relations between you and your mother?" he shot at her in hopes of surprising her and eliciting an unguarded answer.

A flush came to her cheeks. "You will find out or already know," she answered stiffly. "Jeremy informed me that Emma Black has already spoken with you. Mother did not approve of my social life, but not to the point of more than a repetitive, tedious lecture. She had no problem with my professional life. Sales were up each year since I took over. And expenses were down. I brought in several new clients, three firms from Germany and France. After the war, they were eager for our products, and I made an excellent deal with them. Advantageous for us and them."

As she started to rise, Steve innocently asked, "Do you know Barry Jones well?"

Silene sat back down and glared at him. "What do you mean by that?"

He pretended to look at his notes. "We have heard that you and Mr. Jones were having an affair and that your mother was not happy about it."

She rolled her eyes. "I know where you heard that! Look. There was a Christmas party at the nursery. Mother does— did—not like drinking, so she came for a half an hour to be social and left. After that, the band tuned up and the refreshments appeared. I had a little too much to drink. I danced. I stepped outside. Barry followed me and he—I let him kiss me, but when he got grabby, I slapped him and told him that if he ever did that again, it would blow up in his face and I would be holding the dynamite. I was not about to get involved with that 'Jack Keefe.' Wanda, really loaded, came out, knowing what kind of guy he was. Last I heard, when I left, she was threatening to surgically alter him, if you get what I mean. As far as I know, Mother didn't even know about the incident. Emma Black knows that she hated gossip and would never have tolerated it, even if it were true."

She rose gracefully and patted her dress into place. Both men watched the elegant sway of her hips as she walked enticingly from the room.

Buck shook his head and smiled. "Didn't make a friend there, Steve, old man."

Steve looked at Buck's widening smile and the direction of his gaze. "How's your wife, Captain?"

Buck jerked his eyes back, and a slow flush rose from his neck to his hairline.

The interviews with the staff were unhelpful. All of them had been in the dining room or kitchen throughout the evening. Their stories verified some of the movements Steve and Buck had already heard about from Emma Black. None of them noticed any of the guests missing for any length of time, but they were too busy to notice. They were all horrified that anyone could think of murdering Mrs. Chandler. She was kindly. A wonderful employer. Everyone was loyal and loved her. And on and on.

After the interviews with the staff, during which they managed a quick bite of the sandwiches that were brought in, Steve and Buck headed back to Chandler. When Buck drove away to talk with Haney at his home, Steve walked into the hotel. He asked the desk clerk if the Sullivans were in. The manager sent up a bellhop, who returned after a few minutes with an invitation to their suite.

✂ Chapter 8

The elevator took him up to the fourth floor. When he stepped out of the car, Steve saw a tall, sun-browned man with a narrow face beckoning him. He walked over to the thin, well-dressed figure. He had a long face; sunken cheeks; and close-set, piercing hazel eyes. Thick lips were tightened above a weak chin. Steve shook hands with Paul Sullivan and was ushered into the couple's rooms.

Steve introduced himself and took the chair indicated by Paul. "Thank you for seeing me. I'm sorry for your loss," he started. After acknowledging Catherine's quiet thank-you, he continued, "Could you tell me your movements on that night?"

Paul sprang from his seat on the arm of the chesterfield next to where his wife sat. "Do you mean to accuse us?" His dark eyes flashed, and his lips compressed more tightly under his long, sharp nose.

Steve thought, *A man with a temper.* The indignation had come too fast. He paused, thinking it likely that these two had a prepared story.

"Mr. Sullivan, I am not in a position to accuse anyone. At this point, I'm interviewing everyone who was there that night and the family."

The next question was directed at Mrs. Sullivan: "Can you please outline your movements?"

She sat there with worry lines on her forehead and long-fingered hands clutching a mangled handkerchief. She was dressed in a modest black dress, more funereal than Silene's. She was not as tall as her sister and was slightly plump. Her round cheeks had small, bright spots of color. The smudges under her reddened eyes marred what was, Steve thought, otherwise a pleasant face. She waved a hand at Paul, who answered for her, his voice formal and rehearsed: "We met with Mrs. Chandler that evening around four o'clock. We went to tell her about our nuptials. She was very unhappy. I was told to remove myself from the house, and she insisted the marriage be annulled. I was dismissed, and Catherine was told that she was now assigned to the company offices. If we refused to 'disabuse ourselves of this foolishness,' she would ruin us. Cath remained strong, and we left. It was a short interview.

"We returned to the hotel; Catherine lay down. I ordered supper, ate, and retired."

Steve stopped scribbling in his notebook and asked, "Did someone see both of you during the evening?"

Paul responded again. "The waiter, when he delivered the meal."

The inspector looked at Catherine. "Both of you?"

When Paul began to answer again, Steve interrupted him sharply. "Mr. Sullivan, I asked your wife. Please let her answer."

"Catherine is understandably upset. She is delicate and in no state to be brutally interrogated," he defended his wife.

Steve sighed. "A brutal interrogation would be one that is taking place at the police station with bright lights and rapid-fire questions. Unless, of course, you mean the use of large phone directories or rubber hoses. Unfortunately, Chandler is a small town with an inadequate directory, and I left my rubber hose in my other suit. So, I am forced to fall back on the old-fashioned interview. Now, when I ask you a question, you answer it. When I ask your wife a question, she answers it. Do you understand the procedure?"

Paul's thin face was becoming redder and redder under Steve's sarcasm. "Get out, Inspector. Get out now!"

"Paul, darling, he is only doing his job." Catherine turned to Steve. "I am sorry for my husband's outburst. What is it you wanted to know? Oh, yes. As I was lying down, no one saw or spoke to me after we returned to our rooms. I took a sleeping powder soon after I entered the bedroom and slept for the rest of the night."

She made Steve feel like a boor, and he resented it. "So, both of you would be fired unless you divorced or annulled your marriage?"

"I know where you are trying to go with this, Inspector," a minimally calmer Paul said. "But I have a degree in business management from Harvard. There have been several offers from well-established firms—Chevron Oil and Pittsburg Steel, among others. It would be no financial disadvantage if we left Chandler Mills. As a matter of fact, it would be more remunerative."

"All right. Were there any other problems between you and your mother, Mrs. Sullivan?"

"What do you mean by … " started Paul. Steve's sharp glance stopped him and he sat with his thick lips tightly compressed.

His wife patted his hand on her shoulder and replied, "Mother never had any respect for my judgment, Inspector

Walsh. She felt that I was too meek for the business world. That is the reason she exiled me to the Carolinas. And why Paul was assigned as my 'assistant.' He had been the manager of the mill operations here, in Chandler. Not only did that free up the position for Francis, but I was provided an experienced manager. Paul and I fell in love. We married secretly three months ago. We decided to inform Mother while we were both here for the flower show. It was a mistake, obviously."

"Why was your mother upset?"

"Mother has always desired to oversee the business and her family very closely. My marriage had not been sanctioned by her, and she was upset. In time she would have accepted it, and we would have reconciled." She looked tired by the explanation.

After a pause to consider how best to proceed, Steve said, "I would like to speak to you privately, please."

Paul stiffened but kept quiet.

"Any question you have for me, you can ask in front of Paul." She looked up and smiled at her husband wanly. He replied by giving her shoulder a light, loving squeeze.

Steve shrugged and delicately inquired, "There is some vagueness about the reason for your being 'exiled.' Something about an, a ... "

"An affair?" asked Catherine. "Emma Black, our local gossip, told you I had an affair with someone on the estate and Mother sent me away? Possibly to have a child?"

Red-faced, Steve cleared his throat. "Something of that nature."

She smiled. "Emma saw me come out of the stables, followed by a young man, a groom, who worked with the hunters we kept. We were laughing. We both had wisps of hay attached to our clothes. We had not been tumbling in the straw, Inspector. I was rubbing down my horse, Resolute, and Bill was pitching hay from the loft and missed the manger and covered me instead. I suspected it was on purpose. Bill and I had been friends since we were little. Friends and nothing more. She, Mrs. Black, was there to oversee the loading of some manure for the planting beds at her home. If I can be slightly vulgar, Mrs. Black has an affinity for that material because her mind is made of it." She blushed at her daring statement.

Steve and Paul tried to hide their shock, while Catherine gave a low laugh and continued.

"Even though Mrs. Black had her ears blistered, as Daddy was wont to say, by Mother for spreading gossip, I was sent to Carolina for my indiscretion of enjoying a brief moment of humor with a stable boy. Poor Emma. She just could not avoid the temptation to gossip about one of Mother's children. Silene told me at Christmas that year that the vile woman had learned her lesson when my sister amused me with the story of Barry Jones's amorous behavior."

Steve turned to Paul. "Mr. Sullivan, did you resent your demotion to the South? You lost your position as executive at the mill."

"No, Inspector. Not only was I tired of the close management style of Mrs. Chandler, but I found the love of my life. You may not have ever been subjected to that style of management, but having every decision you make second-guessed is uncomfortable for a man of my temperament."

There were more questions but no answers to help with the investigation. Steve thanked Catherine and Paul for their cooperation, picked up his hat, and left. He debated having supper in his room but felt that was a little too decadent for his sensibilities. He took the elevator to the lobby.

As he stepped from the car, a pert brunette called to him from behind the front desk.

"There is a message for you, Inspector." She gave him a bright, friendly smile.

He opened the envelope she handed him and unfolded the note. His heart jumped when he read the signature. This time it was Julie's handwriting. He read: *"Meet me for dinner in the hotel restaurant at 6:00, please."*

He glanced at his watch and saw he had half an hour. That is, if he was going to meet her. Then he ridiculed himself for the thought. Of course he was going to meet her. Who was he trying to fool? Steve wondered whether the meeting would be personal or professional.

Steve and Buck had planned to meet at seven o'clock to compare notes and drive up to the Chandler house to interview the committee members when they arrived for the evening. In the interim, he had planned on taking a taxi to the mill and looking around. Steve argued with himself that Julie might have some important information for him. He debated going back to his room for a drink but decided to sit in the restaurant instead. Steve did not want to talk with Julie with his mind clouded by alcohol.

He asked for a private booth in the corner and asked the maître d' to show Julie back when she arrived. Steve said, "She is a tall, slender woman. She has long blond hair and is beautiful. Blue eyes, nose upturned on the end, full lower lip, and a slight dimple on her chin. Long legs that don't quit, walks like a model … " His voice trailed off into a mutter as he realized he was babbling—an awareness that was confirmed by the amused look on the face of the maître d'. Steve found his heart rate accelerated and his palms damp. He berated himself for feeling like a kid on his first date. Here he was, a cool, steady investigator, feeling like a schoolboy.

He was deep in thought when Julie was shown to the booth. The table rocked when he tried to leap to his feet, and it caught his thighs in the tight space. He managed to grab the small vase containing a rosebud before it toppled over and spilled water on the table. Steve muttered an apology, which the maître d' waved off as he placed two menus in leather sleeves on the table. The waitress stepped up to take their drink orders.

Before Steve could answer, Julie asked for a pitcher of ice water and two glasses. The stout woman gave her a knowing smile, nodded, and left.

She turned to Steve and said, "Well, hello there. Long time no see." Her bright smile had a slight edge of uncertainty. Steve's hope that this encounter represented a thaw in their rocky relationship brightened.

"How are you doing, Julie?" he asked hesitantly. Steve had a sudden urge to dry his hands on his white linen napkin but fought it. He did not want to show how seeing her affected him.

"Pretty well, thanks," she replied. "How have you been?"

They made small talk and looked at the menu until the waitress brought their drinks and took their orders. Leaving the table, she closed the curtains that gave them privacy.

Both were too self-conscious to open them, and they sat there for a moment in uncomfortable silence. Julie moved first, taking a half-pint bottle from her handbag. With an easy, smoky laugh, she poured a drink for each of them and added water to her own glass. Shaking his head, Steve followed suit. She used her spoon to fish out ice cubes for both of them.

"To memories," Julie said, holding her drink up. He tapped his glass against hers and took a healthy swallow, which went down the wrong way. He waved away her offer to slap him on the back and managed to regain his breath. The liquor was no moonshiner's make with caramel coloring. It was probably imported—read: smuggled—from Canada.

The laugh he loved came again. "I would have brought apple juice if I had known that you couldn't hold your liquor."

He snorted and, to change the subject, said, "You wanted to meet. This is social, I hope."

Julie colored slightly. "Of course, but we can talk business, too?"

Disappointed, Steve responded, "You first. What can you tell me about the players?"

"This isn't for nothing. You know what I want in return. Right?" She paused for a moment, giving him a sharp look.

Steve took a sip and equivocated. "I'll give you what I can with the understanding that nothing goes to print until I give the word."

"Done. Let's see. Emma Black is an old gossip. Very little of what she says can be believed—though, like all good gossip, there probably is a kernel of truth in it. She is a small, mean-minded woman. I think her husband died on purpose, myself," she said as she took a stenographer's book from her bag.

After flipping a few pages, she said, "I put down some notes for you. I understand that you have already interviewed Mrs. Black, the kids, and the servants."

He stiffened. *How did she know that?*

Knowing what he was thinking, she smiled, which brought out the cleft in her square-cut chin. Steve shook off the memory of running his finger there. "I have my sources," she said archly.

"A few things you may not know. I met Mrs. Chandler to interview her, and she is a contradiction. She had a sharp mind and had to be in control. Business, family, politics, everything. On the other hand, she was a marshmallow when it came to her husband or his memory. It was one of those marriages of convenience. He went after her for the cotton, and they ended up really falling in love." She gave him a look Steve had no problem interpreting.

"Miss Anna Carlyle is a well-known botanist and artist. She and Mrs. Chandler worked together on several hybrids. Contrary to what you may have been told, Anna was ecstatic to help anyone on her favorite project, which is botany in general and flowers in particular. She helped Mrs. Chandler with the paperwork to register their creations. There is not a jealous bone in Anna's body.

"Professor Lech Poltovski is also a flower lover and has a wide knowledge of historical gardens. He supposedly carried a secret torch for her from the time they met. That is only rumor, mind. Of course, he may have been hiding a secret resentment, but he is against violence. He is a Quaker.

"Mrs. Mary Flowers lost her husband during the war. Her mother was ill, and Mary 'borrowed' money from the show funds for treatments. Mrs. Chandler found out about it. Mary told Mrs. C about her story. For a year, she paid all the medical expenses until the mother's death.

"Then there are Wanda and Barry Jones. They came here at Mr. Chandler's invitation before he died and at Mrs. Chandler's instigation. Mr. C had met Barry somewhere in England, and Mrs. Chandler set them up in business. The nursery is a partnership between the Chandlers and the Joneses. Wanda has a love for the bottle, and Barry has a love for willing women—rumor only."

Their meals came. Buttering a roll, Steve asked casually, "So, what have you been doing when you're off work?" He hoped Julie did not hear the real question in his voice.

Obviously, she did. "No, I'm not seeing anyone. I have no time for that."

"Oh, I wasn't talking about that. Um, you always liked museums and the arts. Have you seen the new French Impressionist exhibition at the Wadsworth?"

Julie smiled knowingly. "Yes, I went with a friend."

Too quickly, Steve asked, "Who?" He mentally kicked himself. For an experienced interrogator, he sounded like a bumbling rookie.

With a low chuckle, she answered cryptically, "Just a friend. You wouldn't know the person. Just someone I met during an interview. You've been pretty caught up in your work. I hear that you rarely get out, socially."

At his surprised look, she continued, "You know a good reporter always has her finger on the pulse of the city."

Steve did not know whether to be pleased that she still seemed interested or irritated that she was keeping track of him. He had a sudden, guilty thought about the woman on the train. He decided that she was playing with him. He could not think of how to continue without making a bigger fool of himself, so he changed the subject. Until he could sort out his feelings about Julie and their future, he needed to stay away from the personal.

He amused her with stories of his last two cases. About a senator, his smuggler son, and a high-speed chase and a judge caught with his pants down and attempted bribery.

Over coffee, they finished going over Julie's notes.

"To summarize: The kids are a mixed bag. Loved father and had problems with mother. Silene is a wild one. Decided to be a flapper during her time at Bryn Mawr. She has a degree in mathematics and economics. She did very well with the sales department, and two years ago was put in charge. She cuts up just enough to irritate her mother but not enough to get her name in the paper, negatively, with too much regularity.

"Catherine Mermet Chandler Sullivan is another story. She was always a serious young lady. She matriculated with a degree in social science. After a stint as her mother's right hand for her charity work, she was assigned to take over the agricultural side of Chandler Mills. Paul Sullivan was moved from manager of the mill operations to assist her. She and Paul fell in love and married secretly. When Mama heard, she insisted that the marriage be annulled or Catherine would be cut off. She and Paul seem to have the strongest motive for killing her?" She made that a question, but drew no response from Steve.

With a shrug, she finished. "Francis Dubreuil. Graduated from Harvard, where he met Paul Sullivan, who was several years ahead of him. On his recommendation, Paul was hired and eventually became manager of the mills when the prior executive retired. Two years ago, Mrs. Chandler shuffled things and Francis replaced Paul. The only dirt on Francis is that he takes trips to Havana twice a year to delve into the fleshpots."

Julie closed the book and handed it over to Steve, making sure that her fingers lingered on his. He hastily withdrew his hand and blushed at the taunting look in her eye.

"Now give," she demanded. "Who are you looking at?" Julie was looking for her quid pro quo. "I want this scoop."

At his hesitation, she said angrily, "Just something I can work into a story. Steve, I will *not* be a social reporter for the rest of my life. This is the best chance I will ever get. I am on the ground, and I can scoop every other reporter. A byline is only good on the first page, above the fold." She crossed her arms and gave him a disgusted look. "I should have known that you wouldn't play fair with me," she huffed.

"Come on, Julie," he replied. "You know I can't talk about the case yet. I haven't even interviewed the whole cast."

"You, you, you … " she snapped, unable to express herself adequately in a ladylike fashion. "You snake. If you give the story to some scribbler that Calvin sends … "

Steve held up his hands in a defensive position. "You will get the scoop. I promise. The moment I make an arrest, I will get ahold of you first." In an attempt to mollify her, he continued, "I will tell you that Emma Black is at the bottom of the list. I shook her hand, and she doesn't have the strength to stick the scissors into a cream pie, much less between Mrs. Chandler's ribs."

Julie glared at him. "Can't you do anything but lead me on? This is getting to be a habit with you, isn't it? Leading me on until you get what you want, then dumping me!"

She jabbed a finger in his direction. "You had just better get ahold of me first, mister. Or the next time there is a story on you, I will make sure you get crucified. I should have known I couldn't trust you. I came here because ... Oh." She grabbed her bag and slipped out from behind the table and flung back the curtains. As a parting shot, she snapped, "Dinner is on you."

Steve put his head in his hands. *Why do I have so much trouble with smart, beautiful women?* he asked himself.

Chapter 9

The inspector had just finished signing the check when Buck appeared at the amused waitress's elbow. There was a grin on his face. "I just saw an angry, good-looking young woman storm out of here. That's how I knew you were here. Made another friend?"

Steve looked up in disgust. "Let's just say intelligent, beautiful women intimidate me and I handle it badly." He wondered how much of his flip comment was true.

He picked up his hat and slid out of the booth. At a table across the room, he noticed a party of young men and women. A tall, well-set-up fellow was glaring at him. The man's antagonistic look followed them from the restaurant.

As they crossed the lobby, Steve asked, "Did you see that well-dressed bunch at the back table?"

Buck nodded. "That's the group Silene Chandler hangs out with. The kid who was giving you the eye is Dean Williams. They're a number, I suppose. Another friend?"

"I have no idea. I never met him." Steve dismissed the incident as unimportant.

They exited the hotel and got into Buck's constabulary automobile. On the way to the estate, he brought Buck up to date on the Sullivan interview. "They seem the best bet so far, but nowhere near actionable."

Buck never took his eyes off the road. "I saw Haney at his home. He had just gotten up and is as surly as you are in the morning. Anyway, I asked him if there was any length of time that he was away from his station when Francis could have left.

"Haney got all insulted and said that he never shirked his duty and that he was awake and alert, and so on. He swore that Francis never left his office until Red came for him, after the murder. I got a long speech on how he never let Colonel Roosevelt down, and he was right behind him during the charge up San Juan Hill."

Steve interrupted. "He was in Cuba? Really? I thought Francis was talking about embassy duty or something."

Buck nodded. "He was there, all right. You have an afternoon? Haney will talk your ear off, unless he is on duty, of course."

He continued with his report: "Also, Silene's friends, Dean Williams and the Steen-Mastersons, vouched for her. They swore she could not have gotten to Chandler and back to Harrotsville in the time she had borrowed Miles's car."

"Were they too drunk to remember, do you think?" asked Steve.

Buck snorted. "Not that they would admit. Dean has a thing for her, and apparently he kept close track until Silene returned. Rumor is that he expects to marry the heiress, though no one knows what she thinks." Buck slid his eyes sideways for a quick glance at Steve and grinned. "Maybe Silene has been talking about you, and that's why he gave you the evil eye just now."

Unexpectedly, Steve felt a twinge of jealousy. He immediately yanked his mind to Julie and banished his thoughts of Silene to some dusty corner of his brain. He told himself that he did not need another woman to further complicate his life.

Steve pulled Julie's notebook from his pocket, and the two officers spent the rest of the trip reviewing her entries. Buck had nothing to add, but he agreed with it, in general.

When they got to the house, Buck dismissed the deputy sitting outside the sewing room door—not Ruth Beckstrom, but a constable he had not seen before. Steve informed Jeremy, who had opened the main door and collected their hats, that he could have the room to clean as soon as they had a chance to look it over again. The butler left to organize the staff. There was little time before the committee arrived.

The new seal was cut and removed, and they entered the room. Nothing had changed. Steve stared at the quilt pinned to the wall, convinced that it was the key to the investigation and willing it to talk to him. He wandered from point to point, reviewing his earlier visit in light of the information he had picked up.

Steve turned when he heard a hubbub in the hall. Mrs. Black bustled in, followed by two women. Buck, by the door, pointed to the plump woman and mouthed, *"Anna Carlyle."* The other was Mary Flowers. Mrs. Black drew up short, causing her companions to jerk to a halt to avoid colliding with her.

"Look at that," she exclaimed, staring at the quilt wall.

"What's the matter, Mrs. Black?" asked Steve. With a frown on her face, she waved a gloved hand at the quilt. "The quilt. Who did that?" She looked accusingly at Steve.

Puzzled, Buck asked, "Who did what?"

She looked at him like he was an obnoxious, troublesome boy. "The quilt," she repeated. "We left it lying on the table; we had not determined the material. Oh," she continued, "Alice must have been trying both."

Steve stepped in front of her, causing her to snap her eyes to his. "What are you talking about?"

"My goodness. When we ended our efforts for the evening, we left the quilt lying on the table. The loops that we use to hang the quilt during the show. We still had to decide. I spoke to you regarding them. Several of us wanted the darker color, and the others, including Alice, leaned toward the lighter. She must have pinned samples of both to get a more clear perspective."

Steve turned around and refreshed his memory of the two sets of strips that had been attached next to the vertically oriented quilt. Twelve-inch strips of light- or dark-colored cloth at the top of the quilt and next to the turned-back section on the lower left, folded over. Now that she mentioned it, Steve remembered the tapestries in the country homes he had seen in England. The tops had looked like crenellations on castle walls. When he approached the quilt, he saw that the loops had not been sewn in. There were four along the top of the quilt. The two on the left matched a lighter piece of the body of the quilt, while the other two matched the border. One of each had a round red patch of cloth, which matched a petal on the central rose, pinned to it. The lower left of the quilt was folded back and pinned to show the reverse of the quilt. Two more patches, one of each, were pinned next to the diagonal fold.

Steve looked back to Mrs. Black. "You're sure that the quilt was on the table?"

"I am not yet in my dotage, young man," she snapped, her bright eyes piercing. "Of course, I distinctly remember that the quilt was resting on the table. The piece was complete, with the exception of the hanging strips. The swatches of light and the olive and magenta border material were ordered on it."

"Didn't you see it the night you found Mrs. Chandler?" asked Steve.

Mrs. Black froze for a moment. "No-o-o. Jeremy kept us from entering. He was blocking our view. He should have let us in so that we could check for signs of life. I was a volunteer during the epidemic and may have been able to help."

The conversation broke off when Jeremy ushered in a slight, older man. Buck greeted him. "Welcome, Professor." The newcomer hesitated in the doorway, nodded at the chief, and looked back at the tableau near the table. "Is anything wrong?" he asked.

Buck patted him on the shoulder. "They're talking about the quilt, Professor."

Before Poltovski could say anything, another couple entered. Steve arched an eyebrow at Buck who nodded. *Barry and Wanda Jones.* They, too, halted. "Here. Aren't we going to finish this off tonight?" asked Barry. Wanda stood with a slightly vacant look on her face, and Steve wondered how far the bottle level had been lowered before they got to the mansion.

"Inspector Walsh and I are here to interview the committee. You are free to do what you want in the sewing room." Buck looked a question at Steve, who nodded. "Mrs. Flowers, will you come with us, please?"

Jeremy arrived with Susanne and Annette, who were carrying cleaning supplies. The butler invited the committee to wait in the dining room while the room was being tidied. "There are coffee, tea, and refreshments available," he informed them.

Mrs. Flowers was obviously flustered at the attention but followed Buck and Steve from the room. They walked silently to Mrs. Chandler's office, and Buck moved a chair beside the door. After seating the woman, Steve circled the desk, sat, and took out his notebook.

Mrs. Flowers was a slight, plain woman who hid her sex behind a shapeless dress and cowed demeanor. At second glance, observed Steve, she might be pretty if she took a little time to dress up. There was no trace of any cosmetics, and her face looked strained because her hair had been pulled into a severe bun at the back of her neck. Her hair was a mousy brown, and when she finally looked at him, he saw that she had large, arresting brown eyes.

"Mrs. Flowers, we need to determine the movements of everyone who was here the night Mrs. Chandler died." He asked her the same questions he had presented to Mrs. Black. Her answers were straightforward, but in the same vein as the older woman's. There was no one she could remember seeing the whole time, with everyone moving in and out of the dining room. She fluttered her hands constantly, clutching a lace handkerchief in her left hand. Her narrow face was strained and her brown eyes wide and worried. There were dark smudges under them.

After writing down her answers, Steve sat back. Something had been niggling at his mind since he had entered the room that morning. Suddenly, he had it. If this was Mrs. Chandler's office, where had her secretary worked? He peered hard at the carpet and saw the signs of a smaller desk and chair at right angles to the large one. A secretary's desk had been removed from the room. "Where was Mrs. Chandler's secretary?" He snapped the question, more to himself than Mrs. Flowers. The overwrought woman began to cry.

"What the ... ? What is the matter?" he asked cautiously, puzzled and slightly alarmed by her reaction. He had never been comfortable with a weeping woman.

Regaining some composure, Mary looked up and replied in a quiet voice, "I was. At least, until ... "

Steve thought he understood. "Until you stole the money." The thought popped out of his mouth before he realized how harsh he sounded.

This brutally bald statement brought another spate of tears, much to Steve's chagrin. "I'm, uh, I'm sorry," he said.

Mrs. Flowers raised her tearstained face and gathered herself. "I had Mrs. Chandler's trust until then. If I hadn't been so desperate I would never have done it. I told her I was wrong not going to her; she had been so good to me. She said she understood, and she was so good to me after," she repeated. Mrs. Flowers, through a waterfall of tears, confirmed the information Julie had supplied. "I needed the money for my mother. She was so ill, and her treatment was so expensive. I convinced myself that it wasn't wrong if it did good and allowed a sick old woman to be comfortable at the end of her time. And I was planning on paying it back. I was." She ended with, "Mrs. Chandler told me during the interview, after the discovery, that she would take care of her own correspondence in the future."

It was obvious to Steve that any trust that had been established between the two women had been shattered. He thought Mrs. Chandler had decided to leave the pieces on the floor. She may have forgiven Mrs. Flowers for the theft, but she was not going to keep the woman in her confidence. It was understandable from the old woman's point of view. In a moment of crisis, Mrs. Flowers had broken the law instead of going to her mentor, the unforgivable sin according to Mrs. Chandler.

Hoping to receive different answers now that she was in an emotionally shocked state, Steve took advantage and reviewed her previous answers. "Could the servants have slipped from the room during the critical period?"

Mrs. Flowers, pale and wan, dabbed her eyes and took a deep breath. "As I said before, Susanne was by the dumbwaiter most of the time. When Jeremy had a need for something, he told her. She spoke into the speaking tube by the dumbwaiter and waited to take what the cook sent up and put it out. There were several platters, the coffee and tea, water—I don't know what else. Jeremy was mostly in the room, leaving occasionally, stepping to the outside doors to see if everything was in order. He was never gone for more than a minute or two. The other girl was in and out. Cook was in the kitchen downstairs. I don't know how she could have gotten from there to the sewing room and back. She could not be sure when more instructions would arrive from the dining room."

"You say that you never left the dining room?"

With slumped shoulders she answered almost too quietly to hear. "Yes. They don't like me. Everyone thinks that Mrs. Chandler was too, well, easy on me." Tears flowed again from the miserable woman. She dabbed at them with the soaked handkerchief. Steve reached into his pocket and extracted his own, which was clean, thankfully, and handed it to her. She thanked him with a weary smile. "They all hate me. I suppose they can have their way now. The committee is sure to remove me."

She looked at Steve with the first look of strength she had shown so far. "I am a good secretary. I am a good person. I made a mistake." She straightened in her chair and gave him a look that dared him to contradict her.

She turned her head and stared at the corner of the room, a sudden anger flashing from her eyes, twisting his handkerchief until it tore in her hands. "That Emma Black. I could just … just … "

"Kill her?" Steve finished for her quietly.

Mrs. Flowers's hands flew to her mouth. Her wide eyes met his. "Oh, no!" she cried, aghast. "No, not that."

Steve leaned back. "That will be all for now, Mrs. Flowers. Stay around the house until Captain Daniels or I give you permission to leave. Will you send in Miss Carlyle when you go back, please?" he asked mildly.

She looked at his damp, rumpled handkerchief and tentatively offered it back to him. Steve waved it away with a grin, and she turned to go. After she had stumbled out of the room, the inspector looked at Buck, who shrugged and said, "I don't think she had any good reason to kill Mrs. Chandler and every reason to wish her a long life. Now, if Mrs. Black had ended up with the scissors in her ribs, I would look at her. And probably everyone else in town, who would show up for the celebration," he added.

✂ Chapter 10

The men looked up when a short, stout, gray woman gave a sharp, businesslike knock on the doorjamb. She wore a gray dress and dark hose. Her square-toed black shoes would have been considered sensible by Steve's grandmother. A matching purse was held tight to her body. Her salt-and-pepper hair was gathered in a loose bun at the back of her neck. Her eyes were pale enough to be almost colorless. The only splash of color was a bright red scarf loosely knotted around her heavy neck. Buck seated her and received a brilliant smile in return. She looked like everyone's grandmother. There were laugh lines around her plump-lipped mouth and friendly, twinkling eyes. Steve swore that he could smell fresh bread and cinnamon, reminiscent of his own Mimi's kitchen.

He lost himself momentarily in the sudden memories of Christmas mornings and then pulled back from the awkward silence with an effort. "Good evening, Miss Carlyle. How are you?"

"I am just fine, Inspector. How are you?" she replied. She twisted in her chair and looked at Buck. "And how are you, Buck? You are looking well. How are Margaret and the children?"

Steve saw that this was rapidly turning into a social event, and he brought the discussion around to the business at hand. "Miss Carlyle. Can you tell me about the night of the murder, please?"

She described the evening much as Mrs. Black and Mrs. Flowers had. Under his probing, she reviewed the committee members' movements after they broke from the quilting. "Mrs. Flowers sat at the table most of the time, but I wasn't there myself the whole evening. The professor spoke to her briefly, I think, and then left. Wanda and Barry left to go out on the terrace.

"I am sorry. I wanted to see how Mrs. Chandler's new hybrids were doing and went out," she finished. "Then the professor and I spoke until Emma came out and gathered me up to leave. The two of us came in her automobile."

Steve stopped writing and looked directly into her eyes. "When did you have time to go upstairs, then?"

She blushed and lowered her eyes. "Inspector! I felt the … the call and repaired upstairs to the powder room. That was immediately after we left the sewing room. When I returned, I exchanged a few words with Alice— Mrs. Chandler—before I went to the sideboard."

"So it wasn't after Mrs. Chandler left?" Buck asked.

"Why, no, Buck. I remember because I wanted to discuss my opinion on whether to use the light or dark hanging strips on the quilt. I knew that Alice always went back to the sewing room after we adjourned. I felt sure that the reason, that evening, was to decide which she liked, though she had expressed her interest in the light when we were all together. You have to understand Alice. She was never someone who forced her opinion on the committee. She felt that all of us should have equal weight in any decision." Miss Carlyle smiled. "Not in the least as she organized her private life and businesses."

Buck continued, "How soon after you spoke did she leave the dining room?"

"Almost immediately. She said she wanted to have another look at the quilt itself. As I said, she always did. Sometimes she would suggest a change to us. That night, I am sure she wanted to consider the hanging strips."

Since she was starting to repeat herself, Steve tried a different tack and asked if she could remember anything else about people's movements. He received a negative answer. She had not noticed the servants all evening, just that they were there and very attentive.

Steve tapped his pencil on his teeth and looked at her before asking, "The hybrids. Didn't Mrs. Chandler only follow your instructions? You are the one who actually created those hybrids. Weren't you angry that she was taking credit for your work? I understand that you didn't even get second mention or any credit at all."

Miss Carlyle gave a cheerful little laugh. "Inspector, I take pleasure in someone who enjoys the same things that I do. I have several hybrid plants to my credit. Alice worked hard, very hard, at running the mill, her charities, seeing to the welfare of her family. She shed a lot of that care when she was with her plants. She laughed, even told jokes. If you had known her, you would understand what a rarity that was. She showed a stern, matriarchal face to the world. Only when she was in the greenhouse or working on her projects was she truly happy. If you could have seen the day it was evident that her attempts had been successful, you would understand.

"I was proud to be part of that. I hold no animosity about the hybrids. None at all." There was finality in her tone, and Steve recognized that same tone from when his Mimi had laid down the law. It was almost a warning that this line of questioning was at an end. Since he could not find any crack in her story, he let it drop.

Steve looked at Buck, who shrugged. "Thank you, Miss Carlyle. We appreciate your help. Will you send in Professor Poltovski, please?" She rose and opened the door.

Jeremy was standing in the hall. He cleared his throat gently. "Sir, I will call the professor, as necessary. I thought refreshments would be in order," he said in his rich, plummy voice. He pushed a cart into the room. It contained a pitcher of water, a full ice bucket, glassware, and napkins. On the lower level of the cart was the familiar coffee service.

With a look of distaste, Steve said, "I think we can drink water and interview people at the same time, Jeremy. Just serve it and Miss Carlyle can fetch the professor."

Buck, looking at Jeremy, inserted, "Steve, I think we should let Jeremy have his way. We can talk about the interviews we have had so far."

Puzzled, Steve waved his agreement, and Miss Carlyle left with a nod. Jeremy closed the door and turned to the two men. Ceremonially, he extracted a large silver flask from his back pocket. He handed it to Steve with a little flourish. "With the compliments of Miss Silene, sir."

The flask was engraved. "Inspector Walsh, won't you come out tonight and dance by the light of the moon? Love, Silene." Buck and Steve laughed at the reference to the popular song. They admired the polished surface and elegant calligraphy. Steve took the flask from a smiling Jeremy and poured a drink into one of the glasses. He looked at Buck with an arched eyebrow.

"No, thanks," Buck said, raising a hand.

"Come on. I'm on duty, too. I won't tell, and one won't hurt you," pressed Steve.

Buck laughed. "It's not that. I took the pledge. I am an official teetotaler. Since after the war ended and I got back. For Margaret, I gave up fighting, smoking, and drinking. Her father was a drunk, and that was one of the requirements before she would marry me." Embarrassed, he added, "Actually, I never liked the stuff anyway. It always seemed to have no effect on me until the last drink, and then I woke up with a raging headache and usually had to get bailed out of the brig. So giving it up was really no hardship for me."

Steve had known a few men who had taken the pledge, but they usually were henpecked husbands or religious folk.

Jeremy had set up the coffee service and handed a cup to Buck. When Steve turned to him and arched a polite eyebrow, he smiled professionally and shook his head. "I will conform to Mrs. Chandler's wishes, sir. If I imbibe, it will be somewhere else. Thank you anyway, sir. Also, that is bourbon; Scotch whisky is my poison." He had been in America long enough not to be surprised at how they related to servants.

Steve extracted a cigarette from the rosewood box and lit it. He took a sip and looked at the glass in admiration. "Silene certainly has good taste in liquor." He respected Buck's decision but was not going to let it interfere with his own pleasure.

Buck brought his coffee and notebook over to the desk. "A few things we didn't get to talk about on the way up here. Neither one of the two taxis in town picked anyone up at the hotel or the mill. No one saw any taxi from out of town, and in Chandler a fact like that is not going to be missed. Gordon, the hotel doorman, was off duty at eight o'clock, but no one had picked up the Sullivans, either one, by the time he left.

"I found a guy in Harrotsville who said he saw Silene Chandler there, driving around in a black roadster. The time was a few minutes after nine, so she didn't have time to drive up here and back."

"How did he remember the night, time, car, and person?" asked Steve. He had interviewed a lot of people who were positive about facts until they were proven wrong.

Buck smiled. "He owns the premier jewelry store down there. He had just shut his store and was on his way to his anniversary celebration. When he stepped off the curb, the car almost hit him, and he recognized Silene because she was one of his best customers. Miss Chandler likes her baubles. She probably got your flask there. I talked to the police chief down there, and the gentleman had filed a complaint, which he withdrew the next day. I imagine he thought that future business trumped the indignity of having to dive for the curb. Anyway, I called the man and he swore he knew the driver and the time."

Steve sighed. "That rules her out." He did not know if his relief was for the young woman or because they had eliminated a suspect. He fixed himself another short drink while he considered the question.

"What about Haney? How trustworthy is he?" asked the inspector.

"Don't even think it," answered Buck. "I told you that Ross Haney takes his job and duty very seriously. He doesn't drink or sleep on the job. If Mr. Chandler had asked him to lie, Ross would have quit. His world is black and white, and I think he would rather die than fail his own sense of honor.

"We test all the watchmen. Try to bribe them, get them to look the other way, or keep them from their duty. Haney, old as he is, punched our man and broke his nose. If Haney said he didn't see Francis Chandler leave the building, he didn't. I would stake my job on it."

Steve looked at his drink in disgust. He stubbed his cigarette out with savage stabs. "So, at this point, we have nothing. Not a suspect. Unless Poltovski or the Joneses confess, the closest we have is the Sullivans, who were miles away at the hotel at the time. And the case against them is weak or nearly nonexistent." Steve screwed the measuring cap on the flask. He tucked it into his coat pocket and patted it before he asked Buck to ring for Jeremy.

Chapter 11

Professor Poltovski tapped lightly and with evident embarrassment on the doorjamb. He stood hesitantly, his coat over his arm and his fedora clutched nervously in his hands. He was stoop-shouldered, short, and thin. The suit he wore was slightly shabby and frayed at the cuffs. The leather patches at his elbows could have been professorial affectation or necessary to cover holes. His face was pinched, and a tic pulsed under his left eye. A prominent hawk nose overshadowed the rest of his face, and his thin lower lip was clenched between yellowed teeth. A green bow tie, slightly askew, circled his scrawny neck.

The two officers rose. "Come in, Professor," invited Steve. "Are you planning on going somewhere?" he asked, indicating the coat and hat.

Poltovski looked at the garments as if he had never seen them before. "No. I had not planned on it," he replied with an Eastern European accent. "Is it planned for me?" he asked nervously.

"I was just wondering why you have your hat and coat."

He answered, puzzled, "They are mine. I take them with me. Is this not allowed?"

Steve dropped the subject and invited him to sit. He reached across the desk to shake hands. The professor looked at the extended hand as if Steve wanted something. Hesitantly, he gave the proffered hand a quick shake and perched on the very edge of the chair before the desk. Steve sat down. The professor stared at him intently, which was slightly disconcerting. Steve did notice that the man clasped his hands together tightly but not enough to hide their faint tremor.

He answered Steve's question on his movements the night of the murder with pauses and hesitations. "I took a plate and some food. I eat—ate—it at the table. I had some tea that the kind Mrs. Chandler had imported for me from Hungary. After that, I went to the garden to sit and enjoy. I talk to Anna a few minutes before. Some went to leave, and then I hear a scream and went, too. Jeremy close door, and we wait for police." He waved a hand over his shoulder toward Buck, who nodded.

"I have answered these questions to the captain. Did I say something bad, wrong?" A nervous pressure seemed to be building within the tense man.

Steve leaned back, thinking. "How did you come to know the Chandlers?"

"Ah. I was a professor of languages in Budapest. Mr. Chandler came for business. I was asked to be translator, though my English was not so good. I teach old languages: Latin, Greek. I read ancient Egyptian, Aramaic, and Armenian. But my English is not so good as now."

Steve leaned forward. "So why did they ask you to translate? I mean, if your English was not so good. Did Mrs. Chandler have anything to do with it?"

"No, no. Mrs. Chandler was not there. Mr. Chandler come alone. It was on business, for selling his cloth. I was ask because I knew the diplomat from United States. He was interest in old cultures and language. Much interest in Egypt. Wanted to dig there. He ask me to help."

Buck shifted in his chair and leaned forward. "Professor, how did you come to teach here in America?" he asked quietly.

The professor twisted in his chair. "Mr. Chandler ask me. I am for freedom of Hungary. I am not loved and was to lose my position. I worry. What is a professor of languages to do? And I am Quaker. My father was in Pennsylvania to work in steel mill for some years and came to be Quaker. I am for peace, and war was close. Mr. Chandler fix for me to come to America and get job with school to teach. He was my good friend. I like gardens. We talk, and I show him my garden in my home. It was fine. I do not know why you are ask these questions." He seemed on the edge of panic and his voice cracked. "The police in Austria-Hungary ask questions so. They are trying to trap one into being guilty. Why are you doing this? Are you trapping me?" He stood up, clutching his coat and hat fiercely to his breast.

Steve leaned back and smiled to reassure the older gentleman. "Please, Professor, sit down. I am not trying to trap you. I am just trying to get to the bottom of the death of Mrs. Chandler. I am sorry if you had problems in the Old Country, but let me assure you, I only want the truth and I need your help finding it."

Poltovski stood a few more seconds before finally seeming to relax a little. He resumed his seat. "I am sorry, Inspector. I am afraid to be sent back. I want to be citizen of United States. I think Francis Chandler does not like me and will have me sent back. It would be bad. My father and mother are Jewish. They want to go to Eretz Yisrael even if they are Quaker. They may be of Jewish faith again, if they get there. Mrs. Chandler was talking to the new government to help."

Steve was confused. "Professor, how long have you been in the States?"

"Oh, Mr. Chandler bring me here in 1914, in April. He pay for ship, and I came to your Ellis Island. I was met and come here. Got job at school. I work hard."

Steve interrupted, "You've been here long enough. Become a citizen."

Poltovski looked embarrassed. "I think that when Mr. Chandler die, I could not be a citizen. Francis say that I would be sent back when his father die. I was enemy to America, and the police would come."

More confused than ever, Steve asked, "What has Francis got to do with your becoming a citizen?" This was getting out of hand, but Steve knew he had to calm the professor down. "Are you worried about your parents or yourself?"

The professor shook his head. "You are confuse, please. When America go to war, Francis say that I am alien from Austria-Hungary, and police will send me back. I was frightened. He say I need his father or a person to say I am good to be citizen."

"Look, Professor. You have been here long enough to be a citizen. They won't send you back. All you have to do is apply. Nobody needs to vouch for you. Just bring your entry papers to the Immigration Office in Hartford." Steve vaguely remembered a section on immigration law at the New York Law School.

"Oh, yes. I know," Poltovski said, nodding.

Steve felt that he had just fallen down the rabbit hole. "Then what are you worried about?"

"I do not worry, now. I speak with Mrs. Chandler and she says to do what you say. And I do it. Now I must worry about my parents."

To get back on track, Steve offered, "I will talk with Silene Chandler, Professor. She may know what to do about your parents' problem." Buck looked as confused as Steve felt.

"What was your relationship with Mrs. Chandler, Professor Poltovski?" He slipped in the question before the professor got him off track again.

Poltovski straightened immediately, as if he knew in which direction this line of questioning was bound to go. "We were friends, Inspector. When Mr. Chandler send for me, they were helping me with job, they find a house to live. When I say when I want be citizen, he help me. Mr. Chandler help with papers. Then he die and Francis talk to me. I am afraid. He talk of sending people back to Europe. I spoke to Mrs. Chandler. One who marries a citizen can be citizen. I like her much. I think she like me and would help. We talked and I ask if she would marry me. I tell her why I want this. She laugh … "

"Did that make you angry? That she laughed at you?" pounced Steve.

"She laugh and say to me I do not worry. Mrs. Chandler say that she would not let them send me away. She say that I have first paper and her lawyer will help with being citizen. I think how powerful she was in government, to make them make me citizen. So I go and will be citizen soon. But my parents, they want to go to Eretz Yisrael and be Jews. They have no money to go. Mrs. Chandler say she will help them."

Back to the parents, thought Steve. He made a mental note to ask Silene for help, even though he knew that he would have to endure her innuendos and flirtatious behavior. He grinned to himself and thought, *Maybe I should call her bluff.* A brief chill slid up his spine. He wondered what Julie would think if she heard about it. Even scarier, what would he do if Silene called his? He shivered again.

Steve's thoughts were interrupted when Buck cleared his throat. The professor was still sitting hunched in the chair. "Thank you, Professor," Steve said. "That will be all." When he hesitated, Steve continued, "I will be sure to talk with Miss Silene about your parents."

A smile almost crept to his lips as Poltovski rose and bobbed his head at the two officers. At the door, he gave a short bow and quickly disappeared as if afraid that he would be called back.

Buck stretched out his legs and observed, "What a poor guy. For my money, I would bet that he has spent his whole life being afraid of something. No way could he have a reason to murder her. She was his only hope, to his mind, for getting his parents to Palestine or Eretz Yisrael or wherever. A little more insight into Francis. He apparently took pleasure in threatening the professor."

Steve shook his head disgustedly. "So, Mrs. Black strikes again. She is one twisted lady. I wish I knew something we could grill her with. Serve her right to be on the hot seat because of some rumor. I tend to agree with you on the professor. And Francis."

✂ Chapter 12

Steve decided to interview the Joneses at the same time rather than try to separate them. He asked Jeremy to fetch another chair once the butler had escorted them into the room. Meanwhile, Buck offered his and stood by the door. His presence behind them seemed to make Wanda nervous, and she kept looking over her shoulder until the interview started. She had a thin, wiry frame. She was a few inches taller than her husband. Lusterless short brown hair topped her round skull. A broad forehead and large, pale eyes that had more focus than earlier dominated her browned, weather-beaten face. A button nose and tiny mouth above a narrow, pointed chin seemed out of proportion to the rest of her. She had wide, muscular shoulders and work-roughened hands, which she kept tightly folded in her lap. Her heavy work shirt, heavy denim pants, and work shoes seemed out of place in the elegantly appointed room.

Her husband looked bulky. A round bullet head with a fringe of ginger hair topped a thick, almost nonexistent neck that spread into wide, muscular shoulders. Thick ginger eyebrows grew in a single line over his deep-set, dark eyes. A bulbous nose, which had met with something hard at one time or another, was a blob in the center of his face. He had thick lips and a round, hard-looking chin. His clothing was a match for his wife's. His shirtsleeves were rolled up to just below his elbows, revealing powerful arms. Thick wrists held massive hands curled into fists. His whole demeanor betokened power and barely controlled anger tinged with fear.

Wanda apologized that they had not had time to change. They had been moving plants to the pavilion all week and were setting up for the show.

Mrs. Jones's head snapped around when Steve asked, "Mr. and Mrs. Jones, the night of Mrs. Chandler's murder, what can you tell us about your movements and the movements of the others on the committee and the staff?"

Barry jumped to his feet and leaned on the desk, supported by his spread sausage-like fingers. "Are you accusing us of this crime? Just because we're foreigners, you can't pin this bloody murder on us." He turned to his wife and said, "Come on, Wanda. I am not about to stand here and be railroaded." His Yorkshire accent became more profound the madder he got.

Steve sighed. *First Sullivan, now Jones,* he thought. With all the rampant rumors about crooked cops, half the time he questioned anyone it seemed they thought he was getting paid to scapegoat them to save the real perpetrator. He gave the man his standard reply: "I am not accusing anyone of anything at this time. It is very likely that I will, but not at this time. Unless you want me to, and then I will happily cuff the both of you and drag you off to Hartford. Now, either hold out your hands or sit down." This last was delivered in a whipsaw voice that rose in volume. Barry was a big man, and when he leaned over the desk in an intimidating manner, Steve squared his feet beneath his chair. He was ready to rise and meet any aggression.

"Be careful, Mr. Jones," he said quietly, looking him in the eye. Steve was prepared to slide his chair back and out of reach. He certainly did not want to get into a fight. Even though Steve gave away twenty pounds and a couple of inches of reach to the nurseryman, he was not worried. He had been beaten and robbed in London when he had strayed into an unsavory part of town. When he had been released from the hospital and returned to his intelligence office at the embassy, his Japanese counterpart had worked with him on the art of jujitsu. Over the years, he had found a trainer to help him continue working on his skills, when he had a chance. However, even though he was confident in his ability to do some damage to Barry, the room was too crowded, and someone was sure to get hurt or furnishings damaged.

Buck, unaware of Steve's skills, had risen slowly and taken two silent steps forward. He had drawn his sap out of a hip pocket and was balancing it in his hand, gauging the distance to Barry's head.

"Barry. Please, sit down. Please," Wanda begged, grabbing her husband's arm.

He glanced at her and back to Steve. Hesitantly, he sat down and held his wife's hand. "Sorry," Barry said gruffly.

Buck repocketed the lead-shot–filled leather bag and backed up to his position next to the door. Barry had never even been aware how close he had come to waking up in a cell with a severe headache.

"Same question." Steve returned to the interview, leaning forward and glancing at his notebook.

While Barry answered, Jeremy entered quietly with a chair. Buck nodded his thanks, and the butler silently closed the door as he left. Barry answered in a calmer tone, "We broke about eight, eight thirty and went into the dining room. I think the last person to leave was Emma. She was talking to Alice about the hanging loops or banding or something. We had decided on the light or dark between us, but not which.

"Wanda and I got something to eat, and when we finished, we went outside."

Wanda inserted disgustedly, "We would rather not hang around with that malicious woman, Emma Black."

"Shh, Wanda," her husband said. Steve noticed that when Barry got excited, Wanda brought him back to earth and vice versa. "Anyway, we went out. The professor was talking to Mary. Anna had already gone outside. I don't remember what the servants were doing. I didn't notice. Sorry."

Steve looked at Wanda. "Is that what you remember?"

"Yes, yes. After we ate, by the balustrade, I went to look at some bayberry plants that we had replaced. We take care of the grounds now, you know. Since Huskins retired."

Barry quickly said, "I went to some new bushes on the other side of the terrace. Alice had a tendency to overwater, no matter how many times we told her we would take care of it when we came out."

"Did you see Anna Carlyle?"

Barry shook his head, and Wanda looked thoughtful for a few seconds before she answered. "Yes, she was sitting on one of the benches by the door. In the shadows. I think she was drinking tea?"

"Oh, yeah," said Barry and snapped his fingers. "Lech came out and was talking to her after I checked on the bushes; then Anna went inside."

"Wait, Barry—wasn't Alice in the dining room? She said something to Anna and left the room. She usually goes back to the sewing room to look at things. I remember Emma wanted to accompany her, but Alice went alone. Then we went out to the terrace."

"Yes, Inspector. That's the way it was. Anna went through the hall when she left Lech. Wanda and I were sitting on the balustrade then."

"Then Miss Carlyle talked to Mrs. Chandler before she went upstairs?" Steve wanted to catch someone in a lie.

Wanda took a deep breath. "Wait. Barry and I went to see the plants after we filled our plates. It was after that I saw Anna speaking with Alice. It had to be after she came back down, unless … Oh, I can't remember now."

Barry put his arm around his wife. "Inspector, give her a minute. It must have been after she came down. When we sat down, after looking at the plants, Alice was alone. Or, she might have been talking to Jeremy or Emma. I don't really remember. But a few moments later Anna stepped into view and said something to Alice."

Steve wrote and asked, when he finished, "How were relations between you and Mrs. Chandler?"

The couple glanced at each other. Finally, Barry said cautiously, "Mrs. Chandler brought us over after the war. She … "

Steve interrupted. "Is this necessary? I am not really interested in how you got here." He did not want another long conversation like the one with Poltovski.

"Well, I think it is," Barry answered diffidently. "To understand the relationship between the Chandlers and us." Wanda nodded encouragement.

Steve nodded for him to continue with a shrug.

"A. J. was staying with our employer in England before the war. General Williams was in procurement for the War Department. Mr. Chandler was over selling products from the cotton mill. After the war, when the general died, we wrote to him. Mr. Chandler had admired our gardens and asked if we wanted to leave and come to America. The death taxes forced the family to sell the property, and we, and Jeremy, did not much care for the new owner. Acted like King of the May.

"Mrs. Chandler wrote back and informed us of the death of Mr. Chandler. She had heard of us from her husband and, to honor his wishes, paid for our passage. We emigrated. When we arrived, she loaned us the money to start the business, as a silent partner. Mrs. Chandler already had a gardener on the property. He had been with the family for years, and she did not want to set him out on his ear, so she refused to hire us here at the house to avoid any problems, as old Huskins had his own staff. That's when she suggested that we start the nursery."

Buck interrupted, "How did you feel about that? Mrs. Chandler not wanting you around and all."

Wanda twisted around. "Oh, we understood. Mrs. Chandler couldn't very well oust the current gov'nor just because we showed up. We were perfectly happy with the business. It gave us a chance to work for ourselves. Make something. Later, when Huskins retired, Alice gave him his cottage on the property to stay in for the rest of his time and started asking us to offer suggestions and work on the property for special projects. We did work for the house and the farms.

"We also had the work at the mill. And we took care of the city parks and other city properties. Alice liked real plants rather than the silk. We took care of the potted plants at the city hall and company properties. We also did work for other families in the area and sold plants and trees and the like."

Barry patted her hand and picked up the train of thought. "Mrs. Chandler put us on the flower show committee. I don't do much on the quilt, of course. I would probably sew my fingers to it if they let me near with a needle and thread." He gave a little self-deprecating laugh. "I was around to do scut work—fetch and carry, bring thread, move the frame around, things like that. A lot of the time, I just talked with Jeremy and waited for instructions. But when the show was being set up or during and afterward, that's when they needed me, to move plants around and such. Also, I studied garden layout, and Lech, Wanda, and I designed the layout of the pavilion."

Wanda quickly added, "We never were late with the payments. The business was doing well. I mean, after the rough time right after the war, but everyone was having difficulties then. Mrs. Chandler let a few months slide here and there, but we paid her up."

Steve flipped back through his notes. He rubbed his nose, trying to think how to present the next question. Finally, he took a deep breath and braced himself for a strong reaction. "This has come up in prior interviews. I understand that there was an incident at the Christmas party held at the nursery … "

Wanda spat out an expletive. "That bloody bi … "

"Wanda," snapped her husband.

She threw an angry look at him and continued, with a rein on her temper. "That would be Emma Black. She is a vicious gossip. I suppose she told you that I drink, too."

"Wanda, let me, please," interrupted Barry. "About Christmas. Yes, I was a little tight, as was Miss Silene, though that does in no way make it all right. There was mistletoe over all the doorways and around the grounds, you know, as decorations for the party, and she was standing under a cluster. I kissed her, and she returned it. I got carried away and she put me in my place. I apologized. Wanda came out then and took me aside and tore into me. She was that angry I acted as I did, but even more, she was worried that Mrs. Chandler would be angry and we would lose the mill and town business. That she would call in her loan and we would lose everything. Alice had a large amount of influence, and she could have ruined the business."

When he paused, Steve asked, "And the drinking?" He was interested in the answer more to ease his own curiosity about how Mrs. Black twisted the facts than to further the investigation.

"My wife," continued Barry, "had an accident while exercising a hunter for a sick groom when she was young. Her horse was startled when a covey of quail burst in front of him, and she was thrown. She spent many months recovering and was given opiates, which she still takes on occasion. Wanda only takes them when necessary, but the pain is so great that, at times, she overmedicates. The effects are much the same as overindulgence in alcohol. Unsteadiness and slurred speech."

Steve nodded. He had seen the results of opium addiction when he was young. A sailor uncle of his indulged on one of his rare visits to the family farm and was told that he would not be welcome again if he brought "that poison" with him. His father had been livid.

"So there is no truth that you went to Mrs. Chandler and demanded that she talk to Silene?"

Wanda looked offended. "Certainly not! Mrs. Black was there at the party, and we knew that *she* would be more than happy to spread her vitriol. As I understand, she did go to Alice and had her ears scorched about something with Catherine and didn't dare bring this thing about Silene up. Barry and I were more than happy to let it drop. I guess Silene didn't say anything either. That one is straight up."

"One more question and we are through for now. Did you see anyone? A stranger or someone you didn't expect to see around?"

Both of them thought a moment and shook their heads. Steve thanked them and threw down his pencil in disgust as they left the room. "Well, from everyone being a suspect to no one being a suspect."

Buck chuckled. "You expected it to be easy? Someone to walk in here and admit everything?"

Steve flicked the cigarette he had just extracted from the box on the desk at the constable. "I can hope. No, but I had hoped for a clue somewhere along the line," he replied as he moved around the desk to pick up the cigarette.

"What next?" asked Buck.

Steve perched on the corner of the desk and contemplated the question. "Tomorrow I am going to look around the plant. Can you get me the medical examiner's report from the sheriff's office? Also, the report on their investigation on fingerprints and the rest of anything in the sewing room. I will need a car, though. Lend me one from your department?"

Buck finished his coffee and said, "Sure. I'll take you to the station and you can take my car from there. I'll use the official automobile for the run up to the county seat to meet with the investigators who were at the house that night. Just don't wreck it. You will have to answer to Margaret while I get on the next slow boat to China."

They bid farewell to the committee members in the sewing room, to mixed reactions. Steve observed that they had decided on the olive and magenta loops to hang the quilt.

Chapter 13

On the way back down the hill, Buck shot Steve a curious look. "I thought you wanted to rattle Mrs. Black's chain."

Steve chuckled. "I was tempted after all the blind alleys she set us up with. Typical of a malicious rumormonger—everything she said had a kernel of truth but was actually a lie. I think she is the only one who is hated by the rest. Anyway, it wouldn't be professional," he said with an air of sanctity. "A woman like that always gets her just deserts when she least expects it. But to tell you the truth, I just couldn't make it convincing. Even she would have trouble believing the gossip I had cooked up."

"Tell Uncle Buck just what you had planned," he entreated with an anticipatory grin.

Steve lit a cigarette and rolled down the window to flick out the match before he said, "Oh, I was going to tell her that I heard that some people said that all three of the Chandler children were hers, and that she had cheated on her husband with A. J. Chandler and begged him to adopt them."

Buck laughed out loud and almost wrecked the car on the narrow drive. "And what was Mrs. Chandler doing while all of this philandering was going on?"

"She was saving the family name. Mrs. Black was probably a long-lost cousin or something. She couldn't abide the scandal, you know, really," he finished, with an atrocious upper-crust accent. "And watch where you are driving. I don't want to be the main guest at my own funeral. My boss would exhume me just to kick my tail for inconveniencing him."

Buck snorted. "You would have a wonderful ceremony. What with all the women who hate you. We would have to hire the hotel's ballroom to hold them all." They came to the gate, waved to Huskins walking his old dog by the road, and turned toward town.

Buck drove to the police station and parked next to his private automobile. Steve opened the door, but Buck asked before he stepped out, "Do you have any thoughts about the case?"

Steve sighed deeply and shook his head. "First of all, the people at the house. Mrs. Black and the professor don't have the strength. With the way his hands tremble, I would guess that he has palsy or something like that. Mrs. Flowers is just too timid. Unless she is the greatest actress in the world, Miss Carlyle just doesn't fill the bill. The servants are out, as far as I'm concerned. They had duties and would have been missed, even for a few minutes. The Joneses said they had been moving plants all week. Wanda was probably taking her medication, like tonight, and was too fuzzy to plan, much less carry out, the murder. That leaves Barry, but he was at the opposite end of the terrace. He was in sight of either Wanda or the professor or the Carlyle woman.

"How would someone get around here where everyone knows everybody else and being incognito is almost impossible? I mean, there are two independent taxis in town, you told me. And you talked to both drivers. Silene, Francis, and the Sullivans would all be recognized. Same thing with borrowing a car—if they could borrow a car, someone would see it and them, or the owner would undoubtedly say something when Mrs. Chandler died. Added to that, Huskins would be around at the gate and would have seen them unless they parked the car and walked in, which would have taken a lot of time and left the car to be seen. And if they couldn't have gotten there using a car, they certainly couldn't have walked in the time frame we're talking about. Silene has an alibi, so she is out. So, if Francis or the Sullivans are involved, how did they get from the mill or town to the house and back? The Sullivans didn't have a car, and Francis would have been seen by the watchman at the mill. That means Haney and/or Huskins would have had to be part of it somehow."

Steve snapped his fingers and grabbed Julie's notebook from his pocket. "Wait a minute." He flipped pages until he came to the write-up she had on Francis. "Francis cycles. Could he have gotten to the house from the mill without being seen on a bicycle?"

Buck gave himself a slap on the forehead. "I must be getting old. Francis wants to be a captain of the United States Olympic cycling team in the next Games. He travels all over the countryside. And, yes, he rides from the house to work on good days, along an old farm road. There is a private bathroom on the office floor, complete with a shower. He has changes of clothes in a closet upstairs."

Steve smiled. "Then the only thing is to prove or disprove that he cycled to the house, murdered his mother and cycled back. All without being seen."

Buck nodded. "The 'not being seen' would not be difficult from near the mill to the side of the house. Like I said, an old farm road runs along the hillside around the town, through thick trees. It's on the far side of the house and mill."

Steve tapped his finger on the roof of the car. "It would all be circumstantial, though. There is no way to place him in the room with the shears in his hand. With as much pull as this family has, we would almost need photographs and film footage, plus an audience of judges. Well, let's prove that he or the Sullivans could have been there and worry about the actual murder later. Ah, I hate cases like this. Give me an old-time shoot-out with gangsters any time."

"Just out of curiosity, what was that gut feeling you were talking about?" asked Buck.

"Something along the cycle lines. Long-distance running. This cycle thing is a lot better. It would get him there and back faster."

Buck asked, "So you've settled on Francis?"

Steve tilted his head and replied, "It's a gut feeling. How he acted during the interview. No emotion, and I got the feeling he was playing with us. Also, he has the weakest alibi. I want to look over the mill and see what's what. But, yeah, he feels right." He continued, "Not that we ignore anyone else, mind you, but I trust my gut."

With a laugh, Buck said, "I hope it's not indigestion."

Steve stepped out of the car and, before slipping behind the wheel of Buck's automobile, said, "Let me know how you make out tomorrow with the sheriff."

"And you have fun digging around."

Steve drove to the hotel, found a place to park, and walked in. When he arrived at the desk, Pete handed him a telegram along with his key. Tearing it open, he read, "Call me. Immediately. Whatever time you get in. (signed) Crowder."

He sighed and looked at his watch. It was ten thirty, much too late to contact his boss. Steve asked the clerk to call him at seven a.m. and have a connection ready at eight o'clock to Bob Crowder at the State Police office in Hartford. He also needed a private office where he could talk. The clerk called the night manager and arranged to have the manager's office made available to Steve.

Steve took the elevator to his floor and changed into his pajamas before collapsing in his bed. He decided that he could give his teeth a break from brushing this one time.

The knock on his door came much too early, and he gave a groggy shout to let the bellhop know that he was up. He stood under the cold water in the shower to finish waking himself. He shaved, made it up to his teeth for the previous night's neglect, and dressed.

On his way through the lobby to the manager's office, he tipped the bellhop to get him a cup of coffee from the restaurant.

He spoke with the manager and was given access to the office, where he sat heavily in the chair, waiting for his call and coffee. The uniformed bellhop arrived first and deposited the tray on the desk. Steve told him to bring a follow-up cup in ten minutes. Halfway through the second cup, the phone rang.

"Steve Walsh, here," he said after picking up the receiver.

"Your call to Mr. Crowder, sir," answered the operator.

"That you, Steve?" came as a bellow down the line. Bob seemed to think the farther away the other party was, the louder a voice was required.

"Yes, Chief," returned Steve, holding the receiver away from his ear.

"I told you to call me when you got in. Where have you been?"

Steve sipped his coffee and replied, "It was late last night, unless you were in your office all night waiting." In the following pause, Steve lit a cigarette.

"No, I went home at nine last night," he grudgingly admitted. "You should have been in before then," Bob said accusingly.

"Well, I wasn't."

Bob growled, "Well, you should have been. What is going on down there? I have been up to my neck in politicians demanding answers. I figured that you would have something by now. You asked for this assignment, and I am really disappointed that there isn't any word from you! Didn't I tell you I wanted daily reports?"

Steve gave the phone a hard look. There must be a lot of pressure if Bob was this close to panic. He seemed to have forgotten that he had shanghaied Steve for this investigation. Steve almost snapped at his boss but was able to check his temper. He was glad that the coffee had come before the call. Bob usually was able to handle the normal second-guessers during an investigation.

"Calm down, Bob," he finally said, a little sharply. "I've only been here a day. Give me a little time. Be fair. Who is this that you can't handle?"

A pause came from the other end of the line. "I didn't say I couldn't handle anything," he said truculently. "I have just had a couple of calls asking about the investigation. The murder was almost a week ago," he exaggerated.

"Who, Bob?" Steve asked, struggling for patience.

His sigh whistled down the line. "Both sides. They want to know what the situation is for the next election. Is the Chandler machine falling apart, or is there someone down there who is going to take over? I had ex-Senator Bradly erupting to the news that this office was botching the investigation of the murder of such an important woman, and there should be a new regime at this office, and on and on. There have been calls from the newspapers, and I have a couple of scribblers here pestering everyone for news. The governor called. He's worried about the next election too. This keeps up, and I am going to take an ax to the phone."

He was almost begging when he continued, "Tell me you have something. Just any little thing I can pass along."

Steve shook his head and lit another cigarette. His third round of coffee showed up as he tried to calm his boss down. "Bob. I haven't had much time here. I am still just clearing out the brush. I have interviewed the people here and have narrowed down the field. There's a new line that Captain Daniels and I are pursuing." He kept it vague. He did not want to give Bob too much detail or he would be getting a lot of useless advice. Bob was a great bulwark against the politicians and press, but he was no detective.

"Come on. One fact. Give me a name, a hint, a ghost of something to spread around. I can't use the 'close to an arrest' comment one more time. Oh, and by the way, I got a call from the governor's aide. He wants to know when the body will be released for a funeral. He is getting pressure from the party. *They* want a big show to get themselves on the front page and their latest scandal off. I know," he continued as if he had just thought of the idea. "Let me send the reporters down there. They could get the story firsthand from you. Say, that's a great idea."

"I wouldn't send those newshounds down here if I were you, Bob," Steve warned his boss. "They wouldn't get anything and would swarm you more than they are doing now when they get back. And I don't want them dogging me and getting underfoot while I am investigating. I can give you fifty dollars' worth of report, but you have the high points now, and all you would do is give money to the telephone exchange company and keep me from doing my job. Now, stiffen your spine and stop panicking. If you can't tell them an arrest is imminent, tell them you have no comment. Or spread some of that manure around that you are famous for," said Steve, letting the irritation he was feeling creep into his voice.

"Okay, I have to go and earn my keep and the third week of my paid vacation. You remember *that*, don't you? Three weeks, paid. Vacation. Good luck, and I will let you know whenever I have something. And *do not* send any of those bloodsucking reporters after me."

"All right, Steve, but if you can't handle this thing, I will have to have one of the other boys sent down there to pull your fat out of the fire." Bob closed the call before Steve could react.

Steve, lips compressed until they were almost invisible, stared at the receiver. He set it down carefully and then finished his coffee and cigarette. He got up and headed for the restaurant for breakfast. While eating his eggs and toast, he calmed down and told himself not to quit until after his three weeks off, at least. He was mopping up the last of the yolk when Julie purposely walked by his table and ignored him when he said, "Good morning."

Chapter 14

Steve finished his breakfast and signed the check. He picked up his hat from the chair beside him and crossed to the front desk. After getting the number from the desk clerk, he borrowed the phone and called the mill. Steve was passed from a switchboard operator to Francis Chandler's secretary. It took a few minutes to make an appointment to meet with Francis at ten o'clock. The large clock on the wall showed him he had more than an hour before he needed to start for the mill.

The sunshine streaming through the front windows drew him out to the street. He decided to walk around the business district and get a feel for the town. He turned left and strolled to the corner, crossed the street, and ambled along the front of the grocery store. Signs showed the items on sale, with some of the merchandise artfully arranged in pyramids of cans and rows of boxes. Fruits and vegetables were arrayed neatly in wheeled wooden carts on either side of the double doors. Further along, meats and fish were neatly placed in iced trays. The offerings looked fresh and, through the glass, trade looked brisk. A butcher nodded and gave him a friendly smile as he lifted a large chicken from its frozen bed. Steve stepped through the door into the cool, well-lighted interior. Shelves were well stocked, and the operation looked well run and prosperous. He had been in a few stores in company towns during his career, and this looked like none of them. A hubbub of cheerful conversation accompanied the bustle.

He exited and continued to the next block. He passed the shoe store and noticed the same care in the displays. Steve recognized some of the brands, and they would not bring shame to any store in Hartford. A woman was helping a young boy choose a pair of Buster Browns. Steve grinned at the obvious disagreement between the lad and his mother, reminding him of times when he had accompanied his own mother. A pang of regret at the estrangement between him and his parents marred the pleasant scene, and he walked on.

The adjoining business had a large watch hanging from a bracket over the door. At the edge of the sidewalk, a green-colored clock tower held a clock face on each side. The storefront was narrow and had only one window. "Felix Zimmerman Watch Repair," painted in gold, decorated the glass. A velvet cloth covered the slanted display area. On one side was a grouping of watches, and on the other a row of gold and silver bracelets, separated by a row of earrings in white gift boxes. Steve noticed that several of the bracelets had blank panels waiting for engraving.

He thought of the flask and entered. A bell jingled when hit by the front door. A man with a fringe of white hair around his bald head appeared from the back room. He was in shirtsleeves, wearing a white shirt with thin pink stripes, with garters around his biceps and sleeve protectors extending from wrist to elbow. His face was short, and thick glasses were set squarely on his hawk nose. Thin, smiling lips sat between sunken cheeks. "Can I help you, young gentleman?"

Steve hesitated, not knowing what to say. He had entered on a whim. Remembering the bracelets, he asked, "Do you engrave here, if I were to need it? Say, a silver flask?"

"Oh, no. We send the item to a jeweler in Harrotsville. He does the engraving, and we can have it the next day. We do not carry any flasks—the Eighteenth Amendment, you know." The old man jerkily pointed a finger at Steve. "You are the inspector from Hartford. Have you found out what happened to poor Mrs. Chandler?"

"Not yet. We are still investigating." He smiled to himself and remembered the advice he had given to Bob Crowder. "Did you know the Chandlers well?"

The older gentleman explained that he repaired the Chandler timepieces as needed. Every other year, he cleaned the grandfather clock with the black walnut case in Mr. Chandler's study. "It was his father's, and he was very particular with it," he said proudly.

"Did you know Mrs. Chandler well?"

"Mr. Chandler was very friendly," he replied, avoiding the question. Hesitantly, he added, "Mrs. Chandler was very good to the town. She was very civic-minded."

Steve got the picture. A. J. was a hale-fellow-well-met kind of guy; his spouse was generous but distant. The type of person you could admire and like, but not one to whom you could warm.

After thanking the man for his time, Steve continued his walk. His thoughts drifted to Silene's generous gift. Taunting gift? Spur-of-the-moment gift? The watch repairman did not carry silver flasks, so Steve assumed that Silene had driven all the way to Harrotsville. Would she do that as a joke? Steve remembered when he had driven all the

way to town on his bike to buy, and get engraved, a locket
for Mary Elizabeth Murray. He had been twelve and almost
missed her birthday party. Steve had been madly in love and
was sure that the two of them would be married and live
happily ever after. He wondered what could have motivated
Silene to drive all that way just to get a gag gift. An expensive
gag gift.

He came to the combination haberdashery and tailor
shop sitting in the center of the block behind the library.
He turned in and heard the sound of the bell. Immediately,
a salesman in a dark summer-weight wool suit approached.
With a generous smile, the diminutive clerk asked, "May I
help you, sir?"

On a whim, Steve answered, "I'm looking for a couple of
shirts and a tie."

"Very good," said the man, pleasantly. He extracted a
tape from his coat pocket and quickly took Steve's measure-
ments, writing the results on a pad. Steve was led to a shelf
of neatly folded shirts arranged in cubbyholes in a rack on
the wall. The quality of the goods was excellent, Steve found
when he fingered the cloth.

The salesman told Steve pompously, "We purchase only
from those companies who use our mill's product. The
thread count is 400, and you will feel how exceptional it
is. This is a fine shirt, and you will be very happy with it, I
am sure."

Steve had not planned on purchasing anything but
ended up with two shirts, light blue and dark brown, with
French cuffs. He added a maroon tie embroidered with tiny
gold horseshoes. He paid and took the wrapped and tied
purchases under his arm.

Out of thin air, the clerk asked fastidiously, "Have you found the person who, who, um, did in Mrs. Chandler?"

Steve fought hard not to laugh at the phrase. "No, we are still investigating. Did Mrs. Chandler shop here?"

"Mrs. Chandler shopped at the milliner's. Mr. Chandler, however, had us manufacture all his suits," answered the fussy little man. "He had rather wide shoulders. Young Mr. Chandler has followed in his father's footsteps. He favors double-breasted suits."

Steve thanked him and exited into the warm summer day.

"Return soon, sir. It has been a pleasure to serve you," called the clerk politely.

Steve saw Julie sitting on a bench in the library gardens, nonchalantly feeding the pigeons bits of bread. He suspected she had not randomly picked that particular bench, sitting as it was across from the haberdashery, when she had to pass several others on her way from the hotel.

He squared his shoulders, suppressed the grin that was struggling to form, and crossed the street. Steve seated himself and waited.

"I do not recall inviting you to sit," she said coolly. She continued to tear a piece of toast to pieces and drop them to the greedy birds, not even glancing his way.

"I don't either. So I invited myself." He hoped the weak humor would thaw her attitude. It did not. "Spoke with Bob Crowder this morning," he said. Julie ignored him. "He is getting a lot of pressure from everybody in the capital." She coughed nonchalantly into her fisted hand and continued to shred the toast. "Wants to send another investigator down to replace me." She hesitated a moment before she dropped another offering. "Also wanted to sic a bunch of reporters on me. Knew that I wouldn't talk, but my replacement would."

Julie removed a napkin from her large purse and extracted another triangle of toast. Steve could see her set her lips as she stared at the unseen bread in her hand. Casually, she brushed her hair out of her eyes and glanced at him. "Why would they want to replace you? Not that I care much one way or the other."

Steve hid his triumphant smile. "He is in a panic and needs a scapegoat. I am on the ground and the prime candidate."

"Oh, I am sure that is not the way Chief Crowder thinks. He knows you are the best investigator he has. Unless, of course, you are in over your head or have lost your touch." Unconsciously, she took a bite with her strong, white teeth.

He laughed. "Nope. He is just panicking. I called his bluff. We will see later today if someone else shows up from the department. Never can tell with Bob. He gets his tail in a crack and he is likely to do anything."

"Did you tell him you are close to finding the murderer?" she asked casually, continuing her fishing expedition. Julie began demolishing the rest of the toast. She pretended disinterest and continued, "What are you planning to do next?"

"Take a ride and look at the mill. Try to find a lead that I can use to crack someone's alibi."

"Silene's?" she asked too quickly.

Steve offered his cigarette case and she snatched a cigarette. He pretended to think about her response while he extracted and snapped a match alight with his thumbnail. Julie dipped her head over the flame, cupping his hand. After lighting his own cigarette, he replied slowly, teasing her,

"You're right. I probably should have another long talk with her. Good idea. Thanks."

Julie's eyes flashed dangerously. "What about the reporters? Is Crowder siccing them on you?" She tried to sound bored, but he knew that if a crowd of scribblers showed up, she would lose her big chance.

"Don't worry. I'll protect your interests, Julie."

He whistled "Buffalo Gals" as he drove to the mill. A cooling breeze tempered the warm sunshine, and he felt right with the world. The guard at the mill gate took his name, directed him to the visitor parking area, and waved him in. Steve pulled in around the side of the massive brick building, gravel popping. The red-painted walls were pierced by windows at the level of the second floor. Below there was nothing but a wide doorway. Looking around the back, he saw another narrower door. Steve thought this was probably the employee entrance. The parking lot was scattered with vehicles.

There was a bicycle rack by the far corner. He casually walked toward it and saw that it was empty. The parking spot reserved for the executive director, identified by a large brass plaque on the wall, was filled by a 1922 Marmon convertible coupe.

He walked to the far side of the bulge that he thought must be the chimney for the fireplace. Steve spotted a set of heavy-duty, dark red painted staples that formed a ladder up to the second-floor window of Francis's office. Crumbs of dark red paint and dirt dotted the gravel below the fire escape. He found a spot where the paint had been scuffed off one of the iron rungs. No rust on the bare spot.

Steve walked around the building. He entered the main doors and crossed to the identical pair of doors at the end of a short hallway. Photos of men and women standing in crowds decorated the walls in large frames. The workers all stared at him from the previous century's picnics or the mill's interior.

Through the second set of doors was a waiting area with a secretary typing busily. She was middle-aged and had an air of efficiency. Her plump, round face looked up expectantly, and she smiled as her fingers froze over the keys. "How can I help you, sir?"

Steve took out his shield case and showed her his identification. "I would like to see Mr. Chandler. I called for an appointment earlier today." He hoped that Francis would be running late and Steve would be asked to wait in Francis's office. Steve wanted to look around a little without an audience.

"Welcome to Chandler Mills, Inspector Walsh. Let me see if Mr. Chandler is available." She turned to an intercom and pressed a switch. "There is an Inspector Walsh to see Mr. Chandler, Frances."

She released the switch and turned to Steve. "Inspector? Would you like to take a seat?"

With a puzzled look on his face, he took a seat on the chesterfield and asked, "That Francis—wasn't that Mr. Chandler?"

"Oh, no. That was Frances Waters, Mr. Chandler's secretary. A lot of people make that mistake. Having two people in the same office with identically sounding names." She went back to her typing, and Steve picked up a March 1923 copy of the *National Geographic Magazine* and flipped through, looking at the pictures of the "Old Spanish Roads in Mexico" and "Land of Montezuma." He heard a double buzz of the intercom and looked up expectantly.

"There will be someone here directly, Inspector Walsh," the secretary informed him, again with a pleasant smile.

Steve thanked her and stood, waiting. The door to the mill floor opened, and a smartly dressed young woman with her hair in a bun and wire-rimmed glasses perched on her upturned nose walked toward him. She held out her hand and introduced herself with a bright smile. "Good morning, Inspector. I am Sally Quinn. Will you come with me, please?"

Sally turned and ushered him into a roar of weaving machines and hurrying people. His guide shouted, "Straight ahead to the stairs. Sorry about the noise." He followed her, dividing his attention between the trim figure in front of him and the organized turmoil around him. They passed a compact wooden office at the foot of the stair. A sign over the door identified it as the watchman's office. Steve saw a metal stairway just beyond. The steps ascended to a catwalk, faced with doors and windows. He saw Francis as they walked past the office window. He was sitting at a massive oak desk speaking on the telephone. Francis raised a hand and nodded at Steve.

A few steps down the walkway, they entered an office occupied by a thin, stern woman who looked like she had forgotten how to smile a decade or two ago. "Thank you, Sally," she intoned. "I will take care of the gentleman now." Sally backed out the door and walked out of sight.

Frances opened an interior door and allowed Steve to enter Francis's office.

Francis stood up. He was dressed in a dark brown double-breasted suit. He wore a white shirt with pale tan stripes and a forest green tie. The coat was unbuttoned, showing a matching vest with a gold watch chain, a gold "C" hanging from it.

"Hello again, Inspector," he greeted Steve. "How is the investigation progressing?"

"I am waiting on the medical examiner's report, and since I had never seen a weaving mill, I thought I would stop by. It was on the spur of the moment. I hope it is not inconvenient."

Francis picked up a mahogany box from the desk and offered a cigar to his guest. Steve refused and lit a cigarette as Francis clipped the tip from his choice and lit his cigar to a smooth draw. Steve looked around the office. It was a large room with a full fireplace on the outside wall, which explained the bulge. Behind Francis's desk were several awards, industrial books, and magazines in an ornate bookcase. A large safe stood in the corner near the window, its door slightly open. On the common wall with Frances's office were several oil paintings. One, an idyllic scene of what looked like an alpine valley, was by R. Steiner. The other was a still life, the corners painted in shadow too dark to determine the artist. Steve noticed a darker space on the wall between the paintings where a plaque or smaller painting had once hung. The window to the outside, next to the fireplace, looked out onto the parking lot and the trees cloaking the low hills.

Steve indicated a trophy topped with a bicycle sitting on a shelf. "I understand you are an enthusiast."

Francis smiled knowingly. "Yes, I am hoping to captain the Olympic road racing team next year."

"Congratulations. It must be tough to get in any training, being busy with the company and all."

"Inspector, I will give you five to one that you know all about my training regimen. Two or three times a week, I ride from the house to the mill. There is a stationary bike in the basement at the mansion for rainy days. The night my mother was murdered, I rode to the mill. The deputy who came and broke the news drove me home that night.

"Now, I'm afraid that I do not have the time to show you around, but I am sure that Silene is available." Before Steve could stop him with some excuse, he depressed a switch and spoke: "Silene, do you have time to show Inspector Walsh around?"

Steve walked over to the window and looked out. Directly below the sill was the first of a set of U-shaped iron bars forming a fire escape down the wall. The iron was painted a dark red that almost matched the brick. When he turned, Francis was standing with a taunting smirk touching his lips and smoking his cigar.

"Yes, Inspector, I could climb out my window and down to where my bicycle is parked," he said. "Across the lot, out of sight from the exit to the old farm road, is a gate in the fence. A few steps from there, a path winds through the forest to a spot near the estate wall. I often ride to work."

Steve sucked in smoke and returned, "And, of course, why would you climb out the window when the door is handier?" He had the answer for which he had come. Steve thought Francis must be very confident to acknowledge the fire escape. He must be sure that no one could prove his guilt. His vague suspicion of Francis firmed into certainty. The only thing missing was that nagging proof.

Francis laughed. "Yes, no reason. When I leave work, I always take the stairs. Ah, here is my sister," he said as Silene walked in the door, a broad smile on her face. Her green eyes sparkled. She was dressed in a smartly tailored linen dress. There was a tasteful pearl necklace around her slim throat. As she approached Steve, he realized that she was almost as tall as he was. She rose on one leg with the other bent, her hands on his arms. There was a quick peck on the cheek, and she said, "Well, it is good to see you. What brings you to my lair?" Her laugh carried a welcome with a hint of playful challenge. A definite change from how they had left things the last time they met.

"He wants a guided tour of the place, Silene. Would you mind showing him around? I have an important call to make. Take him to lunch. Show him a good time," he finished and received an odd look from his sister.

"I would be more than happy to, Francis." She wrapped her arm around Steve's and led him off. When they reached the head of the stairs, he thanked her for the flask and she gave him a dimpled smile. "It was an apology for how I acted."

She gave a thorough tour of all the buildings in the complex. Massive weaving machines roared on the mill floor, while the machines in the facility for spooling thread whirred much more quietly. The projects building where Chandler Mills had produced 3.2 million sterile medical packs containing surgical dressings during the war was now being used to investigate the viscose process for semi-synthetic fibers. Chandler Mills was under license with

Courtaulds Fibres of the United Kingdom to develop the process in America. The whole time, Silene retained a hold on his arm. Steve hoped Julie did not show up to research a feature on the sponsor of the flower show.

Steve weakly tried to beg off Silene's invitation to lunch. He followed her to the family mansion and, in a cloud of dust from the gravel driveway, arrived in a shorter time than he ever wanted to again. "You must have learned to drive from Barney Oldfield," he said.

Silene laughed at him merrily as he helped her out of her 1923 Kissel Gold Bug. She led the way up the stairs and into the house. There was a hive of activity, centered on the ballroom. She was bombarded with questions as she walked. She airily addressed the half-dozen tradesmen clamoring for her attention: "You must speak with Emma Black about any problems. She is in charge."

She waved her hand in dismissal and led Steve through a discreet door in an alcove of the dining room and down to the kitchen. "Cookie," she greeted the stout woman frosting a cake.

Without looking up, she said in a thick Irish brogue, "Miss Silene, if there is anything you want, just get it yourself. And leave the desserts strictly alone. Do you understand? You're not too old to spank." She picked up a large wooden spoon from the counter and waved it vaguely in the young woman's direction.

Silene laughed and set about pulling bread from the box and assembling ham, lettuce, tomatoes, onions, cheeses, and condiments. After she poured two enormous glasses of fresh milk, they sat at the kitchen table and Silene attacked her thick sandwich with gusto. She had no apparent intention of talking while she ate. Steve watched, fascinated. This image was completely different from the spoiled, elegantly dressed, teasing rich girl he had first met.

Silene looked up halfway through the stacked sandwich. She wiped the corner of her mouth with the back of her hand, then her hand on her napkin. "What?" she asked, noticing his stare.

"You're probably eating like a right proper barbarian, young lady," answered Cookie. "Her dear sainted mother tried to teach her manners, but she sets down to the table like a country farmer," she threw at Steve.

"Come on, Cookie. Steve here is a friend. I know how to act in public." She defended herself with an exaggerated pose, holding her glass of milk with her pinky stuck out.

Steve was amazed at the earthiness she showed, and the title of "friend" startled him. He had formed an opinion and she had shattered it. From the cool, indifferent, slightly stuck-up daughter of the rich, she had shown him a different picture. And he was fascinated.

"How are things coming for tonight?" she asked the cook.

"Oh, it will be done all right. You just keep that Emma Black out of my kitchen. You know I won't take any interference." She waved her spatula, scattering frosting.

"I will, Cookie, but if you feel you need to take action, hide the body." Silene's laugh cut off suddenly. She looked at Steve, embarrassed. "I guess that wasn't very funny, was it?"

Silene quickly changed the subject. "You are coming tonight, aren't you? We are doing the annual unveiling of the quilt to the Madding Crowd. The Regional Agricultural Fair committee, the sponsors, big exhibitors, and so on. Starts at seven o'clock. Sorry, no open bar—but I can top off your flask for you," she teased.

Steve looked embarrassed. Maybe because she had shown herself human and he was self-conscious about the expensive gift. Before it had just been a whim from a spoiled, rich brat.

He shook it off and brought up another topic: "When we interviewed the professor, he was a little nervous about his parents in Hungary." He went on to relate what he and Buck had heard.

Silene finished her sandwich and wiped her hands on a napkin. She made sympathetic noises for the senior Poltovskis. "I'll have a word with Senator Bosk and find out what I can do. Francis can be so cruel at times. I can see if any of our ships are in the Adriatic Sea area. I will get them to the British Mandate if I have to hire a boat and sail them myself. But will it be safe for them there?"

"The new Hungarian government is not too fond of Jews and has a lot of quota laws, and there is the backlash against the Kun government. The Poltovskis are Quakers, but there may be someone who remembers them from when they were practicing Jews. I imagine that they will be as safe in the British Mandate as anywhere."

Silene replenished the milk and, despite Cookie's warning, stole two tartlets from the tray. "Okay, time for twenty questions," she said, taking a bite and dribbling juice down her chin. She leaned over her plate and snatched up her napkin and wiped herself clean.

"What questions?" he asked.

She waved her hand in front of her mouth and finished the bite. "I ask you a question and then you ask me a question. It's easy." She settled in her chair. "We ask each other questions, and we both have to answer. Now, me first. What is your favorite color?"

"Green."

"Mine is yellow. A sunny, bright yellow. Your turn."

Steve thought for a moment. "Home cooking or formal dinner?"

"Easy. Home cooking. When it is formal, I feel like a little girl dressing up."

He nodded. "Definitely home cooking."

She mused for a moment. "Travel or stay at home?"

He laughed. "When traveling, stay at home; when I'm home, I want to travel."

Silene snorted. "What a weaselly answer. No fair. I get to ask another one. I like to travel. Read a book or listen to the radio?"

"That's easy: read a book."

"Me too."

They continued, discovering that Silene preferred riding and both liked cross-country skiing. Steve would live in an apartment to hold in check his tendency to fill empty space with "stuff," and she loved a big house. He found he was growing more and more comfortable with the surprising depths he was discovering in Silene.

Silene pointed to the bulge under his left shoulder. "Do you always carry a gun?"

Steve looked down and said, "Been carrying one for too many years to stop. I would feel naked, and there are a lot of bad guys out there."

"Your turn," she said.

"Not until you answer."

She hopped up and raised her arms over her head and did a slow turn. "Where would I keep one?" Steve admired what the snug outfit revealed and hid. He had to admit the gun would have to be about the size of his little fingernail to be secreted on her person. "I can shoot, though. Grandfather and Father thought we all should know. The first time I went skeet shooting, I used Father's gun, and I was knocked on my—well, I fell down," she finished.

"I see what you mean." He hesitated and then blurted, "Married or single?"

Silene's face froze; her grin turned serious. "Haven't been married, but would like to try it with the right man."

Steve coughed nervously, realizing that he had just broken one of his own taboos: he had started asking questions that were too personal. "Maybe with the right woman, it wouldn't be so bad." He felt the familiar knot form in his stomach.

She stared at him for a moment. "Children or none?"

He gulped. "Children." He tried to lighten the mood by quipping, "As long as they don't look like me."

She said quietly, "Me too. A lot or a couple?"

Just as quietly, he said, "That's two questions in a row for you."

Silene leaned forward, her lips slightly parted and asked again, in a voice so low he barely heard her from a few feet away, "A lot or a couple?"

Sweat began to gather on his brow. He could not avert his eyes from the green pools in front of him. "A lot. A baseball team, at least."

She broke their gaze and sat back in her chair, chuckling nervously. "Maybe not a baseball team, but a lot."

Steve dipped his head and looked at his watch. "Getting late. Don't you have to go back to work?"

Ignoring him, her eyes seemed to lose focus. "I was always a tomboy. There wasn't a tree in the orchard that I hadn't climbed by the time I was ten. Mother was always having the servants cleaning me up and putting me in a dress. She always had to have control, and I don't think she really knew how to be a mother. She called me rebellious. I guess it was the only way I could get her attention. I would want my girls to be what they wanted to be." She brought her eyes back to Steve and gave him a vulnerable, serious gaze.

"My dad was easier to talk to. He used to take me around with him when he looked over the farm. He really liked people, all kinds. One time we were walking around the stable and I saw Tommy Green, who had been there forever, sleeping in the sunshine outside the barn. I asked dad why he wasn't working, and he told me that Tommy was retired and didn't have to work. I was puzzled and asked him why he was still here, and he told me that Tommy could stay as long as he wanted, that people were not a disposable commodity. I have always remembered that and even had Tommy help me carve it in a piece of wood for my dad one Christmas. He put it up in his office. Francis took it down."

Steve saw a glint of tears in her eyes and remembered the bare spot on the wall in the office. She dashed them with the back of her hand, tossed her head, and gave him a slightly shaky smile. "Got off track there. Now, your turn."

He thought for a moment and risked a quick end of the camaraderie of the moment. "Are you the tease that you are trying to seem?"

Silene froze for a moment. She hesitated and then said quietly with a hint of sadness, "I'm sorry you think I am a tease. I don't try to be, really. Mother kept trying to make me a lady, and I guess she never succeeded." A sparkle of tears glinted, again, in her downcast eyes.

The conversation had veered from the gay and pleasant to the deep end of the pool. Steve's nervousness with weeping women started to cause his flight instinct to kick in.

"My question, now," she said with forced cheerfulness. "How often do you see your family? Holidays? Reunions? When?"

He wanted to end this suddenly serious game immediately. "I haven't seen my family since I left home when I was sixteen, except for my mom a few times when she came up to Hartford. You may think that your mother couldn't make a lady of you, which I disagree with, but my father couldn't seem to make anything out of me. My brother was the one who always did right. He took to farming and school and everything. The most common phrase in my life was, 'By the time your brother was your age, he could ... ' (fill in the blank)."

She put her hand gently on his. "Looks like we both think we are kind of out of tune with our parents' dreams." She brightened. "Let's form a club. How about it? We could build a clubhouse and everything." She looked at the watch pinned to her dress. "Well, I do have to get back to work before Francis fires me." Steve thought she sounded regretful.

She took his hand and led him outside and gave him another longer peck on the cheek. She looked into his eyes for a lingering moment, got into her car, and roared down the drive.

Steve shook his head and wandered around the house to the terrace, avoiding the interior of the house to bypass the organized chaos within. He noticed the low hedge of several new plants, as Wanda had said. He had to admit that the expanse of greenery, intermingled with brilliant swaths of color, was relaxing. Steve sat on a sandstone bench, wondering if it was the one on which Anna Carlyle had perched the night of the murder. It was close to the mansion wall, but whichever way he turned his head he could see to the end of the balustrade outlining the terrace. The French doors to the ballroom were open, and the din of setup was clearly audible. He froze as the strident tones of Emma Black issued forth. She was complaining that the tables were too close together and the tablecloths were not pressed well enough.

That woman can really complain, he thought. He took out a cigarette, snapped a match alight, and lit it. He almost flicked the match away but held himself back. He looked around the white marble terrace and finally leaned over and stuck the match into a potted plant, burying it with a finger full of dirt packed onto its grave. He slid closer to the large sandstone pot containing the corpse of his match in order to use it as an ashtray. He felt slightly self-righteous; he had heard somewhere that ashes were good for plants.

His feelings about lunch, however, were in turmoil. Silene was much more complex than he had at first thought. Was she trying to con him, or was she serious? She could be trying to influence the murder investigation. She could be bored, and it would be amusing conversation to tell her rich friends what a fool he was. Maybe she would be right. This brought Julie to mind. Did she want to be his girlfriend again? He wondered how much of her antagonism was because of how he had treated her. Or if it was really relief that their relationship was over so it could not interfere with her career ambitions. Did she wish to get him into harness or anger him enough to make him keep his distance? "I hate my life," he muttered, mashing out his cigarette with more force than necessary.

His thoughts shied away from Silene and Julie and leapt down another road. He remembered his younger years on the family farm. He and his father seemed to fight from the time he could talk. By the time he was sixteen, he had decided that his mother would be a lot happier if he was gone and the arguments ended. He "knew" his father would be happier without a son fighting him tooth and nail. His brother would be happier with "the brat" gone. Most important, Steve would be happy getting out from under his father's thumb. He had gone to school one day and never come back. He had left his mother a note and had written letters to her over the years, but he cut his ties and never visited again.

He had headed to New York and shipped out as an able seaman on a freighter bound for Africa. By nineteen, he had money in the bank from cargo and wages. His last trip was back to New York. He confronted George Chase of the New York Law School and convinced him that he could keep up with his studies even though he had never graduated high school. He passed the bar and was recruited by the Connecticut State Police. What he did not know is that his father, at his mother's insistence, had gotten his boyhood friend, Bob Crowder, to offer him the job. His father still refused to contact his son, both of them too stubborn to make the first move. It was only years later that he found out his father's role in the story and was tempted to quit.

Even though his mother begged him to come home, Steve refused. He paid for his mother to visit him, though the tickets he finally sent for his father were never used. These visits always ended with his mother in tears. Steve would be depressed for a week. He was still making his mother miserable ten years after he had left home.

Chapter 15

Steve's bittersweet memories were interrupted by the arrival of Buck Daniels, who joined Steve on the bench and handed him a folder. "Looked for you at the mill," he started. "They said that you and Silene went to the house for lunch. I saw her leave, but with her you can't be sure if she's driving the way she was because she's mad or if it's just her normal style. Mama Chandler should have restricted her to a wheezy Model T or maybe given her one of Churchill's tanks from the Great War."

Steve picked up the folder and looked through the medical examiner's report. A quick review showed nothing to add to what he already knew. The shears were definitely the cause of death, and they were in a position that kept her from pulling them out. She must have lain there for a few minutes in a state of shock, while the murderer probably thought she had been killed instantly. While reading, he gave several grunts in response to Buck's comments. "Huh?" he said when he finished. "I missed that."

Buck was about to answer when Jeremy stepped out with a tray. "I thought you gentlemen would like some refreshments," he said as he placed it on a nearby glass-topped table with a base made from the same sandstone as the balustrade. The two officers took comfortable cushioned chairs. Buck poured himself coffee while Steve assembled a drink. When he tipped the last of the liquor from his flask, Jeremy offered to clean it for him and took it away.

Steve turned back to the report. The sheriff's men had taken fingerprints from the committee members and the servants, including Cookie. There were no unmatched prints in the room, and the shears did not provide any prints at all.

Steve ran through his day at the mill and his conversation with Bob Crowder. "Bob is going to have a coronary, or he will clamp down and ride it out. My guess is that he will start getting mad, fight back, and be fine. Francis was either taunting me with the fact that he could get away from the mill by telling me how he did it, or he was telling me that he knew what I was looking for. Either way, I am pretty sure that he is the one."

"So, which one? Was he admitting his guilt and challenging you to prove it?" asked Buck.

"I think he did it. I'll go so far as to say I'm sure that he did it," answered Steve. "He knows I think he did it, and I know he knows I think he did it." He shook his head in irritation. "Enough of that. From what people said, not to sound like Mrs. Black, Francis is a gambler. He admitted it to us when we interviewed him yesterday. I'm wondering if he looks on this as a game. He thinks he has covered his tracks. Oh, he knows I can make a case for him getting to the house. I can, probably, build a circumstantial case for a motive. Money is always good for that. What I cannot prove is his hand on the shears. I can't even place him in the room." He tapped the folder. "Nothing ties him to the weapon—no fingerprints, no snags of cloth from his clothes, no bits of material from a bike pedal, no oil or anything. He's daring us to prove anything."

"It's worse than that, you know. He's laughing at us," commented Buck. "I don't know about you, but I hate it when people laugh at me. Makes me want to do something to wipe it." He held up his fisted hand and looked at it.

"I hope he's too smart for his own good, 'cause we don't have a thing on him," said Steve sourly. He shoved the folder along the table to the captain. "You going to the shindig tonight?"

Buck pushed out a huff of air. "Every deputy who has a wife will be here. It is the biggest soiree of the year that lets people dress up and mingle with what society there is around here. Everybody is invited, though I have noticed that politicians are a little thin on the ground this year. They are waiting for the shakeout." He looked at his watch. "As a matter of fact, I have to get down to the station to check on things and see to the shift change so I can get home and into a suit and get back here. I really hope that Margaret forgot to have my tuxedo cleaned. A suit is bad enough."

They rose and started down the hall, stepping quickly past the ballroom to avoid any contact with the head of the flower show committee. At the front door, Jeremy handed Steve his hat and the flask. Steve noticed that there had been an increase in the weight of the container, and he raised it in salute to the smiling butler.

"Miss Silene informed me where she sequestered a supply, sir," he said.

Steve followed Buck down the hill and waved at the old man in the garden behind the guardhouse before driving through the gate in the stone wall. He turned off the main road to Chandler and took a rutted track to the old farm road that ran by the house. A look at Francis's route might jog a thought loose, though he doubted it. He turned left and followed the track slowly around town toward the mill. The road wound through a tunnel of old second-growth pines. He stopped several times and opened the door, letting in the summer smell of pines and the sounds of birds. Steve saw the tracks of a bicycle in the dirt. The brush on either side hid the road from casual observation from the town.

He stopped when he saw where a wide trail met the road. Exiting the vehicle, he followed the trail a short way through the trees until he could see the mill. This was, he thought, the path from the mill. He found a wide spot to turn the car and drove back the way he had come. Past the intersecting road from the house, he continued until he found, a little way along, a second trail connected with the road. Leaving the car, he made another reconnoiter that showed him the surrounding wall ten yards from the edge of the trees and brush.

Steve returned to the car and tilted his head back on the seat. He cautioned himself against concentrating on Francis to the exclusion of other possibilities. The problem was, his gut told him that he had the solution. "Now you have to work on the proof." He voiced this last consideration aloud. A hand moved toward the flask. Steve snatched it away with the thought, *Too easy to go down that road. One drink is lonely and wants a friend; then the two of them invite another. Before you know it, there's a party.* He realized his drinking had picked up since he had split with Julie, and his thoughts fled from the obvious reason.

Steve pulled his mind back to the murder and tried to develop a plan to get the proof he needed to nail Francis or any other suspect. He got a glimmer of an idea that needed fleshing out. He concentrated on Francis, proof, and the flighty idea. He pondered the quilt. Everything centered on the quilt and the sewing room. The murderer had to have known two things: what night the committee would meet and that Mrs. Chandler would be alone after the meeting broke up for the night. The one question that kept nagging at his thoughts: Why had the pin been in that spot? It could not have been pointing to who did it. Even the printed tea rose pointed to more than one person. Why would a seriously injured person drag herself to the wall just to leave a vague clue? He knew he was missing something. Something important. He sat up, remembering something Mrs. Black had said. Leaning back, he knew he had the answer to the question of the clue and what it meant. Now, how to get Francis to hoist himself on his own petard?

When a shaft of light struck his eyes, a check of his watch showed him that he had been sitting there for over an hour.

He reversed to the connecting road and drove back to the hotel. A telegram from Bob was waiting for him. When he ripped it open, there was a short, sweet message: "On your own. Solve it. (signed) Crowder."

Steve muttered to himself as he walked across the lobby, "Bob must have gotten over his anxiety attack." He stuffed the message into his pocket and changed direction. He stopped in the restaurant and ordered dinner to be sent up at six o'clock. On the way up to his rooms, he discussed with the elevator operator the dismal showing of Boston, which was sitting solidly at the bottom of the standings, and the likelihood of another New York World Series between the

Yankees and the Giants. "Why da Red Sox ever sold Ruth, I'll never know," the kid lamented.

Steve tossed his hat onto a chair in his room and thought about making himself a drink. He walked to the refreshment shelf and checked himself in mid-reach. With a sense of self-righteousness, he poured a glass of water over ice instead. Fresh fruit was piled in the basket on the table. He selected an apple and returned to the window. "I could really get used to this," Steve spoke out loud, staring out at the hotel garden. Before taking off his shoes and stretching out on the chesterfield, he removed his tie. He settled into a comfortable position with a cigarette in one hand and the water in the other.

He tried to concentrate on the Francis plan that was half formed, but his thoughts wandered to Julie and then to Silene. He finally admitted to himself that he had treated Julie badly. Steve did not know if he was glad that their relationship seemed to have thawed. A wry grin twisted his lips. If it *had* thawed. Maybe she was only being friendly to get a story. Both? What did he feel about her, anyway? And what about Silene? He wished he knew whether she was interested or just amusing herself. Their lunchtime conversation seemed to indicate an interest. Then a twinge of guilt intruded. Should he even think of Silene if he was reevaluating his feelings about Julie? He wished he understood women. He closed his eyes. *I wish I understood myself.*

Shaking his head, he forced himself to consider that night and Francis before his thoughts got a chance to wander again. Steve pictured himself as Francis.

He said aloud, "I climb out the window and down the fire escape. I take the bike and roll it across the parking area and through the gate. I hear the crunch of the gravel under the bicycle's tires. Then I mount the bicycle and pedal along the narrow farm road through the trees. I smell the scent of pines and feel the wind in my face. I ride the bicycle to the house, through the gate. If I am seen, I just park it and go upstairs to bed. Otherwise, I park it out of sight in the carriage house to preserve the illusion that I am still at work. I enter the house and walk normally down the hall. If no one has seen me, I slip into the sewing room and maybe exchange words with my mother and, when she turns her back, stab her. It does not matter if I run from the room. I am caught if anyone from the committee or staff sees me; my cycling outfit is as good as a sign. Even if seen from the back.

"Once I get back to the bicycle, it is a matter of returning to the mill. Though it is unlikely, if a vehicle is on the road, the sound of its motor will give me enough time to hide until it passes. The only real danger is a hiker or another cyclist, but that is also unlikely. The road is away from normal paths and on the estate."

Steve pursed his lips, took a sip, and continued, "The next danger point is if Haney notices that the bike is gone, but he doesn't pass it on his rounds, and the old man would not wander around unnecessarily. I wait to cross the parking lot when there is no chance that the watchman will come out the employee door. I wait near the fence until Haney makes his rounds. That will be safest. I wheel my bicycle back across the lot, park it, and climb up the fire escape. No, I carry it across the lot, both from and to the rack. Then the only sound will come from my shoes on the gravel. Once I am in the office, I take a shower if necessary, dress, and wait until the murder is discovered."

The big question: How to prove Francis had been in the room?

Steve took another swig of water and swirled the ice in the glass. "I really do need a vacation," he muttered.

He settled deeper into the couch and picked up the thread of his thoughts. He picked at the knot again. He knew how Francis had gotten from the mill to the house. He knew how Francis had slipped into the house. He knew how Francis had gotten back to his office at the mill. He could see in his mind the whole process. What he did not have was Francis in the sewing room. A good, or even a poor, lawyer could shatter the circumstantial case he had, and Francis would not have a mediocre lawyer. Far from it—he would have the best legal team that money could buy.

His tentative plan was his only hope. He had one question, and everything hinged on the answer.

With his decision made, he allowed his thoughts to wander along personal paths. He remembered the fun he had had with Julie and the intense conversations about politics and current events they had enjoyed before the breakup. Then his mind slid to the lunch with Silene. He had enjoyed that, too, at least until the game of twenty questions got too personal. That was when the tension began to build. He did not need to share deep emotional childhood memories with a suspect in a murder, even if she was not, technically, a suspect any longer. Of course, she might be a little irritated if he could prove that Francis was guilty and if Steve arrested him. Especially if he was tried, convicted, and sentenced. What an opening line for a date. "Good evening, Silene. I just saw your brother convicted of the murder of your mother. Want to dance?"

One good-looking, smart, and wealthy and, maybe, interested. The other good-looking, smart, and funny and, maybe, interested. They even resembled each other. The same tall, slim figures. One with light tawny hair, the other with darker honey-colored hair. Different personalities, he thought. Julie's temper was fiery, while Silene's was cold, if the interview was any indication. Julie showed no interest in their friends' children, while Silene seemed excited about having little ones. Similar drive to be successful. Neither was a shrinking violet.

He mentally opened the marriage door that he had believed firmly closed. He admitted that he did not want to be a lifelong bachelor. "There," he said. "Steve, old son, you finally admitted it. You want to get married and have a family. Of course, you should have realized it a month or two ago, and the 'who' decision would have been a lot easier."

He sat up suddenly at the knock that announced his dinner, slopping his half-finished water over his front.

Steve debated whether to wear his shoulder holster and carry his cuffs, but he finally decided that he was officially on duty and put on his rig before shrugging into his coat.

Dropping his key off at the desk and informing the desk clerk that he had finished supper, he bought a fresh pack of cigarettes and left the hotel.

His stroll to the car was occupied by looking around the square. He had seen only parts of the town during his drives and the short walk that morning, but he felt comfortable with the feel of the place. Quiet and friendly, similar to where he had grown up. Steve thought it would be a nice place to settle down.

He was relaxed on his drive to the Chandler mansion. He stretched his right arm along the seat and cocked his left elbow on the open window while steering with his fingertips. A cigarette marred the slight smile on his lips. His mind drifted back to the idle thoughts of the girls that afternoon, but he fought them off. "Think of the case, Stevie boy. Only the case," he muttered to himself.

Old Huskins was at the booth, and Steve started to slow down but was waved through. "Go ahead, Inspector. You are almost one of the family by now," the old man cackled.

Steve smiled at the thought. He sped up the drive and surrendered Buck's vehicle to a valet. He adjusted his hat as he walked up the stone steps, still preoccupied with his thoughts.

He crossed the wide, stone-paved court toward the front door. Plants in large clay pots had been scattered along the way. As he passed a full evergreen by the front door, a figure lurched out and grabbed him by the lapels. Even as he reacted, the assailant shouted at him, "Leave my fiancée alone, or I'll make you sorry." Steve crossed the figure's right arm with his left and grasped the figure's left wrist. He twisted and slammed the heel of his right hand into his attacker's left elbow and broke his hold. The inspector spun him around and slammed the assailant into the side of the mansion with a hard shove. The man's face smacked into the sandstone wall, stunning him. Steve spun him around and saw it was the man who had glared at him in the restaurant, Dean Williams. He was a couple of inches taller than Steve, with narrow shoulders and disheveled dark hair. Steve only got a glance at his bleeding nose before his attacker slid, moaning, to a sitting position, with both hands clutching his damaged face.

An older couple, accompanied by a younger man, slowed down and stared at the two men. The gray-haired woman, dressed in a black evening gown with a fur wrap and assorted sparkling jewelry, sounded her disapproval at the sight. "Here, my man," said the young tuxedo-clad gentleman who accompanied them, waving a hand ineffectually.

Steve showed his badge. "Police officer. Can I have your names, in case I need a statement later?"

"My name is Nicholas Martin. I am the Chandler family attorney," he said pointlessly. "These are my parents. What happened here?"

Steve looked around at the slumped figure. "Little accident. You go on in, folks," he said gently.

The door swung open, and Steve forgot everything but the glorious figure in the opening. Silene stood in the light streaming from the interior in an emerald green gown that hugged her gentle curves. It left one tanned shoulder bare. There was a cloth strip of a matching color around her forehead, with a length brushing the uncovered shoulder. The strip was held in place by a brooch of diamonds and emeralds with a short jade-colored feather pointing skyward. An intricate dangle with an emerald stone at its center hung between her sculpted brows. Her mouth, spread wide in a welcoming smile, was made up in dark red matte lipstick. Around her slim throat was a diamond and emerald choker. Her arms, up to her elbows, were sheathed with green evening gloves, and emerald and diamond bracelets scintillated on her wrists. The dress was knee length on one side, while the other covered her delicate ankle. An ankle bracelet of diamonds and emeralds circled her bare ankle, and a pair of matching emerald slippers covered her dainty feet.

Steve stood with his mouth hanging open.

"Steve. I've been waiting for you," she exclaimed, obviously pleased with her effect on him. Her smile faded at the look on the older couple's faces. "What is the matter, Nicholas?" she asked the young man hesitantly. Her glance dropped to her outfit to see if there was a spot or something else out of order. She had spent most of the last two hours getting everything perfect for her guest.

Silene turned to the right at the sound of the injured man calling her in a nasal voice. "Your fiancé doesn't approve of me," Steve finally managed to say in a neutral voice, after getting his scattered wits organized.

She looked at him, puzzled. "I don't have a fiancé. Dean told you that?"

"When he grabbed me and threatened grievous bodily harm," answered Steve, oddly pleased at the news.

"Did he hurt you?"

He chuckled. "Uh, no, but he had a run-in with the side of the house and lost the argument."

Dean had risen and was holding his hand to his nose, leaking large drops of blood on his shirt and tie. Steve took the neatly folded handkerchief from the injured man's pocket and gave it to him after shaking it open.

Dean's lips formed a drunken, vacuous smile. He swayed dangerously and began smearing the mess on his clothing, still staring at Silene. Steve gently took the handkerchief, pulled Dean's hand away from his nose, placed the cloth in the palm of that hand and gently pushed it back into place.

By this time a small crowd had gathered, and Silene took charge. "Just a little accident here. Please, go into the ballroom. We are about to start." She turned to Jeremy and asked, "Will you welcome our guests, Jeremy? Show them to the ballroom, please."

With sidelong stares and whispers, the guests allowed themselves to be herded into the house, leaving Dean, Steve, and Silene. "Will you get one of the valets to come here, Steve?" she asked.

By the time he had returned, Jeremy was standing in the doorway again. Silene asked the valet to look after welcoming guests for a moment. "Jeremy, take Dean upstairs to one of the South guest rooms."

The wounded man tried to bow and said, "Thank you, Silene. Silene, I love you. Will you marry me, Silene?" Steve had to catch Dean before he lost his balance and sat down in the flower bed.

She turned her head away at the stench of his whiskey-soaked breath and looked at Jeremy. "The South guest room near the bath, in case he … "

"Yes, Miss. I will provide him with an appropriate receptacle for emergencies," he answered. He grasped Dean's elbow and led the staggering young man into the house with soothing noises.

"My god," Silene exclaimed. "I hope nothing else goes wrong. He isn't seriously hurt, is he?" she asked with belated concern.

"I don't think there is any permanent damage. He seemed adequately anesthetized and will probably, um, go to sleep. I can always arrest him for slander—him saying in front of witnesses that you would marry a drunk like him," Steve finished with a smile.

Silene gave out a hearty laugh. *Not Julie's,* Steve thought, *but nothing wrong with it.* He shoved that thought down. "So, you don't plan on marrying Dean?" he asked casually.

"Dean is a nice boy. He first told me he wanted to marry me when we were six and taking riding lessons at the pony club. In fact, he has proposed to me many times. I always took it as a joke between friends. No," she said looking up into his eyes, "I am looking for someone else." She was close and inviting, and Steve felt tempted to take her in his arms. He swayed slightly forward.

The moment passed, and Silene wrapped her arms around his right arm in a hug and moved toward the front door. Steve saw her mouth curved in a self-satisfied smile in the hall-tree mirror. The valet took his hat, and, as he turned toward the hall leading to the ballroom, he saw Julie and momentarily froze.

She was wearing a gray-and-black evening dress with a strand of pearls. He had given them to her for her last birthday. Dangling from her delicate ears, visible because her long hair was gathered at the back of her neck in a net strewn with small pearls, were gold earrings. They consisted of a "J" and "S," with the curve of Steve's initial hooked through the hook of Julie's initial. At the intersection of the two was a delicate ampersand in silver. She gave him a straight, expressionless stare. Before she turned away, Steve saw a shimmer in her eye and guilt came crashing down.

He tried to ease his arm from Silene's suddenly tightened grasp, but short of being rough and rude, he was unable to do so. They entered the ballroom behind Julie, who hurriedly made a left just inside the door.

Silene pressed Steve to the right. "Here is Francis," she said. "You two can be bored together." She gave a light-hearted little laugh with a tinge of uncertainty. She walked regally down the aisle of tables, greeting guests as she went, toward the stage set at the end of the large room. The double row of chandeliers caused flashes of light to sparkle from the gemstones she wore.

Steve sighed and looked across the doorway to where Julie was seated, studiously ignoring him. She dabbed at her eyes with the fingers of her white gloves. He looked at his companion and noticed a champagne flute filled with a bubbly amber liquid in his hand. "Have they loosened the rules?" he asked hopefully.

Francis chuckled. "I am afraid not," he answered. "Sparkling apple juice. We produce it on the farms from our own orchards. It is very good. Try it."

Steve, looking disappointed, answered, "No, thanks. Too sweet for me." He moved to the right and began circling toward the stage. Mrs. Black was standing on one end near a group of chairs, and he managed to edge next to her. They whispered together for several minutes. Silene tapped the microphone for attention. Steve nodded to Mrs. Black in thanks and returned to Francis's side.

Seated on one side of the stage behind Silene was the committee. On the other side was a frame with the quilt hanging between the uprights. The reverse side of the quilt was facing the crowd, a broad expanse of black, covered with a pattern of flowers in magenta. Below each flower was a small scroll with its Latin name, in yellow-green, Steve recalled. A large oblong of gold cloth adorned the lower left-hand corner. He could not read what was embroidered there.

"Good evening, ladies and gentlemen. Welcome to the opening of the Regional Agricultural Fair and the A. J. Chandler Memorial Flower Show. I am to be your hostess tonight due to recent tragic events. My mother, I am sure, would have wanted us to carry on. This event, which was dear to her, will now be known as the A. J. and Alice Chandler Memorial Flower Show." A robust round of applause followed this announcement.

She continued with a smile, "Let us all remember that this is a time to celebrate the lives of these two generous and loving people." Louder clapping followed. The crowd relaxed and a murmur of agreement rose.

Silene held up her hands for quiet. "As you know, one of Mother's favorite charities is the Chandler Home for Children. My family—Catherine, Francis, and I—hope you will be generous in your donations tonight." She gestured to bright red boxes resting on tables scattered throughout the room. "We have furnished donation boxes for your convenience. I encourage you to be generous in support of the wonderful children at the home."

Francis leaned toward Steve and whispered, "Mother could support the whole operation herself but thought it would be better if the whole community could be included. Sort of a project that everyone could take part and pride in. A good thing, too. Less of a drain on the family treasury."

Steve nodded in agreement. He wondered if the many charitable projects Mrs. Chandler had engaged in could be the motive for which he was looking. Buck had told him that those works had been generously provided for from the Chandler coffers.

Silene continued, "You all will notice that there is a potted rose on each table. These are cuttings from the new hybrids that Mother and Anna Carlyle had been working on for the past two years. I am happy to announce that they have been accepted and recognized. As a sign of the Chandler family's appreciation of your generosity to our charities, we wish you to share in our mother's greatest achievement. Now, under a chair at each of the tables is a silver dollar. Those lucky few who find them are free to take the rose from their table home as a prize."

There was a general shuffling as the audience members eagerly searched beneath their seats. Cries of happiness and good-natured groans of disappointment rang out as the coins were found and prizes claimed.

"Now, let me present the chorus from the Chandler Home for your entertainment." She moved to an empty chair by the quilt as the curtain parted to show a group of children, arranged by height, standing in the spotlights that snapped on. They were all dressed in white shirts and navy blue ties, with gray skirts or trousers, and all had patent leather shoes that shone in the bright lights.

For the next half hour, the guests were regaled with the songs that Mrs. Chandler loved. Surprisingly, there were cowboy songs, Irish ballads, and early American tunes. Steve saw a wide, childlike grin on Silene's face when they finished up with "Buffalo Gals," though the words had been changed to "Chandler Gals," much to the delight of the audience, which joined in on the chorus. Her eyes were locked on Steve's. The presentation ended with ringing applause, and the children had broad grins on their faces as the curtain slid shut.

"That was wonderful," Silene's voice rang out. "Please give them another well-deserved round of applause." She gestured for a curtain call. The curtain was opened, and the children gave another bow. When the sounds of approbation had died down, Silene swept an arm to include the committee as the curtains closed for the final time.

"Ladies and gentlemen," she cried, "it is my pleasure to introduce—or, should I say, reintroduce—the A. J. and Alice Chandler Memorial Flower Show committee." Steve thought that she would do Barnum and Bailey proud.

"First, Wanda and Barry Jones. They provided, from their nursery, all the wonderful plants you see about you tonight and will see when you attend the show next week. Their generosity and time are greatly appreciated. Thank you, Wanda and Barry." Loud clapping echoed in the room. Steve saw that Wanda was steady when she rose to take her bow. Barry looked uncomfortable in his suit and tie.

"Next, Professor Lech Poltovski. He is invaluable in the design of the show itself. In past years he has brought to life gardens from the world over. Professor Poltovski." More applause. Steve noticed a definite trembling in the man's hands as he nervously gave a bobbing bow to the audience.

"Miss Anna Carlyle. She is the botanist and artist of the committee. She will be the judge for our contest. After years of creating her own recognized hybrids, she helped and guided Mother on her own. We are pleased to include her on the committee and proud to have her as our judge." Joining in the ovation, Steve idly wondered again if Anna Carlyle and his Mimi were related.

"Next, we have Mrs. Mary Flowers. She is the financial master of the committee. Her able handling of the financial matters has kept the committee solvent and financially stable." The applause was muted. Steve thought that the rumors had gotten out. Or maybe it was just Silene's sense of irony.

"Last, but by no means least, Mrs. Emma Black. The beloved head of the committee. Her hard work and dedication are major reasons why this show is so successful." Applause was polite. Steve wondered if this was because of her propensity for malicious gossip.

Silene finished with, "Let us give all the committee a well-deserved round of applause." She led the effort and was answered with thunderous clapping. "After a word from Emma, I invite you to retire to the dining room, where you will find a buffet for your enjoyment. Please feel free to use the donation boxes. Thank you all and enjoy yourselves. Mrs. Black, please take the microphone."

Still dressed in her signature black, Mrs. Black rose, smiling. While Silene took her place beside the hanging quilt, the elder lady adjusted the microphone and cleared her throat. "Thank you for your warm welcome. Each year the committee creates a quilt to commemorate the show. The quilt will be presented to the winner of the show, judged ably by our own Miss Carlyle. Miss Chandler, will you unveil this year's prize?"

Silene gripped the frame and, her jewelry sparkling in the light, spun it on its wheels to show the front of the quilt. Steve leaned forward as if to bring himself closer. Under the bright lights, the border looked darker than it had in the sewing room. The background colors seemed pale and washed out. The only colors that appeared vibrant were the varied reds of the nine roses. They almost glowed beneath the chandeliers.

Steve decided the time had come to act.

Chapter 16

Steve looked around for Buck. He finally saw him at a table on the other side of the room. A woman at the next table, dressed in a bright blue formal gown with her dark brown hair in a fancy pile on top of her head, was looking his way, fortunately, and he caught her eye. He signaled to her, pointing to Buck. The woman questioningly indicated the man, and Steve nodded vigorously. She tapped him on the shoulder and pointed in Steve's direction. Buck raised a hand and bent to the woman next to him. She shot Steve an angry look and turned back to Buck. Steve assumed this was his wife, Margaret. She turned back to the stage, her shoulders stiff with irritation. Buck stood and made his way toward the back wall, edging toward the door between the intervening tables.

When he passed Julie, she clutched at him and whispered a question. He shrugged and pointed toward Steve. She began to rise from her chair but sank back down when Steve violently shook his head. The look she shot him boded him no good when they next met.

Steve turned to Francis and excused himself. He met Buck and led him out of earshot into the hallway. Steve hurriedly explained his plan, and Buck walked back inside and tapped one of his constables on the arm. He bent down and said something, causing the young man to offer hasty explanations to the young blonde sitting at his side. She was dressed in a scarlet oriental sheath with a mandarin collar, hair piled atop her head and held with lacquered chopsticks. An elderly gray-haired matron in a black dress, who closely resembled the officer, asked a whispered question. He answered a query from the fourth member at the table, a tall gentleman in a dinner jacket. A brief argument ensued, and Buck said something and led the constable out.

The tall young man was dressed in a tuxedo that had been in fashion a few years ago. His red hair brightened to a carrot shade when he passed under a chandelier. Freckles made him look much younger than he must have been. There was a jagged scar on his round chin. Despite his gawky, loose-limbed body, he moved smoothly through the press of tables and people.

Buck introduced him. "Red, this is Inspector Walsh from the Connecticut State Police. Steve, this is Charles Brook."

"Pleased to finally meet you, Officer Brook. Sorry to take you away from your family," said Steve, extending his hand.

The constable shook Steve's hand and gave him an engaging grin. "Just call me Red. I was getting bored anyway."

Buck led the constable to Mrs. Chandler's office. Steve returned to Francis's side and touched him on the arm and asked in a whisper, "Do you need to stay here for this? I just thought of something that may help with the investigation."

"Thanks for the excuse. I never liked these events anyway. Lead on," the man replied. His lips were quirked in a sly, knowing smile.

Red stood outside the office door to ensure that the three would not be disturbed. They entered the room to find Buck in his usual chair near the door. Francis greeted him and seated himself in the chair in front of the desk, while Steve circled and took the final chair. He re-created the scene to lull Francis into a sense of self-confidence. If Francis was guilty, as Steve suspected, he must not become aware of how important the upcoming exercise was to the case.

"Mr. Chandler, there is a point of information you might be able to clear up for us. What I would like you to do is remember the sewing room the last time you saw it."

Francis looked puzzled. "I haven't been in there since the incident."

Steve looked thoughtful. "When was the last time you saw it, even for a few minutes?"

"A few days before that. I needed to tell Mother about a production problem at the mill. She insisted that all major issues be discussed with her." He barked a short, sharp-edged laugh. "Do you need to know what?"

Steve shook his head. "No, that won't be necessary. I am going to ask your sisters to go through the same exercise. What I want you to do is close your eyes and remember everything you can about the room. Describe the room in as much detail as possible. There is something about the room that has been bothering us."

A self-satisfied smirk twitched across Francis's thin lips.

Steve kept his own face immobile. He was a decent poker player, and he did not give away his excitement. Steve had worked with enough criminals to know that Francis was hesitating a moment to review his actions on the night of the murder. He would wonder what the information was that Steve was fishing for. After a few seconds he would be sure that he had not taken anything or moved anything that could possibly incriminate him.

This was the mind-set the inspector wanted. Like most self-confident murderers, Francis was sure he could outwit the law. Steve wondered idly why criminals thought they were smarter than the investigators. *Maybe that's because we only catch the ones who aren't,* he thought.

Francis settled himself more comfortably in his chair and closed his eyes. "Going into the room," he started, "on the right is a large fireplace. Centered on the right wall. Flanking that are built-in bookshelves. Most of the volumes are leather-bound editions of classic works: Dickens, Scott, Tolstoy, Emerson. There were other authors, but I don't remember them all. Oh, Shakespeare's plays and sonnets and Homer and some others. I know there were some knick-knacks scattered around. Let's see. On the top shelf there were bronzed baby shoes. Two on one side and one on the other. Mother had them done when we outgrew our first pair. Does it matter whose were where?"

"No, not really," answered Steve to the closed eyes.

"All right. The next shelf down had a picture of Great-Grandfather and President Harrison. They met at the convention where he was nominated for the presidency—Harrison, that is. The next shelf had a small bust of, oh, Shakespeare. Next to the set of his plays and sonnets. Down one more was a glass box with a wedding bouquet in it. Mother's, I think, or Grandmother's. There was a narrow box containing bookmarks that Grandfather had made on the next-to-last shelf, and the bottom shelf had nothing except books. A complete set of Grant's memoirs, and

Longstreet's. That was the left bookcase, assuming everything is still there."

He opened his eyes and shot Steve a taunting look. "Was that what you wanted, Inspector Walsh?"

"Exactly, Mr. Chandler. As much detail as you can," answered Steve, almost regretting his idea. *This is going to take all night,* he thought.

"The right bookshelf. This one had mostly novels. The bindings were all different." Francis droned on with a list of authors he remembered. Steve suspected he was drawing this out to play with him.

"I could give you titles, though I would undoubtedly miss some."

"That's not necessary. Were there any slots that a book was missing from?"

"No. If a shelf wasn't filled with volumes, Grandfather had centered them on the shelf with bookends. Mother and Dad did the same. To carry on, the next lower shelves contained books for us when we were young."

To forestall another interminable list of authors, Steve interrupted, "Did you notice any gaps?"

Francis shook his head. "No, these shelves were packed with books. Are you sure you don't want me to try and remember the authors?" he asked with false innocence.

"No, we don't think that is necessary, unless there was a book missing." Steve fought for patience. "Please, go on."

The taunting smile flitted across Francis's lips again. "The fireplace mantel had silver candlesticks on each end, six silver antique cups from England, and a large portrait of my great-grandmother on the wall above. There were a set of brass fireplace tools—a shovel, tongs, a poker, and a brush with black bristles. The andirons were black iron, with the uprights shaped like dragons.

"On the wall facing the door there were rows of plaques, pictures, and a pair of swords that some of my ancestors carried in various wars. Do I need to describe every picture and plaque?" he asked.

Steve sighed to himself and replied, "No. They had been there for a long time, and if any of them were missing the faded spot would show."

Francis continued with a hint of condescension, "Underneath these was a cedar chest that Mother brought up from South Carolina. It was a trousseau chest, a tradition for Southern girls to collect things they would need when they got married—linens, little treasures, and things like that. There was a standing lamp and a plush reading chair with antimacassars on the back and arms. That's where we spent a lot of time reading. All three of us children were readers. Catherine used it as a place to escape Mother's constant criticism.

"Next to the chair, on the other side, was a record cabinet that had a built-in player, and underneath was a slotted cabinet that held a collection of records upright. Mother believed in the classics for us, though she listened to a variety of low music. There were Mozart, Tchaikovsky, Handel, Chopin … "

Steve interrupted, "The records are not necessary, Mr. Chandler. They were behind the cabinet doors."

"Well, all right," he said smugly. "To the left of the door was what Mother called the 'quilt wall.' The committee pinned up the quilt on the wall. There were rectangular pieces along the top and at the lower left corner, where the quilt had been turned and the backing was visible. They weren't attached. It looked like they were trying to decide on which color to use."

Steve interrupted him. "Could you describe them, Mr. Chandler?"

Francis sighed. "I don't know much about quilts, you know. The quilt was pinned on the wall and, let's see, the strips were about the size of a folded dollar bill. The loops through which the brass pole was threaded to hang the quilt on the frame were pinned up around the quilt. You saw it tonight. They chose the dark color."

"I get the picture. But you said the cloth for the loops was not attached?" said Steve.

"No, tonight they are attached, of course. The last time I saw the sewing room, they were just pinned to the wall around the quilt. They were obviously trying to decide which color to use, at least that is what I assume. Two dark pieces were on the left side at the top and two light-colored pieces on the right. Next to where the corner of the quilt was pinned to show the backing, there was one light and one dark piece, one of each color. Odd that I can remember so much detail."

Steve shot a look at Buck and said, "I have done this before, and relaxing with your eyes closed is a tremendous aid in recall. I understand the layout of the quilt. Please, go on. The quilt was pinned to the wall."

"Not to the wall, exactly. The middle third, above the chair rail, was sheets of cork. That is what the quilt was pinned to. In the corner there was a quilt frame, made of poplar from Chandler Lumber. Mother had it made. It folded up flat. The wheeled base pivoted and was locked in place. There were small brass horseshoe-shaped pieces at the top of the uprights that the rod rested on to display the quilt. There was a large table in front of the cork wall. Scattered near the quilting table were chairs."

"Was the large table against the wall?" asked Buck, speaking for the first time.

Francis lifted his chin and replied, "No. It was far enough from the wall to allow walking around. To work on the quilt when it was pinned to the wall, you understand. And so they could sit all around it, to sew, I suppose."

Buck nodded. "All right. Thanks."

"Well, the chairs could also be arranged so that they all faced the same way. That was the arrangement when I interrupted Mother. Like a classroom, where they discussed something about the quilt, I imagine. There was a table near the quilt frame that was stacked with precut pieces of cloth. These were ready for the quilt or extras. The quilt looked finished to me. A box held pincushions. I think they had a band so they could be worn on the arm or wrist. This table was against the wall but allowed room to get around the other table.

"Let's see. Another table stood by the door. It contained a silver tray with those things that stuck on your finger so the needle wouldn't hurt. Thimbles. Thimbles were scattered on it. There was another tray with scissors laid out according to size. A large thread box was the last item. We supply them to the stores that carry our thread." Francis continued with a detailed description of the contents.

"The chairs were usually lined up in rows on the right side of the doors when they weren't being used. Mother had the servants set up the room before the committee arrived.

There was a chesterfield and other overstuffed chairs with occasional tables arranged in a group in the middle of the room on the large Persian rug Great-Grandfather brought back from one of his trips to the Far East.

"When Mother wanted refreshments brought in, Jeremy would wheel in a tea cart. They usually held their business meetings there. Mother hated us to come into the room. We had messed up the quilt one year. Silene moved around the swatches pinned to the wall and they had to redo the layout before they could finish the thing.

"That's about all I can remember. Did I give you something you wanted?"

Steve blinked twice, having almost fallen asleep at the near-monotone voice. "Yes, that is what we are looking for." He glanced down at his notes. "Just a couple of clarifications. One, you don't remember any other memorabilia on the bookshelves? Two, was there a record on the turntable? Sleeve? Three, was the quilt pinned up horizontally or vertically? Fourth, were the dark strips of cloth on the left and top of the quilt and the light ones on the top right and one of each along the side of the quilt where it was folded?"

Francis hesitated, closing his eyes again and thinking for a moment. "Um, there was only what I mentioned on the bookshelf. If there is anything else there now, someone put it there since Mother died—I mean since I was last there. I didn't enter the room far enough to see if there was a platter on the record player. I didn't notice any sleeve and don't remember there being any music. Then again, I was only interested in an answer to my question and getting out. The quilt was pinned up vertically, the narrow ends at top and bottom. Yes, the strips were as you described them."

Buck looked at Steve and rose. The constable took his handcuffs from his pocket and silently started across the carpet. Just then, there was a commotion outside and they heard the voice of the deputy, "You can't go in there. Wait. Wait." Then the door burst open, and Silene and Catherine were framed in the doorway. Behind them were Paul Sullivan and the hapless Red. Steve felt sympathetic for the constable; you do not manhandle the powers that be.

"Francis," snapped Silene, "we expected you on the stage. What are you doing here?"

"Silene, dear," her brother replied in a bored tone. "This is your show. Yours and Catherine's, if she wants to be a part of it. I find it tedious and boring. Inspector Walsh asked me in here and had me doing an exercise in what I think is futility."

Silene turned to Steve with an irritated look on her face. "Take a day off," she snapped. "This is important, more important than a few more silly questions that could wait."

Steve drew himself up to his full height and glared back at her. "*Miss Chandler.* I am conducting a murder investigation—an investigation of the murder of your mother. I will be happy to drop the whole thing if you have no interest in finding her murderer."

Silene paled and her eyes widened. Her breast rose and fell with her emotions. After a moment, she took a deep breath and calmly said, her voice icy, "Inspector. I have the utmost interest in finding who killed my mother. I apologize that I gave you any other impression. Please let me know when you have completed your present interrogation. I would like my brother to attend the social portion of the evening, at least."

She turned, her back ramrod straight with her anger. Steve said quietly, "Please stay, Miss Chandler. Mr. and Mrs. Sullivan." Steve noticed Jeremy appear over Red's shoulder. "Jeremy, will you please have Mr. Martin come in?"

They waited in tense and unfriendly silence for a few minutes until Jeremy returned. Buck ordered Red to close the door and see to it that they were not disturbed.

Steve held his chair for Silene and, with an angry look, she took the seat. The scent of her expensive perfume caused him a slight dizziness before he straightened. Francis offered his chair to Catherine and moved toward the door where Buck stood. Francis sat himself in Buck's chair and crossed his legs, brushing imaginary dust off the thighs of his trousers.

Mr. Martin looked puzzled. He still held his buffet plate, which he set down on the desk. Steve started, "Thank you for coming here, Mr. Martin." His gaze swept the room. "As you probably know, I was sent from Hartford to investigate the murder of Mrs. Chandler. It all centered on the quilt and the flower show committee. Or so it seemed."

Silene gave a most unladylike snort and lit a cigarette.

Steve looked her way and continued, "Unfortunately, everyone had an alibi—not unbreakable, but solid enough. The committee members were all in the dining room or out on the terrace. The servants were busy doing their duties, and none of them had the opportunity. Silene was out with her fiancé and friends." His jab caused her to sit upright and subject him to a fierce, angry glare. "Catherine and Paul were at the hotel. Francis was at the mill, and the watchman swears that he never left. By any normal means.

"However, it is known that Francis often, especially in the summertime, rides his training bicycle to the mill. He wants to be a member of the United States cycling team for the next Olympiad and constantly trains. I understand that there is a stationary bicycle in the basement exercise room. On the night of the murder, Francis climbed down the fire escape to where his bicycle is usually parked. He took it through the fence by way of a gate. His usual route to the house was hidden by the trees and the dark. At the house, he used his key and opened the gate. He knew approximately when the committee broke for the night and went in for refreshments. He knew that his mother always went back to the sewing room to view the night's work. He probably saw her walk down the hall, or if he was later than he expected, he saw the light from under the sewing room door. It took only a moment to open the hall door, hurry to the sewing room, and enter silently while his mother was there. Even if she noticed him, she would think nothing of it. She would tell him not to interrupt her or something of the sort and turn back toward the quilt wall. At that moment, Francis took a pair of scissors off the table and jammed them into her back. Then he retraced his steps and waited in his office, having changed back into his suit from his biking togs, until Constable Brook came for him. It was almost foolproof. If anyone had seen him, what could have been more normal than him using his bicycle to get from the mill to the house? In fact, this may not have been his first attempt. Something may have interrupted him on other occasions."

By the time Steve had finished, everyone in the room was staring at the accused. During the presentation, Francis had calmly extracted a cigar from his pocket. He had snipped off the end and lit the tobacco. He smiled a self-satisfied smile and said calmly, "Very interesting, Inspector. A fine story. Very believable. One problem, though: no proof. I admit I could have climbed down the fire escape, but I didn't. I freely admit that I use the gate and take the trail through the woods; it is the easiest way to get there. I do use my key to open the gate at the house. I park my bicycle in the garage before going into the house. Now, to your fiction. Did anyone see me enter the gate at the time in question? Did anyone see me enter the house at the time in question? Did anyone see me, supposedly, stab my mother at the time in question? You have no proof, Inspector.

"Nicholas," he turned to the lawyer, "is this inquisition and accusation actionable? I want to teach Inspector Walsh that this is not Mussolini's police state. *We* still operate under the Constitution."

Mr. Martin looked between Francis and Steve, hesitated, and answered, "I will look into it first thing in the morning. First thing. I think you have actionable reason, Francis, but wait until the morning. In the meantime, I advise you not to say anything more in his presence."

The attorney turned to Steve and said, "Inspector, I must insist that you terminate this session immediately. And please remove any constables who are not invited to the events of the evening.

"Buck, I think it would be advisable if you and your department, invited or not, leave until I can look into this."

Francis rose with a superior smile directed at Steve and reached for the door handle. Before he could open the door vacated by Buck's back, Steve said quietly, "Will you let me answer your question before you go, Mr. Chandler?"

Turning, Francis gave him a puzzled look.

"Your question of proof," explained Steve.

Francis took his hand from the door, turned, and drew on his cigar. He slowly blew out a stream of smoke and gave a condescending tilt of his head in assent.

"As to putting you in the room at the time and place, you did that. You told me yourself when you described the room. Do you remember that you gave Buck and me—oh, and Constable Brook through the crack in the door—a word picture of the quilt wall?" He opened his notebook. "You described the quilt on the cork wall. You said that there were four pieces of light and dark cloth on the top of the quilt and there were two pieces of cloth next to the turned-back portion on the bottom left? Mr. Chandler, those strips were not on the wall until Mrs. Chandler pinned them and the quilt there after the committee adjourned for the night. The loop material and quilt had been left on the table. That is what she was studying that night. She was trying to decide whether she wanted the light or dark as the loop material. Mrs. Black confirmed it when she and the rest of the committee were allowed back in the room to finish the quilt for tonight's presentation. She confirmed again, tonight, that the quilt had not been on the wall for two weeks, including the night you interrupted with your question. It was on the table being sewn together and hand quilted.

"Since the murder, it has been sealed in the room, with a constable stationed at the door, thanks to Buck. You couldn't have described the quilt wall unless you were there that night after the meeting. You crept in. You took the shears. You viciously stabbed you mother. You left her to die on the floor. But she didn't die immediately. I think she lay there, thinking, in pain, gathering her strength. She was a tough, strong woman. Your mother must have known that your plan was nearly foolproof and that the only way to prove you were the murderer was to point out the only item in the room that was moved after the committee left. It must have seemed like a long shot, but she did the only thing she could: She struggled to the wall and stuck the pin into the quilt. Your mother brought the quilt itself to our attention—not the color, not the pattern, but the tea rose and the quilt itself. Maybe she knew that your own contempt for others would hang you. Maybe she knew that the flower would get us on the right trail. Whatever her thoughts, she pointed to you. Your mother identified you, and you fell into whatever trap she intended to set.

"Francis Chandler, you are under arrest for the murder of Mrs. Alice Chandler," he finished, motioning for Buck to take him. The accused murderer paled and collapsed in the chair with Buck's hand on his arm. Francis, a stunned look on his face, dropped his cigar on the rug, where it smoldered until Buck snatched it up.

Catherine began to weep and fell into Paul's arms. She covered her face with her hands, and her husband held her protectively, his arm around her shoulders.

Silene rose slowly, a stricken look on her face. "No, no, Francis. You didn't." She took two steps around the desk and stopped. She supported herself on the desk with her palms. Steve barely made it to her before she collapsed. He helped her back to her chair and bellowed, "Jeremy!" The butler pushed through the door, nudging Buck out of the way and sticking his head into the room. "Is there a doctor out there?" Steve asked, and the butler disappeared.

"Brook," said Buck through the door. When the deputy entered, the captain ordered, "Take Mr. Chandler out the side way and take him to a cell. No one is to talk to him with the exception of Inspector Walsh or myself." Buck snapped a handcuff bracelet to Francis's left wrist and Red's right. On the way out, Buck nodded to another constable who was in the gathering crowd and jerked his head in the direction the other two had gone. "They need a driver, Correy."

The doctor arrived. He was a tall, rotund man in a black suit. He reminded Steve of a clergyman. He stopped in surprise, stared around the room for a moment, and moved rapidly to Silene. He pulled smelling salts from his bag and waved the bottle under her nose. She coughed and looked up. Her eyes locked on Steve, who was bending over her, and she blinked in surprise. She smiled, then remembered what had occurred and sat up so suddenly that her forehead smacked into his nose. Steve yelped in pain and grabbed his handkerchief to clamp on his face. Silene bent over and began to weep into her hands. Steve awkwardly patted her bare shoulder.

The doctor pushed Steve away and ordered, "Everybody out." Jeremy escorted Annette in to help, if needed, and informed Steve that he had made excuses and shown the guests out. "Mrs. Black, of course, was the last to depart," he reported in a flat voice, but Steve detected a smile in it.

"Mr. Martin, would you like to accompany us to the constable's office? Captain Daniels and I would like to interview Mr. Chandler in a more normal venue, and I am sure that you are anxious to speak with him yourself," Steve said.

The lawyer said, "Of course. Let me see to my parents, and I will be right with you."

No sooner had the officers stepped out the front door than they were confronted by Julie. A very angry Julie, Steve noticed.

"I'll see you at the station," he said to Buck and turned back to the reporter. "Julie, I would love to let you have an interview, but it isn't over yet. Give me a chance to wrap it up, will you?"

"By the time you have it all wrapped up, the rest of the press world will be here, getting the story, and I WILL BE LEFT OUT. YOU PROMISED, YOU … "

Steve, desperate, grabbed her shoulders and smothered her mouth with a hard kiss, stopping the flow of words. Then, like a thief in the night, he ran for Buck's car.

Chapter 17

Two days later the town was inundated with reporters, as Julie had predicted. It was like a pack of sharks in a feeding frenzy. They had descended on Chandler since the word had gotten out that the spectacular crime had been solved. All of them demanded to speak with the accused, with the officers, with the family. They pestered everyone in town. A few gave them interviews out of frustration or a desire to get their names in the papers or on newsreels.

Steve expected the newshounds to break out pitchforks and torches when they were refused the interviews they demanded. There were several newsreel cameras set up in the street, forcing traffic to be rerouted. One reporter had managed to get his hands on a uniform and pretended to be an officer to get into the cells in the basement of the building. And, to make matters worse, Julie was mad enough to chew nails.

Francis had held out during the first day of grilling. By the time he had gotten to the constable's office, he had regained his aplomb. He sat in his chair in the close, gray-walled interview room, looking calm and trying to stare them down. Steve, playing the bad cop, had snarled out questions and threats. Buck, because he knew the man, played the good cop. Whenever Francis looked like he might be on the point of anger and sullen silence, the captain would pull Steve away and offer the prisoner a cigar or a drink or give him a moment's respite. He spoke gently to him, with sympathy and friendship.

Once or twice, Buck lashed out at Steve. He would push the inspector out of the room, seeming to defend Francis. When the murderer calmed down and let down his guard, Steve would come storming in again, barking questions and accusations.

Though he hated the job, Steve kept it up. He suppressed his distaste, knowing they were interrogating a man who had viciously slaughtered his mother. He knew that even with what they knew, a good attorney might be able to convince a jury that the case was circumstantial and bring in a decision that would free Francis. He was frustrated that the prisoner seemed to bend but never break.

Francis was allowed only three or four hours of sleep. When they woke him up out of a sound sleep and started peppering him with questions, he tried to gather his previous arrogance around him.

There was a break when the shift changed and Ruth Beckstrom replaced the officer who had been taking notes. She brought in coffee and rolls from the Chandler bakery. Steve noticed that Francis was showing cracks in his self-assurance. He hesitated when answering their questions, and his voice had lost its sharp edge. By ten o'clock in the morning, he was sitting forward in his chair, and his hands were trembling when he held his cigar. When another hour had passed, his coffee mug was rattling gently against the wood surface of the table as he lifted it. Steve had had no more sleep and was on the verge of losing his temper for real.

Francis's personal attorney was a senior partner in the firm of Bucklin, Bucklin, and Sawyer in Hartford. He had taken the morning train down and constantly tried to end the interview, saying, "Can't we do this another time? The poor man is distraught. I need to speak with my client immediately." The florid-faced man was dressed impeccably in a dark suit and raspberry red tie. His silver hair was perfectly coiffed, and his shave had been so close that his round red cheeks were shiny. He had a commanding voice, and even Steve was impressed by his presence. He noted the contrast between Mr. Martin and the Hartford powerhouse and knew that even a short interview between the client and his attorney might stiffen Francis's spine.

"My client has a right to speak with his attorney," he demanded. "I insist that you desist with this brutality and remove yourself from the room."

Steve lit a cigarette with forced calm. He looked at Bucklin Senior and waved out the match with quick flicks of his wrist. "As soon as we are finished. Until then, sit down." He would be happy to give him a copy of Francis's statement as soon as Francis had signed it. He returned to the interview after dropping his half-smoked cigarette on the floor and smashing it with a twist of his foot.

As the clock edged toward noon, Francis buried his head in his hands and began sobbing. Bucklin jumped to his feet and tried to raise his objections again. Steve realized the attorney was aware that Francis had reached the point of surrender. When threatened with ejection, Bucklin angrily sat.

Ruth straightened and took down his confession.

"It, it was like you said, Inspector," he said in a tone that begged for understanding. "I tried the week before, but the old man, Huskins, was wandering around, and I had to call it off. He came out of the dark when, uh, after I had parked the bicycle near the carriage house. The next week it was clear, and God help me, I must have been mad." He buried his head on his arms, which were crossed on the table. Buck held up his hand to forestall any more questions from Steve, who took a deep breath.

"I'm sorry, Francis," Buck said gently, a sympathetic hand on the weeping man's shoulder. "Take it slowly. Get it off your chest. You'll feel better."

Bucklin, who had been sitting in the corner, fidgeting with his briefcase, suddenly rose to his feet and snapped at his client, "Mr. Chandler, do not say another word." He turned to Steve. "Inspector, I demand you stop this." The turn this was taking was clearly worrying him.

Francis looked up. He seemed to get a grip on his emotions. "No, Sam, I want to get this off my chest." He had to hold his cup with both hands before he could take a gulp of coffee. Francis said, almost to himself, "I've got to clear my conscience." He stopped and stared sightlessly at the far wall. Steve wondered what he saw there.

Buck leaned over and whispered kindly. "Mr. Chandler—Francis—we are almost done. Please, just tell us what happened. Believe me, your mother can rest peacefully if you unburden yourself. I know that it is tearing you apart."

Francis took a deep, shaky breath and said in a dead voice, "That night, I climbed out the window, got my bicycle, and rode to the house. I parked the bicycle in the carriage house. I made sure that Huskins was not around. Once there, I snuck into the house and stabbed Mother. After, I ran. I thought I heard someone coming. I retraced my way to the mill, climbed back to the office, changed, and waited until someone brought me the news. That was the worst of it. Just waiting. She was looking at me when I was leaving; her eyes were wide open. I could see her face, accusing me, condemning me. God forgive me." His head dropped back to his arms.

Bucklin sank into his chair in resignation. Steve knew that he was already calculating his next move. The investigator reviewed the interrogation but could not find any openings they could have given Bucklin.

Buck continued, gently, "Was there any coercion by the Chandler Constabulary or the Connecticut State Police representative?"

Francis covered his face with his hands and shook his head, but Buck insisted, "You have to say it, Francis. Just tell everyone. You are doing the right thing."

There was a muffled "No" from the murderer. A collective sigh of relief went up from Steve and the other officers in the room. Bucklin was writing furiously on a notepad.

As Ruth started to rise, Steve waved her back down. "Francis," he said, not quite as kindly as Buck, "why?"

Francis lowered his hands. With a confused look he asked, "Why?"

"Why did you do it?" Steve expanded. "Why did you kill your mother?"

The sorry figure seemed to tense and, finally, sat up straight. He met Steve's eyes and replied, "Gambling debts. I owed a syndicate in Havana over $50 thousand, and they were pressing me. I knew that they would ruin me. My social position. I was seeing Miss—uh, a girl. We were talking marriage. Her family was on the verge of merging their company with Chandler Shipping on the weight of that. If they had found out about my gambling, they would have ended the deal. They were from an old Puritanical family. They thought drinking and gambling were unforgivable. For months, I had been managing to scrape enough money together to pay their ruinous interest, but recently they were insisting that I pay it all.

"I went to Mother, but she said that it was my problem. She wouldn't give me a loan. There was another time when Father paid my debts, when I was much younger. When I was at the university, I stole a few dollars from my fraternity. Mother was livid. She said that I must pay for my mistakes, take responsibility for my actions. Even if it meant prison. 'Be a man,' she said. She refused to let me liquidate part of the trust fund that my grandfather left me. She had control until I was forty. FORTY. Did they think I was a child? If she died, the three of us would receive the money immediately. Don't you see? I had to do it!" His words exploded from him in an indignant flood.

Ruth rose and started to close her notebook. Francis suddenly spoke again, his voice tinged with anger: "All the money she wasted. Always giving money to other people. Not her family. Oh, no, we didn't deserve anything from her. Those old fools who couldn't work anymore. Sitting around, everything paid for. Dad's stupid plaque, 'People are not a disposable commodity'—what rubbish. That was the first thing to go. The Children's Home. A bunch of snotty kids abandoned by their parents. She gave them my—our—money. Wasted it on ignorant brats who weren't worth it. She should have let the state take care of them. And the flower show. Every year a memorial to Father. Like he could enjoy it. Or the idiots who showed up. They didn't know a rose from stinkweed.

"I know how much it cost. Special printing. The setup costs alone were hundreds. The disruptions were costing the family thousands. The show itself, more thousands. The cost of the committee. And to what purpose?" By this time, tears of self-pity were streaming down his cheeks. "A damned quilt! Pieces of rags sewn together so some dirt grubber could hang it on the wall." He laughed bitterly. "It even betrayed me. I was building the company!" His voice rose in anger. "I was making this family the money she wasted on her causes, especially the flower show and quilt!"

He dropped his head to his clasped hands, drained. "I needed that money more than she did. She was such a greedy, miserable … " His shoulders drooped, and he raised his head and appealed to the room: "You understand, don't you? Don't you? You must! She forced me to do it. Even the quilt hated me. That rag turned on me!" His voice cracked. "I wish I could burn it."

Ruth nodded when Steve whispered, "Did you get it all?"

Steve followed the recorder out of the room and turned to Buck. "I'm tired. I'm going to get some sleep." He paused for a moment, then crossed to Bucklin's chair and lifted him from his seat and led him, protesting, to the door. Steve did not want him to get another chance to sway Francis before the confession was signed.

Buck nodded. "I'll stay here until he signs his statement and then do the same. Poor Francis. Poor, miserable Francis."

"Poor Alice Chandler," Steve retorted. He escorted the lawyer to a chair in the waiting area outside the front desk. After telling the sergeant on duty to make sure Bucklin stayed put until Buck sent for him, he squared his shoulders and watched Ruth sit down at a desk. He stood there wearily as she assembled carbon paper between three sheets of paper and started typing the confession. Steve shook himself and turned toward the front door.

He ran a gauntlet of reporters who surged toward him as soon as he stepped out of the building. As he shoved through them, they shouted questions and tried to cajole him into giving them some answers. He did not even give them "No comment"; he just shouldered through.

He started the car and slowly edged through the crowd in front of the constabulary building. It gave way, and he continued on to the hotel. Looking in the rearview mirror, he was relieved to see that no one was following.

Steve got his key from the desk and stumbled toward the elevator. When the operator tried to make conversation, he shook his head and slumped against the car wall with his eyes closed. The trip up seemed to take forever. He tugged his tie loose and unbuttoned the collar button of his shirt. Three attempts with his key, and he was inside. The first thing he noticed was Julie's perfume faintly scenting the air. He glanced around and saw her sitting in one of the armchairs, with a brittle smile. Steve groaned to himself and threw his hat at the table and missed. He stared at it and decided that it would be too much trouble to retrieve.

"Okay, fella, its payback time," she said. Julie extracted a cigarette from a case in her handbag. She tapped it on the silver case while she waited for him to scrabble in his pocket and snap a match to life. Immediately, she slotted the cigarette in an ashtray on the adjacent table at her side. With a pencil and pad in her hand, she said, "So, give."

"Aw, have a heart, Jules," Steve begged. "Give me a couple of hours of shut-eye, and you can wring me dry."

Relentlessly, Julie pointed to the chair across from hers. "First question: Did Francis confess?"

With quiet resignation, Steve sat and went over the last three days as she scribbled rapidly. He described the night of the murder. He covered the investigation from the first day to the tableau in Mrs. Chandler's office. Briefly, he sketched the interrogation. Under Julie's pressing, Steve topped it off with the reactions of the Chandler sisters for a human interest angle. Julie wrote for an hour before she was satisfied that she had it down accurately, frequently interrupting him with questions.

She rose to leave. When she reached to stub out the cigarette, she found that it was out and only a long, gray line of ash was left. Picking up her coat, hat, and bag, she bent and gave Steve a peck on the cheek. "Got to get to the telephone exchange and make a connection to the paper. Calvin has been frothing at the mouth to get this, and he was getting ready to cast a curse on you."

Steve was suddenly galvanized with alarm, the fog in his brain lifting abruptly. "Julie, this is strictly from an anonymous source. Bob will spit rocks if my name is mentioned."

"Oh, don't worry. I've done this before," she said airily.

When she had left, Steve sat in the chair, debating whether to sleep there or struggle to bed. He jerked off his tie, levered himself out of the chair, and headed for the bedroom. Halfway there, a hard knock sounded on the door, and he groaned. He reversed direction and opened the door to two detectives from his office. Morgan and McQuarry stood there, Morgan grinning and McQuarry glowering.

They took off their hats and stepped in. Morgan whistled as he looked around. "I knew I should have been nicer to old Bob. Maybe I would have been given these plum assignments."

McQuarry grunted.

"What do you guys want?" asked Steve, trying to keep the weariness and irritation out of his voice.

"The chief sent us down to take Francis Chandler back to Hartford. Before you mess it up," snarled McQuarry.

Morgan shot his partner an exasperated look. "Everybody, and I mean everybody, wants the circus to happen in Hartford. The opposition party wants to have a public crucifixion of one of the machine's own. The machine wants to show that no one is above the law to get ready for the next election. Neither side thinks the Chandler organization is going to be a player anymore. So, we take the doomed man home."

McQuarry, refusing to be ignored, added, "You talk to this Daniels character and get Chandler released as soon as possible. We got paper to take him with us."

Steve was just tired enough to lose his departmental discretion. "Listen, clown. I didn't do a thing except solve this case. I dragged Crowder's chestnuts out of the political fire. You got a problem with that, McQuarry?"

"Whoa, whoa," interjected Morgan, stepping between them. "We are all friends here, right?" He turned to Steve. "Look. Crowder sent us down here to get Chandler. Are you gonna work with us? We drove down here, and we want to drive back with a prisoner. Look. Everyone knows you did a great job on this case." He stared the belligerent McQuarry down.

Steve sighed. He had made his report the morning after taking Francis into custody. The conversation seemed like a speech that Bob was writing to extol his own virtues and take as much credit as possible. His last command was to get a confession, no matter what it took. Bob made it sound like rubber hoses and other kinds of torture would be overlooked. "You guys go down and get something to eat, go sightseeing, whatever. I have been up for a couple of days and nights and need some sleep. I want a chunk of shut-eye before I fall down.

"I'll meet you in the lobby at three o'clock." He took a sheet of letter paper from the desk and scrawled an introduction across it. "Give this to Captain Daniels, who is not a character and who can, undoubtedly, keep you here for a week fighting paperwork if you get under his skin. Be nice, McQuarry," he warned. As an afterthought, he looked at Morgan and said, "Have the front desk send a wake-up at two thirty, will you?"

Morgan took the paper and turned to the door. He paused. "Thanks," he said. "C'mon, Jerry, and let me do the talking, will ya?"

Steve locked the door and debated a drink before sleep. He decided against it and moved wearily toward the bedroom. As he reached the threshold, another, lighter knock sounded. He tossed his coat onto the chesterfield. "I died," he snapped before turning and retracing his steps. He wondered if there would be a deep groove in the carpet from his pacing by the time the day was done.

Unlocking the door, he pulled it open and his weariness disappeared. On the doorstep was Silene, looking wan and tired. She had on a pair of cream-colored linen slacks and a white puffed-sleeve silk blouse. Her short blond hair was tousled. There were dark circles under her eyes, which were red from crying. A tremble in her lower lip made his stomach lurch with sympathy. She was obviously hurting and vulnerable. "Can I come in?" Without waiting for an answer she stumbled in and into his arms.

Steve kicked the door closed and held her. Her body gave little jerks as she sobbed, and he felt her tears dampen his shoulder. "He won't see me. He won't even see me." He awkwardly stroked her hair and nervously murmured platitudes.

Silene finally pulled herself away and tried to smile. "I guess I am a mess," she said, touching her hair with quick movements.

"Oh, no," assured Steve quickly. He looked into her eyes and he felt a sudden urge to take the girl back in his arms and soothe away her pain.

Instead, he led her toward the chair Julie had occupied just a few minutes ago. Impulsively, he turned slightly and sat her in his chair. It was as if she would sense Julie's departed presence. He squatted in front of her and held her hands. "Can I get you something?" he asked solicitously.

She shook her head wearily. "I just needed someone to talk to. I really should go, let you … " Her voice trailed off.

Normally, Steve would jump at any excuse to rid himself of a distraught female, but with Silene, he tried to think of a way to make her stay. "I was just going to rest for a moment. You look like you could do with a little sleep, too. Look. Why don't you take a nap with me." He realized what he had said when he saw the startled look in her eyes.

"No, no. What I meant is you sleep in the bed, and I'll sleep out here on the chesterfield. I didn't mean you to think I wanted to sleep with you."

He tried to extract his foot from his mouth when he saw the look his last statement brought to her face. "Wait—I do want to sleep with you, but … " He quit while she threw back her head and gave a hearty laugh. She stopped to catch her breath, her hands pressing against her chest. Her amusement seemed to have changed her demeanor. She wiped her eyes with the heels of her hands, and a gleam of life came back to them.

"The chesterfield is too short," she said as she took his hand and led him to the bedroom. She sat on the edge of the bed and removed her shoes. Steve was having a difficult time taking a breath. There were so many rules that could be broken if things continued as they seemed to be going.

Silene smiled and flipped back the covers on her side and slid into bed. She turned to the other side and pulled the comforter off the pillows, leaving the sheet and blanket tucked in. Turning onto her side, facing the middle of the bed, she was immediately asleep. Steve took off his shoes and crawled onto the bed and pulled the comforter over himself. "Nice solution, Silene, when there's no bundling bag around," he muttered as he dropped off.

Chapter 18

Steve groaned when the knock came. It had probably not been the first one. It was too loud. He glanced quickly at the peacefully sleeping Silene. "You must have been beat," he observed. She was "purring gently," as his mom would have said, insisting women did not snore, even quietly.

He stumbled to the door and opened it to prevent further assault on his ears. "Right, right. I'm up," he whispered to the surprised bellhop. Steve pressed four bits into his palm and quietly closed the door and turned to lean his back against it.

His heart lurched when he saw a figure in the bedroom doorway. Silene stood there, raking her long, strong fingers through her tousled hair. When her mouth spread wide in a jaw-dislocating yawn, she quickly used them to cover her tonsils. Steve laughed and she smiled.

"I needed that," she said, smothering another smaller yawn.

"You are entirely welcome. Anytime, Silene." He sighed. "Here we go again." He looked at his slightly rumpled guest. "I should start carrying a salt shaker to make my foot taste better."

She let out a belly laugh. "I needed that, too." She continued more seriously, "Mother is being buried on Sunday." She hesitated and lowered her eyes to the rug and played with the fringe with her toes. In a faint whisper, she asked, "Could you come? I, I would like you to be there." She added hastily, with a quick glance at his face, "Catherine, too. And Paul."

Steve doubted that Paul wanted him anywhere near the mansion or the town of Chandler, but he let it go. He hated going to funerals. His grandmother had looked like a wax statue in her coffin. Nothing like the warm, laughing Mimi he had known. But Silene looked so young and vulnerable. "Not a problem. I have to get back to Hartford and report, but I can be back by Sunday." He looked around the suite and continued, "But with a smaller room. If I keep staying here, I am going to be tempted to put my name on the door, and I can't afford the place on my salary."

Silene looked up. "You could stay at—I mean, the company is taking care of the bill here until the case is complete. We offered that before you came. With Robert Crowder's office. I don't think it would be complete until the victim is buried, would it?" Steve wondered what she had left unsaid. Had she been about to invite him to stay at the house? He started to protest, but she hurried on. "You would be our guest. The Chandler family. I—we—invited you, after all."

He chuckled at the convoluted logic and nodded. His eyes flipped to his watch, and he rushed past her. "I have got to get ready to meet McQuarry and Morgan at three o'clock. Stay as long as you want." His face burned with embarrassment at her laugh. "What kind of steak sauce goes with raw foot?" he asked as he entered the bathroom and closed the door.

While he was shaving, he heard a tap on the door. "Steve, I'm leaving. Thanks for everything. You have been great."

He called back, "My pleasure—I mean, you're welcome." He grabbed for a towel to stem the flow of blood from the wound he had just inflicted on himself. He finished shaving and brushing his teeth. He tied his tie on the run and made it to the lobby just after three.

McQuarry looked as sour as ever and stood with his hands clenching. Morgan nodded to the restaurant, and they were shown a table by May. She seated them and set out menus. They all ordered coffee.

To forestall a lot of grumbling from McQuarry, Steve asked, "How did it go with Captain Daniels?"

"Pretty well," the truculent detective admitted. "Chandler signed the confession, and his lawyer was jawing to him about lawyer stuff. The captain finally had time for us and was about to give us an argument, but Bucklin—yeah, I recognized him, and it was mutual—started making demands that his client should be tried locally." Steve recalled that there was an unpleasant history between the two. Three years ago, McQuarry had leaned on one of Bucklin's clients and broke his arm. The judge had thrown out the confession, and it had cost the detective a promotion and resulted in a week's suspension. "He probably figured the jury would be friendlier than in Hartford. That seemed to convince Daniels that a change of venue was the greatest thing since air, and he put in a call to the county seat. Everyone seemed to think that getting this thing far away from here and dumping it on the state attorney general's office was the smart thing to do." Steve knew that "everyone," to McQuarry, included only law enforcement. A lawyer's wishes were beneath notice.

"So we can use the paper we brought to move him back to Hartford. Right now, we are waiting for them to get the evidence together, and we will be off. Daniels said it would be about an hour, since Chandler's mouthpiece has dropped his objection."

Steve led Morgan and McQuarry through the heat, down to the constabulary office, and parked. Fighting their way through the still-hungry press, they ignored the shouted questions and grabbing hands. Buck met them at the front door, looking harried. "I'll be glad when this circus follows Francis to Hartford."

Ruth extended the transfer papers across the desk to Morgan, with a pointed look. Buck rolled his eyes and whispered to Steve that McQuarry had said something derogatory about female cops. Typical of the large, opinionated detective. Morgan scrawled his signature and straightened up. "What now? Is there another way out of this place? I would hate to have to fight through that again." He jerked a thumb over his shoulder at the door.

Buck nodded and answered, "We can take him out the back. There may still be some reporters there, but nothing like the mob out front. We'll put him in one of our cars and drive him to the north side of town to the park."

Steve looked at his fellow detectives and said, "Let me handle the reporters outside."

Bucklin Senior, who had approached unnoticed, suddenly spoke up. "Detective Morgan. I will accompany you in your car back to Hartford. I have to protect my client's interests." He stared pointedly at Morgan's partner.

McQuarry reddened. Before he could react, Morgan stepped in. "Sorry, Mr. Bucklin. I can't give you a lift. It's against department policy. I will personally guarantee that Mr. Chandler will arrive in the same condition he leaves here."

"All right, Detective. If *you* guarantee it," Bucklin conceded, smoothing his silver hair. Steve recognized the gesture. The attorney used it as an unconscious sign that he considered his point made to a jury.

A few minutes later, Buck and Ruth left, escorting a handcuffed Francis. Bucklin would accompany them to Chandler Park, and they would give him a lift to the station to wait for the evening train.

After the members of the Connecticut State Police left the building, Steve held up his hands and announced to the waiting press, "You might as well wrap it up, ladies and gentlemen. Mr. Chandler is staying the night. He will be transferred to Hartford tomorrow by Detective Sergeants McQuarry and Morgan. That's it."

The officers waded through the scribblers and past the sound trucks and got into their cars. Steve watched McQuarry and Morgan turn off toward the park to pick up Francis and head for Hartford. No chase started after them, and he figured he had fooled the press—not something they would easily forgive. He foresaw a string of uncomplimentary stories in his future. Especially after the scoop he, as the anonymous source, had given to Julie.

Chapter 19

Steve sat in the guest chair in Bob Crowder's office. He had gotten back to his flat the previous evening. The dishes had been washed, the sheets changed, and the soiled linen carried away. Swept carpets, swept floor, and all the dust banished. The smell of wood polish and cleansers permeated the rooms. *I will sell the furniture and eat nothing but oatmeal before I get rid of Mrs. Colletti,* Steve told himself.

On his way to the office in the morning, Steve dropped off his laundry at the cleaners, telling them that he would pick it up on Saturday. After the usual drama, the little Frenchman agreed, with Gallic resignation, to have his things ready for him.

He took a cab to work and headed to Bob's office. He got a glower from Ida Clark. Mrs. Clark being the best bellwether of Bob's moods, Steve assumed he was in for a rough time.

Bob was trying to crack his nerve, but Steve just sat and idly worked on his smoke rings. The chief looked up from the news story he was reading and growled, "How did Julie Boroni get this story, Steve? I mean, there is quite a bit of detail. Things that I trusted you not to divulge. You got this assignment because I trusted you. And now you disappoint me. A pretty reporter bats her eyes and shimmies up to you, and you spill your guts. That's not how I trained you.

"I took you under my wing and worked with you like you were my own son. Then you throw it all away. My trust, your pride, your professionalism—all of it. Simply thrown away." His voice took on a note of sadness.

"You would have made my Mimi proud, Bob. You have that quality and tone down almost perfect. That woman could make you feel guilty even if you didn't do anything. She would make you beg her for forgiveness for drinking water. But she would never lower her head. Mimi would pin you to the wall like a bug with her look. You need to work on it, Bob. You really do." He smiled as he blew a perfect smoke ring in Bob's direction.

Bob glowered. He changed direction. "McQuarry said that you weren't too cooperative when he and Morgan went down there."

Steve shot him an irritated look. "McQuarry can jump in the river. You know him; nothing makes him happy unless he can tear someone's playhouse down. I got them Chandler as soon as I could and decoyed them out of town. Have him file a complaint."

"Well, he doesn't like you very much," added Bob, lamely.

Steve snorted and ruined the smoke ring he was working on. "That doesn't make him a member of some kind of exclusive club or anything. Nobody's going to raise any statue to me, and I don't much care. You want a politician in this job; find someone whose only vocabulary consists of 'Yes, sir.'"

Bob rubbed his mouth with his ham of a hand, but Steve caught the smile the gesture tried to hide. He pulled a paper from his desk and tossed it toward Steve, who only gave it a quick glance. The pale blue color of the cover identified it as a subpoena. "You have to be here for the duration of the trial. That means no vacation for that duration. They are going to start selecting jurors Monday. Until then, I want you to write up your report. Get it to me by Friday. And use a typewriter this time. Your handwriting would embarrass a two-year-old. Now get yourself out of my office."

Steve knew from his reception that Bob was pleased at the rapid and successful outcome of the investigation. Best of all, there could be no repercussions from either party. Even the news story would only see the press grumbling about an anonymous source.

Without a comment, Steve rose and picked up his hat from the table at his side. While he was settling it on his head, Bob said, "Oh, by the way, the state attorney general wants you at his office on Saturday morning. You and his team will be going over your testimony all weekend."

"Saturday only. I have plans for Sunday, and I won't be available. My testimony won't change, and I don't like to be coached. I will speak my piece in my own way, in my own words, in my own style. I'll tell the attorney general that I won't disappoint him. There is not a whole lot of leeway in the case."

"You say," snapped Bob. "Both of us know what a snake Bucklin is, and he has a big enough staff to find a way to discredit the witnesses."

Steve left without another word. Rather than use his desk at the office, he decided to work on the report at home. He found the battered typewriter at the bottom of the closet in the spare bedroom. Several hours later, he had the written version of the report finished.

He broke for supper at La Tavola di Felice, owned and run by Giovanni Conti. Steve had gotten him out of a dangerous situation, and he had never forgotten it. Every time Steve entered, Giovanni would rush up, shouting in Italian, welcoming him. The chubby little man would pull him down for a hug and kiss on either cheek. He would always lead him to a table in a private room with thick, heavy curtains. His wife, Francesca, would bring out a bottle of wine and three glasses, and they would sit and have precisely two glasses. She would put the cork back in the bottle, after pouring Steve a third glass, and bang it home with the heel of her hand.

Giovanni would make the same joke every time: "Don't tell no cops about this, Stevie boy. It's a secret for you and me."

Somewhere along the line, they got the idea that Steve's favorite was veal ravioli, chicken Marsala, and spaghetti Bolognese, and they supplied them all. Francesca served him personally and refilled his wine glass constantly. "Steve. Why you not married? I can introduce you to a nice Italian girl."

"Mamma Conti, you are the only one I want. Run away with me," Steve shot back at her, holding his hands over his heart.

She would giggle like a schoolgirl and slap his shoulder. She continued their conversation like they were reading a script: "I could never leave my Giovanni. Unless, maybe, you got rich?"

While he ate, he smiled at the memory of the first time he had put on the act. He had practiced the line for days before using it, perfecting the Italian on Mrs. Colletti. When he had first said it, Francesca had let out a roar of laughter and had to sit down as she tried to catch her breath between gales. Steve had flapped his napkin in her face, and that struck her as funny, too. She got louder and sounded like the seventh wave breaking on a shore. Giovanni came rushing in to see what was happening and, between laughs, she managed to tell him what Steve, who caught only part of it, had said.

The chef rushed from the room to return a few minutes later with a carving knife. It was the size of a small saber, the wooden handle worn and scarred and the steel blade dull except for the edge, which sparkled in the light. He struck a pose, knife raised, head tilted toward the ceiling, and fist on hip, looking like a plump Mussolini in a long white apron. He said, in English, "You will never have my Francesca while I live. Draw your sword!" He threw a tiny paring knife on the table. His wife had erupted in further roars of laughter, rocking back and forth and dabbing at her eyes with double handfuls of her apron.

Steve covered his head with the napkin and said, "I am safe now; no one can see me."

Suddenly, Francesca stopped making any sounds. Steve removed the napkin and looked at her in alarm. She was sitting with her left hand over her breast and her right waving at them to stop. Her husband was pounding her on the back, trying to help her breathe again. Finally, she took a deep breath. "*Basta, basta,*" she gasped.

"Sì, sì, mamma," Giovanni said, a worried look on his face. "We will be enough. Sì, sì."

Francesca dabbed her streaming eyes. She rose and slapped Steve with her apron. "You are a bad boy," she said with attempted dignity, which was marred by her continued chuckling. Giovanni shooed the staff away from the doorway, where they had been attracted by the uproar. They had never achieved the same level of laughter since, but Francesca loved the comedic act.

At the end of the meal, a waitress would enter bearing Steve's dessert. Behind the girl's back, Francesca would shape an exaggerated hourglass with her hands and make a crude Italian sign and nod eagerly. Her intent was to make Steve laugh at her antics and embarrass him, if not convince him that the girl would make a perfect wife. Giovanni would then follow the server, eyes wide, trying to look like Barney Google, and pour thick Italian espresso.

As part of the game, he tried to pay them. "Mah," spat Giovanni. "You don't pay for nothing here. You want to pay for something, go down to that garbage scow, *La Dolce Vita*, down the street." He would then take the proffered bill and stuff it in the handkerchief pocket of Steve's coat. "And then you never come back and insult me and my family again." Francesca would stand there looking disappointed and sad, shaking her head in mock dismay at Steve's rudeness. They would find a bill tucked under his coffee cup and give it to the servers as a tip.

With apologies, Steve would back out the door, duly chastened.

Back home, he gave the mess on the kitchen table a dirty look and turned on the floor lamp in the living room. He stretched out on the chesterfield with his book lying open on his chest. His mind drifted from Susan to Julie to Silene, and, somewhere along the way, he fell asleep.

✂ Chapter 20

Steve stuffed the finished report into his well-used briefcase on Friday morning and walked in the summer heat to the office. Steve cheerfully greeted Mrs. Clark. He looked for a crack in her unassailable manner, but she shot him the hard look she reserved for insolent young men. Steve winked insolently and could have sworn he saw a hint of a smile. He walked back to Bob's office door, arched his eyebrows at her, and received a stern nod.

Steve opened the glass-paneled door and entered. "Here is the report on the Chandler case, Chief," he offered. He flicked the clasp on the briefcase and drew out the folder. With a flourish, he placed it on the desk and took a seat.

Bob spent a few minutes reading the report and tossed it on the desk. "Okay. The state attorney general wants to see you at nine o'clock tomorrow morning." He looked over his glasses and continued, "And Sunday, too."

Steve shook his head and smiled wearily. "I told you that I will be in Chandler on Sunday. They have invited me to the funeral—the family, I mean. I keep telling you that my testimony is going to be straightforward, and I hate being coached."

Bob scowled. "That you will have to take up with the attorney general. This is a tough one and you *will* cooperate, Steve. Full cooperation. Understand?"

"Yep. Understand perfectly. Do you have any message for Captain Daniels?" he asked, making his own position clear.

"Get out of here," Bob growled wearily. "I've got work to do."

Steve rose and left. He tossed a cheerful wave at Mrs. Clark and received a glare in return. The smiles of the two girls from the secretarial pool cheered him up as he left.

Having rushed to get to the state attorney general's office a little after nine, Steve spent the next half hour sitting in the well-appointed waiting room. The pale carpet and rich leather couches and chairs were tastefully lit by lamps sitting on expensive tables. Obviously, the attorney general did not have the same budget constraints as the Connecticut State Police. The room was lined with shelves holding law books in leather bindings with gleaming gold accents. Paintings of past attorneys general hung between the shelves. In a place of honor, the stern face of President Harding looked down. The picture stirred thoughts of the Veterans Bureau scandal, which was still being investigated by Congress. Cramer had committed suicide and Forbes had fled to Europe. The opposition papers were making hay with the resulting mess. While Steve admired Harding's handling of the postwar recession, as a veteran he was disgusted at the administration's handling of this affair.

The secretary was a petite redhead who murmured into the intercom on her desk. She told Steve that Mr. Franklin would be with him almost immediately, nearly convincing him with her sincere, hushed tone. He sat in one of the butter-soft leather chairs.

Steve thumbed through several magazines, growing bored. He pointedly checked his watch and was just as pointedly ignored by the secretary. After being rebuffed when he tried to initiate a conversation, Steve closed his eyes and fought off the urge to doze. After thirty-two minutes, by the clock on the wall, Mr. Samuel Bucklin Sr. exited. He wore an expensive dark-blue pin-striped three-piece suit and a bright red tie. Silver hair perfectly combed and a haughty look on his florid face, he walked through the office with regal indifference. His companions were undoubtedly junior attorneys from his office, brought along to cow the state. He gave a curt and grudging nod to Steve. One of the juniors opened the door as if ushering out royalty.

Paulie Franklin stood at his office door, wiping his hands on a handkerchief. The state attorney general was a tall, rail-thin man with thinning, dark hair in a deep widow's peak and gray eyes. Steve wondered if the sharp, angular planes of his face could slice bread. His thin lips formed a tight, humorless smile as he motioned to Steve.

After nodding to the two assistant state attorneys in the room and shaking hands over introductions, Steve sat in a deep armchair whose leather felt as good as that of the seating in the waiting room. Franklin seated himself behind his acre of desk and started shuffling papers. "Inspector Walsh. We would like to spend some time going over your testimony. Because of the importance of the case, Judge Towers wants the trial to take place as soon as possible. Mr. Francis Chandler was arraigned this morning and, as you saw, we had a preliminary meeting with his attorney, Mr. Bucklin Sr. Not surprisingly, he has filed several motions." Franklin's long, slender fingers tapped a stack of legal documents. "They are contending that you coerced him into admitting guilt. That the venue should be changed away from Hartford. They have also filed a complaint against Captain Daniels and the Chandler Constabulary. He insists that they are not a recognized police force, only a group of strong-arm ex-military thugs, and had no jurisdiction. You are accused of criminal tactics and not giving the attorney access to his client. He wants the confession thrown out, and without that, the case will prove almost impossible."

Steve received a nod when he extracted a pack of cigarettes from his pocket and raised an eyebrow at the state attorney general for permission. After lighting up, he leaned forward, his elbows on his knees. With one hand, he ticked off the points on the other: "In order of importance, Bucklin knows that capital cases are tried in Hartford. You must have told him that." Franklin nodded. "Second, he was in the room with Chandler from the time the shyster arrived on the train. Next, Francis wanted to show us how smart he was and insisted on talking with us over Bucklin's advice. At first, he was smug and answered all our questions. He tried to fudge about what he admitted in the interrogation at the house. Sure, Buck—Captain Daniels—and I worked on him, not physically, but using normal techniques. At no time did we touch him. Bucklin tried to get him to shut up at every opportunity.

"When he finally broke down, he was only too eager to tell us how he did it and why. He again ignored Bucklin when Bucklin told him not to speak. We had a recorder and witnesses, and he signed the confession of his own free will. Look at the transcript of the interrogation. Two detectives transferred him to Hartford, and you have had two people from your office sitting outside his cell on a suicide watch.

"As for the Chandler Constabulary, the sheriff has certified the training and experience of the force. There are three deputies with military police experience and training, and all but one have had some military training. I would put them up against any small-town police department in the state."

Steve settled back in his chair. "The trial venue problem is up to you. You want to crucify me, go ahead. I did nothing unlawful, and I didn't let anyone else do anything unlawful. Bucklin would be a great witness for you, since he was there most of the time." Steve leaned back in his chair, barely containing the irritation he felt.

Franklin used the intercom to ask his secretary to bring in fresh coffee. He turned back to Steve. "Yeah, that's what I thought. Bucklin is trying to throw smoke around. All right, I will handle the motions. They do not look like too much to me, depending on what the judge has in mind.

"Now, I want to go over your testimony. Start at the beginning with your arrival in Chandler … "

The three state attorneys spent the next six hours throwing questions at Steve in rapid fire. He took his time and gave his story in chronological order, leaving out only the private moments with Silene and with Julie. He was concise and orderly, referring to his notebook frequently to refresh his memory. The attorneys' interruptions did not faze him or cause him to stumble. They broke for lunch and then continued through the early afternoon. By four o'clock, Steve felt wrung out and tired. A couple of times he had to rein in his temper and take a deep breath, especially when the questions drifted close to slandering his relationship with

Silene. The two daughters had been accused by Bucklin of conspiring to murder their mother and placing the blame on their brother. Steve carefully dismantled any attempt to shift the blame from Francis to another suspect. He went over the alibis of the committee members, Silene, and Catherine. Steve thought Bucklin's accusations sounded like one of Emma Black's creations.

Before Franklin called it a day, Steve informed him that he was returning to Chandler for Mrs. Chandler's funeral. Franklin looked over his notes and told him to go ahead. "I expect you at the courthouse Monday for the preliminary hearing on the motions. The judge will probably have some questions for you."

Steve had enough time to pick up his laundry, pack, and make it to the station for the evening train to Chandler.

Silene was waiting for him at the station. She waved enthusiastically and gave him a happy smile. A tight hug matched the wave. Clasping his arm, she walked him to her car. Despite her apparently cheerful demeanor, Steve suspected she was upset. She was chattering about the weather, her car, and other irrelevant topics in an uncharacteristic manner.

They drove to the hotel at her usual breakneck speed and with several close calls. Steve wondered whether the endangered citizens had an instinctive sense of self-preservation when they knew she was behind the wheel.

The doorman was at the curb when they screeched to a halt. Steve started to thank her for the ride when she jumped out and threw the keys to the uniformed doorman. "Park it for me, will you, Sam?"

She stood waiting on the sidewalk for him. Tall and elegant, even in jodhpurs and boots. Her red silk blouse moved in the light, warm breeze, and she played with the silver bauble on the chain around her slim throat. There was a nervous half-smile on her patrician lips, and her eyes hesitated to meet his.

With a sigh, Steve exited the car and pulled his bag from the back. As the car drove away, he asked, "What's going on, Silene?"

Her face flushed under her tan, and she clasped her hands in front of her, twining and untwining her fingers. "I don't want to go back to the house right now. There are too many people, saying nothing. I need a—a moment. Just a drink, and you don't have to say anything. I'll leave when you want—I promise." Her voice was quiet and almost shy.

He picked up his bag, took a firm hold on her arm, and ushered her through the door to the lobby. After retrieving his key, they moved to the elevator. The operator stared at them until Steve cleared his throat, and then sprang into action, his face red. The lad tried not to turn and stare, but he stole glances at their distorted reflections in the brass panel in front of him. His passengers looked straight ahead and said nothing.

At his floor, Steve allowed Silene to precede him out of the elevator, and they walked silently to his room. He opened the door and ushered her in. While he took his bag to the bedroom, she crossed to the window and stared out distractedly. Steve returned to the living area and stood for a moment looking at her slim figure. Silene had her left arm crossed under her chest and gripped her right arm above the elbow. The bauble whispered along the chain in a steady rhythm.

"Bad day?" he asked.

With a sad, quiet laugh she turned and walked slowly over to him. Both arms reached around his chest and tightened. She laid her head on his shoulder. Steve stood there awkwardly for a moment and hesitantly held her. He hoped she was not crying but swiftly realized she was. He should not be too surprised, he thought. Her mother had been murdered and her brother arrested, and still everything had to be held together—something with which Catherine was of little help, from all he heard.

He led her to the chesterfield and seated her before crossing to the table and building them drinks. A fresh bottle of whiskey and ice had been set out. Steve poured the alcohol and added an ice cube to each. A shot of soda finished the task. He remembered his talk with himself on the farm road, and his drink was more soda than alcohol.

The crystal glass clicked against her teeth when she took her first sip. She gave him another shaky laugh and attempted a smile. "Thank you," Silene whispered and took another sip.

Steve sat next to her, and she grabbed his free hand with hers. The long, tapered fingers clasped his almost in desperation. He realized that she was at a breaking point and needed a release. She gave a shaky laugh when he asked with a purposeful double entendre, "Do you want to go to bed and take a nap?"

She leaned against the upholstered back and let out a deep breath. "I wasn't sure you would let me in, after the fool I made of myself last time, Steve," she said with closed eyes. "I seem to turn into a weeping mess every time I see you lately."

Steve squeezed her hand, and she continued. "I needed this. Things have been so hectic. Preparations for the funeral, all the calls and telegrams. I love Catherine dearly, but she doesn't handle these things well. Paul tries to help, but he is so worried about Catherine and the baby."

"Baby? When did that happen?" a surprised Steve asked.

"Catherine? I guess you wouldn't know. That's why they came up. To tell Mother about it, but she was so upset about the marriage, they never got a chance. It is due in about six months."

"Sorry to interrupt. Go ahead."

"Where was I? Paul. He goes down to the office and is trying to keep the mills going.

"I have a good staff, and my second-in-command is handling things on the sales and merchandising end, thank God. Everyone is looking to me to do *everything* at the house, for the funeral, wake, everything. I could have sent one of the people from the farms to pick you up, but I needed to"— she hesitated and changed her mind before finishing—"get away." Silene avoided his eyes by taking another sip.

"Stay here as long—oh, here we go again. Stay here. I will get another room. Get a good night's sleep. Things will work out. I will help where I can. There. If I speak in short, slow sentences I won't put my foot in my mouth."

Silene moved and threw her arms around his neck, spilling her drink. She kissed him short and hard. Before he had a chance to respond, she pulled back, a smile on her face. A genuine stretch of her mouth, not hesitant or shy. She rose and grabbed a cloth that was folded next to the ice bucket. With quick dabs, she mopped at the spill.

"Thanks, Steve. I am better now. I don't know what it is about you, but you know what to do to make things better." She looked at him from under her perfect brows. "One of these days, Steve, you are going to break out of that shell and find there's someone who can really appreciate who you are."

He sat there with his mouth open and watched her walk out of the room. Her back was straight and her step sure. She was ready to face the world again—the strong, assured woman he had always seen. Silene paused at the door and blew him a kiss over her shoulder.

✂ Chapter 21

The next morning, Steve was awakened by a stray shaft of sunlight shining through a gap in the curtains. He pried opened one eye enough to see that the clock showed nine fifteen. He rolled over and reveled in the fact that he would not have to get up for at least another hour.

After another few minutes, though, thoughts of Silene, Julie, and Susan drove him to the shower. He managed to shave without doing too much damage. With teeth brushed and hair combed, he decided that he would survive the day. He dressed and went in search of breakfast. His shoes stood gleaming by the door where he had placed them the evening before.

Steve detoured to the front desk. He asked the clerk if he would send someone up to retrieve his black suit and have it pressed. He flipped a coin to the bellhop before turning to the restaurant.

The room was crowded. Dress was somber, and he recognized a few individuals as being high in the party. There were several who looked like businessmen and businesswomen.

As he glanced around, he saw Buck enter the room wearing his tailored uniform. The captain pulled out a chair and ordered coffee from the waitress. "How are things, lover boy?" he asked innocently.

"Cut it out. She just picked me up from the station," Steve snapped irritably.

"Come on. She met every train that came in yesterday. You have smitten our little Silene," he said with a grin.

Surprised, Steve tried to collect himself. He had not even thought about how she knew which train he was on. "She was just being nice. Skip that 'lover boy' stuff or you'll get smitten," he snarled with mock seriousness, showing a clenched fist to the laughing Buck.

Their orders came, and Steve brought Buck up to date on the status of things in Hartford. The constable's brow clouded when he described the motion in relation to the Chandler Constabulary. "I may do a little smiting myself if I ever see that shyster again," he said angrily. "I'll put my boys against any force in the state."

Steve inserted innocently, "And girls?"

"Don't you start. All my officers. Ruth can outshoot most of what's out there," Buck retorted. He took a sip of coffee and grinned. "Touché."

Following breakfast, Steve visited the constabulary office. He greeted Ruth and Red. After a half hour of shop-talk, he returned to the hotel to change for the funeral.

Streets had been closed off for the funeral procession. He lit a cigarette as he stepped out of the hotel. The day had warmed up, and the light breeze did little to dispel the heat. He tugged his hat more firmly on his head and started for the Episcopal church down the street in company with most of Chandler.

The church was a formidable pile, taking up half a city block, with the graveyard next door. A low stone wall surrounded the plots, with lightly weathered gravestones and marble monuments dotting the grounds. In the center of the well-manicured lawn stood the Chandler crypt, freshly washed and gleaming in the sunlight.

The crypt was open, and Steve smiled at the angel standing above the doorway surrounded by mounds of flowers. Its left hand was resting on a stone shield, and the forefinger of its right hand was pointing at the sky, where its face was also turned. From what he had heard about Old Man Chandler, Silene's grandfather, the statue was probably telling Saint Peter that someone important was on the way and to polish the Pearly Gates.

The hearse, a shiny black wood-and-glass horse-drawn carriage, sat in front of the steep stone stairs. It was hung with black crepe, and the four horses had black tack, with black ostrich feathers that bobbed as they moved their heads. The solemn driver was dressed in a black suit and wore a silk top hat with a wide black ribbon band. The tails of the ribbon hung down his back.

The streets were packed with people, many from the town and farms. Everyone had been given the day off, it seemed. Even the hotel had closed for the duration of the funeral.

Behind the hearse was a 1923 Franklin Town Limousine. The chauffeur held the door and helped Silene out. Steve's heart lurched. Her chic dress fit her like a glove. Not tight and showy, but elegant. A round black hat perched on her golden hair, and a veil hung in front of her strained-looking face. The driver released her black-gloved fingers, and she moved aside, clutching her small handbag.

Silene looked around and saw Steve. She immediately moved to his side and placed a hand on his arm, a change from the death grip he was used to. "Stay with me. Please,

Steve," she whispered. He nearly protested that he was not a relation, but he nodded reluctantly and patted her hand.

They led the family up the stairs and into the church. A black crepe bow hung at the end of each pew, and black ribbon was strung across the rows reserved for family. Dark-suited ushers led the Chandlers down the broad nave.

Steve, who had not spent as much time in church as he—and his parents—thought he should, tried not to gawk like a country tourist visiting the big city for the first time. Light streamed through the stained-glass windows depicting biblical scenes. Sparkling colored light, contrasting with the solemn occasion, tinted the scene. The graceful arches held up the soaring ceiling painted with depictions of scenes from the Old and New Testaments. Surrounding a central piece portraying God on his throne, attended by cherubim and seraphim, were illustrations of biblical stories. Moses faced a burning bush. Joshua stood before crumbling city walls. Jesus sat upon a stool, while behind him listeners thronged. A stark scene of the Crucifixion faded into light, airy visions of the Resurrection and Ascension. Above the windows stood the Apostles, with scenes from their travels. An evil-looking Judas was shown slinking away at the end of the line. On the opposite wall, David, Solomon, Ruth, and Abraham were only a few of those immortalized. Scrolls and verses identified the figures. On the wall behind the altar, Christ was shown with his right hand raised and his left holding a shepherd's crook. Pastoral scenes of peacefully grazing sheep framed him. Steve was impressed at the detail, and Silene had to urge him along. He glanced at her smiling lips as she whispered, "Dad spent a year searching for the artist. It took almost three years to paint, and Dad came here every week on his way home from the mill."

The coffin was sitting in the center of the transept, surrounded by a sea of flower arrangements. More bouquets covered the chancel. A large easel held the painting of Mrs. Chandler that Steve had first seen in the woman's office. The gilt frame was draped in the same black crepe as was present throughout the sanctuary. The rector stood next to Bishop Brewster at the altar, surrounded by deacons and clergy. Father Williamson from the Catholic church, which rivaled the Episcopalian building in size, was standing on the bishop's other side. He was dressed in traditional funeral vestments. The pews filled; even the choir loft was packed. The side aisles held more mourners, and Steve knew that the steps and sidewalk in front of the church would be filled with those who could not fit inside.

During the ceremony, Silene never released Steve's arm. She wept silently, and he handed her his own handkerchief when hers became a wad of damp linen. With the eulogies droning on and the sisters weeping on either side of him, Steve realized why he avoided funerals. Though neither of them spoke, there were plenty who did. Senators, representatives, governors, and every other politician who managed to get on the roster. Business associates and friends of the family. Apparently, Silene had drawn the line, and the flower show committee was not included.

The warmth and drone had nearly lulled him to sleep when the congregation rose.

The family followed the pallbearers out, down the stairs, around to the graveyard, and into the crypt. Every square inch of the cemetery was covered with mourners, as were the sidewalks. Once the graveside ceremony concluded, the crypt doors were closed. The large ornate iron key sealed the lock with a click of finality, and the attendees passed the family, extending their condolences. Steve earned curious looks as he stood by Silene. He smiled awkwardly and nodded to the few people he knew and accepted introductions to their wives or husbands.

Annette, Susanne, and Cookie gave his arm a squeeze as they passed, and Jeremy gave him a formal nod in greeting. Buck tossed him a knowing look and introduced Steve to his wife, a short, plump woman with red eyes and nose. She, obviously, had been a true mourner at the ceremony, not just a polite attendee. One of the last sympathizers caught Steve's eye, and he groaned inwardly. Julie, sent by the paper to cover the event, extended her sympathies to the family and gave him a stony look, shifting her gaze pointedly to Silene. Maybe it was a coincidence, but Silene's hand tightened on his arm as she thanked Julie by name. The two women had met when Julie interviewed the family regarding the flower show. From the looks that passed between them, Steve saw that battle lines had been drawn.

When the family was alone and the clergymen had gone to change out of their vestments, Steve found himself at the limousine. He helped Silene into the automobile and, as he started to step back, felt her tug on his hand. Short of yanking his fingers away there was no way he could refuse her silent invitation. He stepped in and settled himself on the seat next to her. Catherine and Paul Sullivan entered and settled in the rearmost seat. He could almost feel Paul's glare burning into the back of his neck.

No one spoke on the way to the mansion and the reception, which Steve desperately wished he had been able to avoid. It looked like he was in for the duration. He sighed and stared out the front window past the driver. He thought about his disaster of a love life after the look Julie had given him and sighed again in resignation.

A large buffet had been arranged in the ballroom. A catering firm had been engaged to allow Annette, Susanne, Cookie, and Jeremy to attend as guests. To make matters worse, in Steve's view, the drinks rule still held. Coffee, tea, juices, and other nonalcoholic beverages were all that were available. The family lined up again by the door, and the tedious process of welcoming guests began. Silene, her old grip renewed, was gracious, and Catherine made low murmuring sounds. Steve wondered if Paul's look of disapproval was the only expression he owned. Julie politely shook Silene's hand and turned away, back rigid, lips tight. Steve's gaze followed the reporter. When he turned back, Steve saw a sad, lost look in Silene's eyes.

The smug and knowing expression on Buck's face made Steve feel like taking a poke at him to relieve the irritation. One of the politicians could not help whispering in his ear, "Looking for Crowder's job, huh, Walsh?"

When the greeting line broke up, Silene walked the room, speaking to her guests. Steve's arm felt numb, but she kept her hold. Jeremy brushed by him, and he felt a weight drop into his coat pocket. An exploring hand found the shape of a metal flask. He immediately steered Silene away from her current conversation.

"Where are we going?" Silene inquired, surprise on her lovely face.

"Quiet," ordered Steve.

"But, my guests … " she protested.

"That's not quiet," he said and continued walking, folding her hand around his sleeve. Steve kept a strong grip on her hand and dragged her along.

He exited the ballroom and continued determinedly down the hall. Steve finally turned into Mrs. Chandler's office. As he expected, there was a tea cart in the room. It contained several glasses, an ice bucket with tongs, and a bottle of seltzer.

He released her hand and walked to the cart, fishing the flask from his pocket. Silene closed the door behind them with a grin. She perched on the desk and retrieved two cigarettes from the rosewood box. Picking up the heavy silver lighter, she lit them and traded one of them to Steve in exchange for the drink he offered.

"Miss Chandler," he said, raising his glass in salute.

She kicked off her shoes and rubbed one foot with the other. "Mr. Walsh," she returned and took a large drink. "Oh, my feet hurt," she complained.

Steve loosened his tie and unbuttoned his collar button. "Some woman got her revenge for high heels by inventing the necktie."

He finished his drink and turned to replenish his glass. "Take some more of Uncle Steve's Patent Medicine," he said.

"I am going to recommend you for sainthood," she said with a sigh, holding out her glass for a refill. "I haven't had an opportunity for this. You saved my life!"

"If I did, I am your responsibility forever, according an old Chinese custom." Realizing what he had said, he hurriedly continued, "It wasn't me. Double Jeremy's salary."

When he turned, he saw the speculative look in Silene's eye.

"Your brother is pretty depressed," he said to avoid the territory into which they seemed to be wandering.

She gave him a determined look and said firmly, "Francis is a murderer. It is difficult to face, but he killed Mother. We, as a family, will publicly support him, but Catherine and I have no intention of viewing him as a brother ever again. We will not see him, except in the courtroom, and we have been to Nicholas Martin to determine how we can keep him out of our lives." She took a hard, angry drag on her cigarette and exploded the smoke out. Steve thought her look boded no mercy for her errant brother.

A sharp knock interrupted them, and Paul stuck his head around the door he had opened without invitation. He ignored Steve and gave Silene a stern look. "Silene, you have guests who are looking for you. Catherine cannot be expected to do everything." The door closed more forcefully than necessary.

Silene hopped off the desk and slid into her shoes. "I had better save Catherine from her constant labors," she said sarcastically.

"Look, Silene," Steve began, but she interrupted him.

"I know. I have monopolized all your time," she said, a slightly guilty note in her voice. "Go ahead, Ju … um, your friends are waiting." Though she smiled brightly, there was a resignation in her glistening eyes that caused a lurch in his stomach.

"It's not that." He spoke to her back but did not know if she had heard him. Steve rarely cursed, but he spat out a few choice words as he followed her out.

Buck agreed to lend him his car, despite the threat in his wife's eye. As he drove down the hill, Steve said to himself, "There are a real lot of women who just don't seem to like you, Steve."

When he got to the hotel, he ordered supper to be brought up to his room and requested a wake-up at six o'clock in the morning to give him time to catch the early train. In his room, he fixed himself a drink in the tallest glass he could find.

He sat in the dark after supper, changing his beverage of choice to water. He stared out the window into the night. He focused on his reflection in the glass and muttered, "Steve, old son, time to grow up. On the one hand, you have Julie. On the other hand, you have Silene. On the third hand, you could be a bitter old man with a mangy cat." He organized his thoughts as he would in a case. First, he mentally created a list, carefully considering everything he knew. When he finished with Julie's list, he created one for Silene. He had only known her for about a week, so this list was shorter and less concrete. The last list took longer to create. Steve had to argue with himself over several points, as to whether they were pros or cons. He had to put several under both columns, with "being alone" the most difficult for him. Steve enjoyed his freedom, but less so his loneliness.

At the end of his analysis, he managed to amputate the third hand. Steve was left with Julie's and Silene's lists and a surprisingly lighter heart. There was only one more question to face: Would either one have him? He might have to resurrect list three after all. In the wee hours of the morning, he went to bed.

Chapter 22

Steve was half awake when the knock sounded. He had spent a rough night drifting up slowly through the thick mud of his restless sleep to toss and turn until he slid into oblivion again. He wearily climbed out of bed and tried to ignore the headache brought about by the lack of sleep. He called through the door, "Okay, I'm up. I'm *up*." In the welcome silence that followed, he struggled back across the room.

He took a headache powder and tried to pretend he did not look as bad as the mirror reported. After a shower that was almost too hot to stand, he scraped the fuzz out of his mouth. Some of the fog dispelled as he dressed and threw his clothes in his suitcase, with no regard for mixing clean with dirty or folding. His suitcase was closed before he noticed his mismatched socks.

Steve dropped his key off and left a tip for the staff. Looking regretfully at the restaurant, he let the doorman signal for a cab, not wanting to drive himself to the station. Steve handed the key to Buck's car to Sam and asked him to drive it down to the constabulary office.

The taxicab ride to the station seemed like riding a rocking boat on rough seas. Steve realized that one headache powder would not be enough. The train whistle blasted as he picked up his ticket and hurried, painfully, across the platform to scramble up the metal stairs. He found an empty cabin and collapsed onto the seat. After a couple of deep breaths, he heaved himself in the direction of the dining car. *If I have to, I'll show my badge and arrest whoever has failed to make coffee,* he pledged as he rocked down the corridor.

After breakfast and enough coffee to jump-start his thoughts, he returned to his seat. He lit a cigarette and stared at the passing countryside. His thoughts drifted back to the conundrum of the previous evening. Steve assumed that both women were interested, ignoring the seeming arrogance that that implied. Julie had signaled her interest by wearing the earrings at the quilt unveiling and by her obvious irritation at seeing him constantly in Silene's company. Silene's actions could not be misinterpreted. Her picking him up at the station. The visits to his room for comfort or sanctuary. Her attitude when she left him at the wake.

Steve realized he had to make a decision about whether he felt more for the fiery Julie or the calmer Silene. These thoughts occupied him during the hours to Hartford. The exercise exacerbated his headache.

Steve jumped to the platform and hurried to the cab-stand. He hopped into the first available vehicle. He ordered the cabbie, "Courthouse. Step on it."

The driver looked over his shoulder at his fare. "Look, buddy. The city has a little rule about turning the streets into racecourses. They feel that pedestrians should have a chance to get where they are going. It looks bad in the newsreels when they show bodies littering the streets. They frown on it so bad, I could lose my license. Now, you want to go to the courthouse in this cab or not?"

Steve reached into his pocket, the movement showing the cabbie his shoulder holster. Before his surprised expression could change to panic, Steve flipped open his identification and badge. "Does this help?" he asked. "There is a murder trial, and I need to get there fast."

The driver gulped and pulled out into the street. He stamped on the accelerator, and they roared down the street. After his first hesitation, he grinned and gunned the cab. As they weaved in and out of traffic, horns and shouts followed them.

Steve sat back and tried to relax. He upbraided himself for not leaving the previous evening. If he had enjoyed himself last night, he would at least have something pleasant to think of. Instead, he had a headache and was going to be late. He tried to enumerate everyone who would be unhappy with him but quickly lost count.

A city cop picked them up two blocks from the courthouse, but a quick word and a flash of his badge got him enough professional courtesy to keep the cabbie out of trouble when they stopped in front of the justice building. He paid off the driver, who said, "Any time you need a cab, just ask for Buddy Reilly. I could do this all day." He gave Steve a salute and drove sedately off.

The inspector raced up the stairs and shoved through the doors. At the information desk he asked where the Chandler trial was taking place and dropped off his baggage. He walked hurriedly to the courtroom and pushed open the door, straightening his tie and removing his hat.

The courtroom was empty except for a bailiff. He looked at Steve. "Bucklin asked the court for an adjournment. Franklin and his team are in Meeting Room 3, waiting for you. Oh, and Steve, Judge Towers said something about witnesses not being available. Keep your head down. He's in a foul mood. He hates to have his time wasted like this."

Steve thanked him and headed to Meeting Room 3.

He found Franklin waiting impatiently. "Where have you been? Towers was looking for you."

Steve answered, "I was in Chandler for the funeral. Didn't get out until this morning."

There was a chuckle from one of the assistant state attorneys, and Steve flushed. Franklin snorted and continued, "Bucklin came in this morning and asked for a delay. Said he was in conference with his client. Judge Towers was less than amused that one of his flunkies delivered the message. At one o'clock the judge wants everyone in court, quote, 'even if you have to get there on a gurney,' end quote."

"What's the story?" Steve asked.

Franklin scratched his chin. "Anything from a change of plea to an incapacity defense. I've got two of my attorneys trying to find out, but no go. Be back at one. And, Steve, be here," he warned.

A runner knocked on the door with a message for Steve: "Get back here. Bob Crowder." Usually, the shorter the note, the angrier Bob was. Steve excused himself, picked up his suitcase, and headed for the street.

When he entered the office, the first person he saw was McQuarry. He had a sneering smile on his face. McQuarry raised one hand with his index finger extended and his thumb cocked. He brought the thumb down. Steve knew that anything that made McQuarry playful meant ill for Steve. He continued toward Bob's office, rubbing his forehead.

Mrs. Clark watched him cross the room. She pointed to the water cooler and slapped a headache powder she retrieved from a desk drawer onto the corner of her desk. Surprised, Steve halted. He stared at her and, hesitantly, drew a paper cup of water. He did not question her instinct that he had a headache, but her action. His eyes still on her, he crossed the space to her desk and added the powder. With a small smile creasing her mouth, she handed a letter opener to him. Steve expected her face to crumble from the mouth twitch; he refused to even consider that Cerberus could smile. He used the opener to stir and handed it back. Steve drank the mixture down and sighed.

"Thank you, Mrs. Clark. You are an angel."

She snorted and said acerbically, "The condemned man has a hearty last meal." Steve stared at her as he crumpled the cup and dropped it in the trash. Mrs. Clark making a joke—this was more disconcerting than McQuarry's mime.

The magic moment passed and the world swung back into its normal orbit. She nodded her head toward Bob's door. "He's been waiting."

Steve walked into the office and closed the door. He started toward the rickety wooden chair that served visitors to the office. He was stopped by Bob's angry voice.

"I didn't ask you to sit, Inspector," he snapped.

As Steve turned slowly toward his boss, a section of a newspaper flew at him and spread, scattering. It was followed by another and another until the floor was adrift in newsprint. He sighed and picked up a sheet before he sat. Steve read the headline circled in red pencil: "Mystery Man at the Chandler Funeral." Another read, "CSP Sends Mourner to Comfort Family." The *Hartford Morning Post* heralded "Impartial CSP?" with the subheading of "Inspector Walsh

Courts Heiress." It carried Julie's byline. He sat wearily and waited for the eruption, willing to take his medicine.

"What in the Sam Hill did you think you were doing?" Bob bellowed, rising and leaning over his desk, supported by his fists. "Turning this office into a laughingstock? You go off gallivanting with that girl. The state of Connecticut is not your private bank! Your vacation is not going to be two weeks but twenty years! You and that little … "

"That's enough, Bob," Steve warned. His voice was soft, but there was no doubting the steel that edged his words. He had been quiet and humble when his boss's anger had been directed at him, but when Bob started attacking Silene, he had stepped over a line, and both men realized it. Steve rose from his chair and stood rigidly, his hands clenched into fists.

The two men stared at each other for a full minute. Bob looked away first, though he disguised it as a search for his chair. He sat angrily and waved at Steve. "Sit down. Sit down. I got a little carried away. Sorry," he finished gruffly.

Steve slowly lowered himself back into his chair, but he did not relax. His hands gripped the arms, and his knuckles were white. "I've got to get back by one o'clock," he said tightly.

Bob rubbed his bald head. "Pick up the papers, will you?"

"No," answered Steve through his teeth. He realized how childish this was and straightened the mess and set the badly folded press reports on the corner of the desk.

Bob sighed. "Okay, okay. You're upset. I understand. I am not too happy myself. I don't need one of my investigators to bring the organization into disrepute. There are going to be calls for your resignation." His voice started to turn hoarse, and he brought himself under control with an effort. "We have to work together to fix this." Bob had made his point and was ready to be reasonable.

Steve relaxed a little. He extracted a cigarette and lit it. "I messed up. I won't try to make excuses. You have to fire me, suspend me, take me off the case? Okay, I understand and won't fight it. Just concentrate on me when you blame someone. Please. Now. Fix what and how?" he asked.

The chief snorted. "Bucklin is going to use this to cast doubt on the case. He's going to say that you were so busy having an affair with Miss Chandler that you failed in your duty as an investigator. He'll say that the two of you colluded to frame her brother so you could … whatever … with her." The last came out lamely.

"Okay, Bob. First, I am not having an affair or 'whatever' with Silene Chandler. You keep that up, and I'm going to bust you in the nose," he said lightly, trying to ease the tension.

"See? Right there. A woman-hater like you getting so upset like that over a rich skirt. I don't just sit around with my head stuck in the sand, you know. She's been up to your hotel room, you squire her around like a—a—a lovesick hound dog."

Steve was stunned. He could see Julie's fine Italian hand in this. She must really be mad to have torpedoed him like this. In keeping with his thoughts of the last couple of days, he wondered if she would be this angry if she were not interested. Julie could have mentioned his name as the source for her earlier story if revenge had been her motive.

He leaned forward and supported himself with his elbows on his knees. His anger had evaporated. "Yeah, I see your point. How much damage has it done?"

Bob's face lost its choleric hue. "I guess we can ride it out. There might be some embarrassing questions during the next budget cycle, but that's months away. The important thing is the trial. Get together with Franklin before the court convenes. Work out some plan. Tell him I'll back him up, whatever he decides. You may have to eat crow over this. Be contrite. Grovel, if you have to."

Steve glanced at his watch. "I've got to get back. I'll talk to Paulie." He looked up at Bob. "There is nothing to this. She needed a tree to hold onto. There is nothing between us."

Steve rose and turned to the door. He said forcefully, "There is nothing to this."

As he closed the door, he heard Bob say, "Who are you trying to convince, Stevie boy?"

Chapter 23

Steve's fingers tapped his knee on the ride back to the courthouse. He was mulling over the situation. He wondered if the party organization would take Silene's side. Would it still keep its head down if a Chandler were being attacked? Steve sighed. He knew they would not want to antagonize Francis only to find him exonerated and in a mood for revenge. Especially if Silene were involved in a frame and they defended her honor.

Steve found the state attorney general in the same conference room. "I need to talk to you, Paulie," he said.

Franklin tapped the paper resting on the desk. It had been turned to the society page and the story circled. "You bet you do. This could be big trouble."

The state attorney general read Steve the riot act. He outlined the problems that they would face during the trial. Steve endured the lecture silently, knowing he deserved every word.

"Listen, Paulie. I talked with Bob. He said to throw me to the wolves if you have to. I'll admit I acted unprofessionally and will resign. I know Francis did this, and anything that can be done to damp this down—go for it."

"It is not as easy as you make it sound, Steve." Franklin's voice rose in irritation. "The whole confession may be thrown out. Without that, this case unravels and—"

In the middle of the tirade, a knock sounded on the door. One of the junior attorneys answered it and had a short conversation with the visitor. Several times they heard him ask, "Are you sure?" The attorney shut the door and stood with his back to the panel.

"What is it, Craig?" snapped Franklin.

"Oh. Judge Towers wants you to return immediately. Chandler wants to change his plea to guilty. Bucklin brought him the news."

They hurried back to the courtroom and arrived as Towers entered. While the members of the press rushed in and hastily took their seats, he gaveled for order.

Attorney Bucklin announced his client's change of plea and affirmed it when the judge asked him to reiterate. "Your honor," Bucklin said, "against my advice, Mr. Francis Chandler desires to save himself and his family the pain of a trial. He wishes to throw himself on the mercy of the court."

Judge Towers gaveled loudly to quiet the sudden buzz.

"Mr. Chandler?" he queried. Francis raised his head, face pale. "Mr. Chandler, is this your wish?"

Francis got shakily to his feet. "Yes, your honor," he answered in a gravelly voice. He took a drink of water.

Before he could continue, Towers interrupted. "It has come to my attention that there may have been some irregularity in the investigation that may cast doubt on the State's case. I think you should consult with your attorney before you make this decision."

The defendant stubbornly shook his head. "It doesn't matter, your honor. Nothing changes what I did. The confession is true." Francis dropped into his chair as if his legs could no longer support him. "I want to change my plea to 'guilty.' I—I murdered my mother." He covered his face with his hands.

After some further questions and the scheduling of the sentencing, the press made a rush for the door before Judge Towers could gavel the proceedings closed.

"Three weeks is a long time, Steve. Look. Take a week and come back. You would be completely bored moping around for that long."

Steve was sitting in the chief's office. With the trial over, he was due his vacation. Bob Crowder was not letting him go quietly.

"Anyway, there is a case I need you to handle. It came up while you were working down in Chandler. There is another outbreak of 'murder whiskey' like in 1919. More wood alcohol–laced booze. A dozen people were brought to the hospital, and three more died. I need my best man to take this over. We have to shut this down. You would be saving lives," he said, looking over his glasses, trying to gauge the impact.

He pulled another folder from the pile scattered on his desk. "These are reports of cross burnings in the immigrant ghettos. The governor is running on law and order again and wants the KKK shut down. We had a couple of Poles beat up pretty badly."

Another folder slapped on the other two. "Illegal liquor. They are making it by the bathtub load in New Haven and shipping it here. Bad stuff. Blindness."

Bob spread his hands. "There is a new freighter loaded with booze offshore in the international zone. The Feds are demanding our help to stop them smuggling it in. Who else can I trust?"

Steve sat patiently in his chair, legs stretched out. The standing ashtray next to him was nearly full, and a haze clouded the room. He had been sitting in the uncomfortable chair for over an hour while Bob harangued him, browbeat him, cajoled him, and begged him.

He looked at Bob and said, "No. You promised me three weeks. If I come back after a week, I will never see another day. What is it with you needing me every time some little thing goes wrong? Doesn't anybody else work around here? McQuarry is champing at the bit to prove how smart he is. Why don't you strap a box of dynamite to his back and have him blow up the freighter? No. Three. Weeks. Vacation."

Bob dropped his head and folded his hands on his desk. Before he could start the process of making Steve feel guilty, the subject jumped out of his chair and grabbed his hat from the rack. "Don't even start, Bob. You already cost me my reservation in the Poconos with the Chandler case. I had to find somewhere else to go. Plans are made, my laundry is done, and my suitcase is packed. Sayonara. Adios. Ciao. Au revoir. Auf Wiedersehen. I'm going, going, gone."

"Where are you going to be, if someone needs to get in touch?"

"On vacation," Steve said. He shut the door on Bob's shout and left the building.

He caught a taxi to the station. Steve found his first-class cabin. He pulled the cord for the steward and ordered a pitcher of water, ice, and a glass. He assembled a drink from Silene's gift. He thought about her as he sipped his drink and watched the world go by.

Epilogue

A young woman walked with Steve down the platform. She had accepted his proposal of marriage. They were to meet his parents, though he was not aware of this fact. This was a plot between Steve's mother and his fiancée to heal the rift between two stubborn men.

Steve's fiancée had taken it upon herself to write to her future mother-in-law. Between the two of them, they had planned the reunion. Mary Walsh simply told her husband that they were going to Hartford. Though he had groused and complained, he started packing. Steve's fiancée believed he would be relieved at being forced to make the move toward reconciliation.

It was easier to get Steve to the station; his fiancée told him that she was meeting friends coming in on the train. When Steve stopped abruptly, she knew that he had seen his father. She felt the tension in the arm she held. Ignoring the expletive he spat, she continued dragging him forward. "You did this, you traitor," he snarled at her, though his lips twisted in a slight smile.

A large gray-haired man with a battered fedora and a rumpled suit stood next to a short, stout woman with a round, friendly face, tracks of tears on her cheeks. Steve's mother turned and waved merrily, propelling her husband reluctantly forward.

When they finally faced each other, both Steve and his father had their hands in their pockets. Despite the bustle around them, silence surrounded the group. A minute went by while the women stood by with knowing smiles on their faces. Mary winked at the young woman on Steve's arm, who laughed. She drove a sharp elbow into his side and he yelped. Sighing, he stuck out his hand. Steve said, "Well, Dad, looks like we've been snookered. Welcome to Hartford. I'd like to introduce my fiancée, Silene Chandler."

About the Author

Mark Pasquini was born in Eureka, California, to a large and rambunctious family. He studied history and business at Humboldt State University and went on to a career in computer technology that took him from Seattle to Frankfurt, Germany. Now retired, he has settled down in Cartersville, Georgia. Mark has always been interested in writing and started out writing short stories as a hobby for his children, nieces, nephew, grandnieces, and grandnephews. Inspired by a challenge from his sister, the world-famous quilter Katie Pasquini Masopust, Mark began to write the Steve Walsh Mystery series. He is currently working on the next volume of the series for your enjoyment.